Journey Man

Knights of Black Swan 9

by Victoria Danann

Print Edition

Published by 7th House Publishing
Imprint of Andromeda LLC

Read more about this author and upcoming works at
VictoriaDanann.com

SUGGESTED READING ORDER:

1. *My Familiar Stranger (Black Swan 1)*
2. *The Witch's Dream (Black Swan 2)*
3. *A Summoner's Tale (Black Swan 3)*
4. *Moonlight (Black Swan 4)*
5. *Gathering Storm (Black Swan 5)*
6. *A Tale of Two Kingdoms (Black Swan 6)*
7. *Solomon's Sieve (Black Swan 7)*
8. *Vampire Hunter (Black Swan 8)*
9. *Carnal (Exiled 1)*
10. *Journey Man (Black Swan 9)*

ALSO BY VICTORIA DANANN:

Prince of Demons (A Black Swan novel)

Shield Wolf, Liulf (New Scotia Pack 1)

Wolf Lover, Konochur (New Scotia Pack 2)

Two Princes (Sons of Sanctuary MC, 1)

Thank you for continuing Elora Laiken's epic journey with this book. I invite you to keep up with this and other series by subscribing to my mail list. I'll make you aware of free stuff, news, and announcements and never share your addy. Unsubscribe whenever you like.

Victoria Danann

SUBSCRIBE TO MY MAIL LIST

http://eepurl.com/bN4fHX

Website

victoriadanann.com

Facebook Author Page

facebook.com/victoriadanannbooks

Twitter

twitter.com/vdanann

Pinterest

pinterest.com/vdanann

AUTHOR FAN GROUP

facebook.com/groups/772083312865721/777140922359960

New York Times and USA Today
Bestselling Romance Author

Winner BEST PARANORMAL ROMANCE SERIES –
Knights of Black Swan
THREE YEARS IN A ROW!

Prologue

What has happened since Elora Laiken arrived in Loti Dimension.

This series is also a serial saga in the sense that each book begins where the previous book ended.

There is a very old and secret society of paranormal investigators and protectors known as The Order of the Black Swan. In modern times, in a dimension similar to our own, they continue to operate, as they always have, to keep the human population safe. For centuries they have relied on a formula that outlines recruitment of certain second sons, in their early, post-pubescent youth, who match a narrow and highly specialized psychological profile. Those who agree to forego the ordinary pleasures and freedoms of adolescence receive the best education available anywhere along with the training and discipline necessary for a possible future as active operatives in the Hunters Division. In recognition of the personal sacrifice and inherent danger, The Order bestows knighthoods on those who accept.

BOOK ONE. ***My Familiar Stranger:***

The elite B Team of Jefferson Unit in New York, also known as Bad Company, was devastated by the loss of one of its four members in a battle with vampire. A few days later Elora Laiken, an accidental pilgrim from another dimension, literally landed at their feet so physically damaged by the journey they weren't even sure of her species. After a lengthy recovery, they discovered that she had gained amazing speed and strength through the cross-dimension translation. She earned the trust and respect of the knights of B Team and eventually replaced the fourth member, who had been killed in the line of duty.

She was also forced to choose between three suitors: Istvan Baka, a devastatingly seductive six-hundred-year-old vampire, who worked as a consultant to neutralize an epidemic of vampire abductions, Engel Storm, the noble and stalwart leader of B Team who saved her life twice; and Rammel Hawking, the elf who persuaded her that she was destined to be his alone.

BOOK TWO. ***The Witch's Dream:***

Ten months later everyone was gathered at Rammel's home in Derry, Ireland. B Team had been temporarily assigned to The Order's Headquarters office in Edinburgh, but they had been given leave for a week to celebrate an elftale handfasting for Ram and Elora, who were expecting.

Ram's younger sister, Aelsong, went to Edinburgh with B Team after being recruited for her exceptional psychic skills. Shortly after arriving, Kay's fiancée was abducted by a demon with a vendetta, who slipped her to a dimension out of reach. Their only hope to locate Katrina and retrieve her was Litha Brandywine, the witch tracker, who had fallen in love with Storm at first sight.

Storm was assigned to escort the witch, who slowly penetrated the ice that had formed around his heart when he lost Elora to Ram. Litha tracked the demon and took Katrina's place as hostage after learning that he, Deliverance, was her biological father. The story ended with all members of B Team happily married and retired from active duty.

BOOK THREE. ***A Summoner's Tale: The Vampire's Confessor***

Istvan Baka was captured by vampire in the Edinburgh underground and reinfected with the vampire virus. His assistant, Heaven McBride, was found to be a "summoner", a person who can compel others to come to them when they play the flute. She also turned out to be the reincarnation of the young wife who was Baka's first victim as a new vampire six hundred years before.

Elora Laiken was studying a pack of wolves hoping to get puppies for her new breed of dog. While Rammel was overseeing the renovation of their new home, she and Blackie were caught in an ice storm in the New Forest. At the same time assassins from her world, agents of the clan who massacred her family, found her isolated in a remote location without the ability to communicate. She gave birth to her baby alone except for the company of her dog, Blackie, and the wolf pack.

Heaven was instrumental in calling vampire to her so that they could be intercepted and given the curative vaccine. Baka was found, restored, and given the opportunity for a "do over" with the wife who had waited for many lifetimes to spend just one with him.

BOOK FOUR. ***Moonlight: The Big Bad Wolf***

Ram and Elora moved into temporary quarters at Jefferson Unit to protect mother and baby. Sol asked Storm to prepare to replace him as Jefferson Unit Sovereign so that he could retire in two years. Storm declined, but suggested twenty-year-old trainee, Glendennon Catch, for the job.

Litha uncovered a shocking discovery about the vampire virus by accidentally leading five immortal host vampire back to Jefferson Unit. Deliverance struck a deal with Litha to assist Black Swan with two issues: the old vampire and an interdimensional migration of Stalkson Grey's werewolf tribe.

In the process of averting possible extinction of his tribe, the king of the Elk Mountain werewolves, Stalkson Grey, fell in love with a cult slave and abducted her with the demon's assistance. He eventually won his captive's heart and took his new mate to the New Elk Mountain werewolf colony in Lunark Dimension where the wolf people's ancestors had settled centuries before.

Throughout this portion of the story, Litha's pregnancy developed at an alarming rate. Since there had been no previous instance of progeny with the baby's genetic heritage, no one knew what to expect. The baby arrived months ahead of schedule. The birth was dramatic and unique because Storm's and Litha's new daughter, Elora Rose, "Rosie", skipped the usual delivery with a twelve inch ride through the passes and appeared on the outside of Litha's body.

BOOK FIVE. *Gathering Storm*

Book Five opened with Storm and Litha enjoying quiet days at home at the vineyard with a brand new infant. Sol shocked Storm with the news that he was getting married to Farnsworth and asked Storm to help Glen run Jefferson Unit so that he could take a vacation – his first ever – with his intended. Storm agreed, but when Rosie reached six weeks her growth began to accelerate drastically.

Deliverance was to pick Storm up every day, take him to Jefferson Unit so that he could spend two hours with Glen and supervise management of Sol's affairs, then return him to Sonoma, but the demon lost his son-in-law in the passes en route to New Jersey. Every paranormal ally available was called in for a massive interdimensional search. Finally, Deliverance was alerted that Storm had been located.

The demon picked him up and dropped him in Litha's bedroom, but it was the wrong Storm. B Team, Glen and Litha all undertook a project to do a makeover on the fake Storm so that nobody would find out that there was a huge flaw with interdimensional transport.

Jefferson Unit was attacked by aliens from Stagsnare Dimension, Elora's home world, with nobody there to offer defense except Elora, Glen, the fake Storm, Sir Fennimore, the non-combat personnel and the trainees.

BOOK SIX. ***A Tale of Two Kingdoms***

The book opened with a look behind the metaphysical scene. It seemed that the strings governing Earth-related operations were being pulled by a group of misfit adolescent deities who were, eons in the past, given the planet and its derivative dimensions as a group project.

Kellareal led the elves and fae to discover the truth that they were once the same people, but were separated in the distant past because of a tragic estrangement of siblings. After believing that they had escaped the politics of their families, Duff and Song were captured and separated. With the angel's help, however, they were reunited. Meanwhile, Aelsblood, Ram's older brother was removed as monarch and his son, Aelshelm, succeeded as king in name only under the agreement that Ram's father, Ethelred Mag Lehane Hawking, would reign in Helm's place until he was old enough to decide whether he would join the family business and accept a career as king.

BOOK SEVEN. ***Solomon's Sieve***

Sol crossed the veil, but raised so much hell in the afterlife that the Council was persuaded to place his essence in the body of a Black Swan knight that had recently been vacated. He returned to Jefferson Unit with every intention of concealing his true identity, but intentions often go astray.

Dr. Mercy Renaux was a professor of archeology hired to investigate a vampire tomb unearthed in Bulgaria. She took the job thinking she would change her life and find something to blot out the guy she couldn't forget, Sir

Rafael Nightsong, bad boy member of the infamous Z Team.

She found him even harder to forget when Raif's team was assigned to escort her on a mission to contain irrefutable evidence that vampire existed. After being trapped inside a mountain together and presumed dead, Mercy and Raif decided the spark that had exploded a New York speed date could be used to ignite a more pleasurable and lasting connection.

BOOK EIGHT. *Vampire Hunter*

Ram's book is partly *My Familiar Stranger* retold from his unique point of view with chapter insights from other significant characters. The story begins the first time he runs away to the wild magic of the New Forest at age ten, follows his recruitment by Black Swan along with his training to be a vampire hunter, tells the story of the death of his first partner, and his romance with Elora Laiken.

CARNAL. Exiled 1

Though *Carnal* is part of a different series, it is a spinoff of Black Swan. Rosie Storm was the shared character and the principal character in *Carnal.* A few references to events that occurred in *Carnal* appear in this book. Note that it is listed prior to this book on the suggested reading order.

New to Black Swan…

If you're new to Black Swan or haven't read the series for a while, we have provided an index of characters, terms, places, and things at the end of the book. The Swanpedia.

Happy Reading!

JOURNEY MAN

For five years, Glendennon Catch had knocked around the globe as a floater, filling in wherever a team of vampire hunters was down a member. He'd buried six good knights and watched the life take its toll on countless others. He'd drunk his share of whiskey and bedded so many women he would hate to hear the count, but he'd never gotten over his first love. And, if he had a chance for a do-over, he wasn't sure he wouldn't have chosen Rosie Storm over The Order.

Elora Rose Storm had spent five years nursing a heavy heart, while on a cross-dimensional mission to make the world a better place, especially wherever she found human/animal hybrids being mistreated. She'd seen horrors, righted wrongs where she could, and matured into a powerful witch/demon with altruistic leanings.

After all that time, unbeknownst to each other, both were headed home. To Jefferson Unit.

Chapter One

Kristoph Falcon was one of only a handful of trainees who had ever been assigned to a Jefferson Unit team right after graduation. Not only that, but his entire team had been in his graduating class. Normally trainees would spend years with seasoned knights before being given the responsibility of team patrol, but three of the four members of K Team, so dubbed by Rammel Hawking because they were 'kids', had participated in a legendary run down of two vampire in Manhattan while they were still trainees and unarmed.

If that wasn't remarkable enough, two of them, Falcon and Wakenmann, had been decorated for heroics when J.U. had been attacked by aliens, also when they were still trainees. The two of them were the only *prospective* knights in the long and illustrious history of the centuries-old Order of the Black Swan to earn medals.

K Team consisted of Falcon's partner, Rolfe Wakenmann, aka Wakey, Sinclair Harvest, aka Sin, and Kellan Chorzak, aka Spaz, though in present day he wasn't likely to be called that by anyone other than his teammates. As it turned out, the awkwardness that had earned him the nickname of 'Spaz' as a young teen was a harbinger of masculine blossoming into a six-foot-four frame that was big-boned enough to support a truly impressive musculature.

The four of them had grown up together and knew each other well enough to think they might achieve the elusive 'team telepathy' that had been reported by a few quartets over the centuries.

In less than a year, Kris Falcon would be able to claim that he'd lived half his life on the J.U. premises. He had a routine. Rise. Shower. Dress. Have breakfast. Double check the duty roster. And the best part of his day, stop by the Operations Office to say hello to Mademoiselle Genevieve Bonheur.

Mme. Bonheur had recently become Chief Operations Officer after functioning as assistant to Farnsworth for six years. Farnsworth had retired to pursue some personal interests that included cooking, painting, collecting sea shells, and spending time with her daughter when possible.

On Wednesday of every week, Falcon arrived with fresh flowers for the Operations Office. Flowers would normally be delivered to the O.O. So he made a point of being at the entrance to intercept the delivery truck just so he could carry the bouquet personally, saving and savoring Genevieve's smile for himself.

With widespread floral mutation, it wasn't that easy to get flowers with a lovely fragrance anymore, but he shopped florists until he found one that grasped the concept of money being the least important factor along with the stipulation that they would only present a bouquet with an intoxicating perfume. Falcon believed no price was too high to experience seeing Genevieve bury her face in a bouquet, close her eyes with pleasure, and make sounds of delight.

He had the maintenance crew come in after O.O. hours on Tuesday nights and remove the past week's flowers so that the office would be ready for a new splash of color and scent the next day.

After repeating this process for so long, Falcon had developed a discriminating eye when it came to floral arrangement. If the other knights knew that, he'd never hear the end of it. So he took care to keep his interest in horticulture private. Oh they knew that he bought flowers every week. They just didn't know how much care he put into the details.

He'd developed personal preferences for particular flowers, along with how he liked them paired with varieties of greenery and how he liked them arranged. More importantly, he'd learned what Genevieve liked. She smiled graciously even when she didn't particularly care for something and would thank him effusively no matter what, but over the years he'd learned to read the nuances well enough to know exactly what would cause her spirit to do a high handstand.

On that particular Wednesday he'd given the driver an extra big tip when he picked up the armload of flowers set in a large square clear-glass vase. Falcon knew it was just the thing to elicit a big reaction. He walked a little faster than usual, anticipating the way she'd stand up, walk toward him with her high-beam smile, reach for the flowers, bury her face in the petals, take in a big breath, make sexy-sounding noises of delight, and turn her mesmerizing caramel-colored eyes his way. First she'd say, "Thank you, Sir Falcon. They're lovely." Then she would turn her head toward her desk and say, "I think I'll put them here. What do you think?"

He would return her smile and say, "Whatever you want." Then he would add, "I have tomorrow night off. Would you like to have dinner with me?"

He knew the chances were slim that she would say yes. She would almost certainly say, "I like you very much, Kristoph, but I'm too old for you and I'm not looking for a lover. There are so many beautiful girls who would love your attention. You should ask one of them."

He would say, "It may be true that others would say yes, but it's you I'm asking. And I don't agree with your conclusion that you're too old for me. Remember this. When you're ready for a lover, you'll want one with youthful vigor in the prime of his ability to give."

He would grin.

She would laugh, shake her head, set the flowers on her desk and fluff the arrangement which, in his mind, could never compete with the life and beauty she emanated like a halo shining all around her.

That exchange had taken place two hundred and sixty-three times. Yes. He'd gone to the trouble of counting. Black Swan had taught him many things about aspiring to being a person of worth and one of those was that a person of character does not give up. He'd engaged in that dialogue with Genevieve so many times that the lines were rote, like actors who had done a very long-running play on Broadway. He didn't bother to ask himself why he continued to try. He knew why. Because a chance at something, anything, with Genevieve Bonheur was worth that much effort. And that much patience.

Sir Sainregis called out as Falcon passed his way to the O.O. "Still at it, Falcon? You need to get a new hobby. That woman is your lost cause."

He looked around to see who was within earshot. When he confirmed that the Sovereign and instructors were nowhere near, he said, "Fuck off," and continued without breaking his stride. He didn't care if people thought he was a love-sick fool. Maybe it was true, but if it was, it was his business and nobody else's.

By the time he turned the corner into the Operations Office that Wednesday, he couldn't suppress his smile a moment longer. It only took a second to scan the room. She wasn't there. He glanced at the wall clock. She was *always* in the office at that time of day. The only person present was the trainee who'd been assigned runner duty that morning.

"Where's Mademoiselle Bonheur?"

"I don't know, sir. No one has been here this morning but me."

Falcon set the flowers down on the counter that separated the administrative area from personnel. "Have you notified the Sovereign's office?"

"No, sir."

"Why not?"

"I… uh, didn't think of it." Falcon stared at the kid

long enough to make him nervous. The trainee looked at the phone on the desk that used to belong to Farnsworth and reached for it. "I'll call them now."

"No," said Falcon. "I'll tell them myself."

"Okay." Falcon looked at the boy sharply. Discipline wasn't just something to do. It was crucial to grooming prospective knights who wouldn't someday turn and flee at the first sign of fangs. "I mean, yes, sir. Thank you, sir."

Falcon's mind was a jumble that matched the uneasy feeling developing in the pit of his stomach. Like most people who worked for Black Swan, Genevieve took her job seriously. The Order didn't tolerate personnel who didn't understand the importance of the work and give it a priority. If she wasn't at work, which had never happened before, and hadn't made arrangements to cover her position, the logical conclusion was that there was something to be concerned about.

The Sovereign's office perpetually maintained a staff of two twelfth-year students who served as admins for the office. One in the morning. One in the afternoon. It was a sought-after prestigious post for a trainee, even though working for Rev would never be described as 'fun'. It was a resumé plum similar to a law student clerking for a policy-making judge.

Jamie Kirkpatrick was the trainee on duty. So far as anyone knew, he was the first elf to ever hold the position. Elves were not usually inclined to serve or accept attitude without giving it back. You might say they were usually unsuitable, personality-wise. Jamie looked up and acknowledged Falcon when he came in. "Sir Falcon."

"Are you aware that the Operations Manager didn't show up this morning?"

The elf scowled. "No one told me. Let me check with the Sovereign." Rather than using the interoffice comm, he rose, walked over and knocked on the boss man's door.

"What!" Rev practically shouted.

Jamie was unfazed. "Mademoiselle Bonheur didn't come in today. Did you know she'd be otherwise occupied? Sir?"

Rev saw that Falcon was standing behind his admin, looking like he was also waiting for an answer to that question. Rev shook his head. "News to me," Rev said to Jamie before shifting his eyes and shouting, "Falcon!"

Kirkpatrick stepped aside to let Falcon take his place in the doorway. "Yes, sir."

"Did you bring this news to our attention?"

"Yes, sir."

"I see."

"I, ah, don't have her phone number, but it's very unlike her to no show. Maybe you could give her a call?"

Rev matched the intensity of Falcon's gaze as he said, "Mr. Kirkpatrick! Call the lady and find out what's going on."

Falcon heard a, "Yes, sir," behind him.

"I'm sure there's no worry," Rev said. "It's probably Bastille Day or some such and she forgot to call."

"Not to disagree, sir, but the reason why she's head of Operations is because she doesn't let details slip through cracks. Or take holidays that aren't cleared. Ever. Sir."

Rev knew that was true, of course.

Falcon turned toward the admin desk when he heard Kirkpatrick speaking, but quickly realized he was just leaving a voicemail asking her to call the office as soon as she received the message.

Kirkpatrick returned to Rev's doorway. "No answer, sir. I left a request for a phone call as soon as possible."

Rev nodded at the kid and said to Falcon, "Come in and close the door." Falcon did as he was told and came to stand in front of the Sovereign's desk. "So you're close to Bonheur?"

Falcon debated how to answer, finally deciding that, where the Sovereign was concerned, honesty was the best bet. "Not as close as I'd like to be, sir. But I know her. Fairly well."

Rev nodded. "I agree that she wouldn't alarm us without good reason."

He was already up and moving when Falcon said, "Maybe we could check her quarters? Make sure she's not sick?"

"Exactly what I was thinking." Rev passed Falcon as he exited his office. "Kirkpatrick. What is Ms. Bonheur's apartment number?"

Kirkpatrick's fingers clicked on the keyboard. "241."

As soon as Kirkpatrick had spoken the number, Rev was moving toward the elevator.

"Permission to accompany you, sir?" Falcon asked, keeping pace with Rev.

"Given."

THE SECURITY BOX on the wall next to Genevieve's door

read Rev's face. When combined with the push of a black button that served as a master key to everything that could be locked in Jefferson Unit, the apartment door clicked open.

He pushed through, but didn't enter without announcing himself. "Ms. Bonheur? Reverence Farthing here to see you along with Sir Falcon. Are you here?" There was no response. "Do not be alarmed. We're coming in to check on you."

The two men entered Genevieve's apartment. Falcon's breath hitched when he saw it. The furniture was covered in prints of floral crewel on a white wool/cotton blend. The balcony shutters had been left open and sunlight was streaming in. A crystal pedestal bowl with fresh fruit sat on the kitchen bar. The effect was feminine, pristine, upscale, and, to Falcon, a little magical. As he would have expected, knowing Genevieve, everything was in its place as if she'd been expecting a photographer from "Architectural Digest".

He passed through the living room to the bedroom. It was the same as the outer room in both style and occupancy status. Beautiful and empty. The bed was made. He rushed toward the bathroom. Again, everything in its place. Fluffy towels folded neatly as if awaiting an honored guest. He opened the drawers close to the sink.

He opened the door to her walk-in closet and found that it had been redesigned to be both attractive and functional. It even had a rod with a shorter hanging space for shirts and blouses over a seat with drawers where she could sit to pull off boots or pull on leggings.

The important thing was that everything was there, including her luggage which fit just above the closed cabinetry.

Falcon could feel it when Rev came to the closet door.

"She's not here," Falcon said without turning around. "And she didn't plan to be away."

"You're sure?"

"There's fresh fruit in the kitchen. Her luggage is here. So's her makeup. And you know how women feel about that."

"Indeed I do. You seem kind of young to know that much about women." Rev took in a deep sigh. "You know her social circle?" When Falcon didn't answer, Rev said, "I'll call my wife. Find out who her close friends are. Somebody will know something. Until we find out, don't be jumping to unwarranted conclusions."

Falcon thought that was easy for the Sovereign to say. He nodded, but felt like the lead weight in the pit of his stomach was getting heavier by the hour.

"You need to get your mind on duty because you're up tonight," Rev continued. "Let patrol take your mind off this. I'm sure there's a plausible explanation."

"Will you have someone call me if one of her friends knows something?"

Rev's expression softened. "Count on it."

FOR FIVE DAYS thereafter Falcon continued to stop by the Operations Office just to stare at her empty desk. On the sixth day, he was surprised to see Farnsworth at her old station.

He looked from Genevieve's empty desk to Farnsworth and said, "What is it?"

"I'm just filling in. That's all."

"What do you know?" She jumped a little when his frustration exploded into a shout. "TELL ME!"

"Watch your tone, Falcon."

He narrowed his eyes. "That's Sir Falcon."

"Don't you try and pull rank on me. I remember when you were being taken to see the Sovereign for classroom pranks!" On processing the worry on Falcon's face, Farnsworth backed down a little. "We don't know where she is. She had a day off. Somebody said they thought she'd gone shopping in the city. That's all we know. I'm just filling in until she's back."

Falcon turned to go, but Farnsworth stopped him at the door.

"Falcon. I *will* call you if I hear anything."

He nodded solemnly and tapped the door jamb twice before leaving.

Chapter Two

When Glen's foot touched the tarmac as he deboarded the jet at Fort Dixon, he felt the idea of 'home' settle around him. Unfortunately it felt more like a shroud than a favorite fleece blanket. The last time he'd been there his heart had still been intact. He was thinking… correction, hoping, that Rosie would soften the consequences of her ultimatum and decide that what they had was worth a compromise here or there. When he'd been given his first assignment, he'd been sure that he'd be getting leave and seeing her in the near future. But after a year's worth of phone calls to her parents, who hadn't heard from her and didn't know where she was, his hopefulness and outlook for the future had begun to fade.

The second year, hopefulness had turned into emptiness.

The third year it became hopelessness.

The fourth year it became bitterness. And that was the filter through which he viewed his 'homecoming' to Jefferson Unit.

Not much had changed. It was familiar right down to the look of the serviceman waiting by a jeep to take him to J.U.

"Take your bag, sir?"

He looked at the driver and thought it was a little silly to wear camouflage on an air base in New Jersey, but he knew the soldier didn't have a choice about what he wore. He was probably close to Glen's age, but that was just on the outside and looks can be deceiving. Glen was pretty sure he was at least fifty years older on the inside.

"Sure." He handed his duffel over and pulled himself into the Jeep.

"Been having nice weather."

Glen just grunted and turned his head away in the universal gesture of I-don't-want-to-talk.

The driver took the hint and said nothing else until they stopped in front of Jefferson Unit. Glen sat in the Jeep staring at the front door for a few seconds, not really motivated to get out and open a new chapter to what had become a lousy excuse for a life. He tried to remember the guy who had once functioned as temporary Sovereign. At twenty years old. Glen supposed that remnants of that kid must still reside somewhere inside, under countless layers of things he wished he'd never seen. But he hadn't been in touch with that person for what felt like an eternity.

There was a time when he would have chatted up the driver and had the guy inviting him out for a beer by the end of the five minute ride. He'd been easy to get along with, had a tendency to bring out the best in people, wasn't big on judging, and liked things pacific. You might think that was a gift, and in some cases it might be. In Glen's case, however, it had been a curse. Because his affability was the very reason why he'd been tagged to be a 'floater', one of just six such knights in the whole of The Order of the Black Swan.

If Glen had been asked to write a job description for 'floaters', he might have said they were accursed souls, doomed to wander the earth without roots, home, or lasting connections. Unfortunately, no one with the authority to make changes had ever, in the near five-hundred-year history of Black Swan, asked a floater how he felt about the assignment.

With a sigh he pulled himself out of the Jeep and took his duffel, which held everything he owned. He had no place that he could call his residence, no car, no furniture, no pets... What he did have was a lot of money in the Black Swan 'bank'. Since he'd spent practically none of what he'd earned for five years, he'd be considered a wealthy guy by most.

"Thanks," he said to the driver without looking at him.

"Sure thing, sir."

Glen walked purposefully toward J.U.'s state-of-the-tech security entrance wondering if he'd see people he'd known from before. He wondered how he'd appear to them and what they would think when they realized he wasn't the same person they'd known. Storm had called a few times. Glen had let it go to voicemail. Each message was the same; a recorded inquiry about how he was and an invitation to visit them on leave. He'd never returned any of the calls. Same thing with Elora.

He punched in a series of codes, talked to the tech officer on duty, gained entrance to the security lobby, then stepped through the inner door which put him on the outer ring of the Hub. It was early afternoon, one of the busiest times of the day at Jefferson Unit. The knights had awakened and come down for breakfast at one or two. The students were transitioning from academics to physical training.

Glen stood where he was and surveyed the hustle and bustle, the bright clean atmosphere, the energy that, oddly enough, might be called happy. Jefferson Unit was like a crown jewel of facilities and he should know. He'd certainly seen enough of them. He watched with as much anonymity as if he was in Grand Central Station. No one noticed him standing there. If they did, they left him alone.

After a couple of minutes of observing how Black Swan's elite lived, he walked toward the elevators and waited for a car that would carry him down to the Sovereign's office. A lot of his former faith in himself had been forcibly overhauled over the past five years, but one thing remained the same and that was that he knew the way to the Sovereign's office. Definitely. As he waited the fingers of his free hand juddered against his jeans-clad thigh. Sometime during the past few years, he'd begun to find it difficult to simply be still.

Rev's door was open when Glen entered the outer office. The Sovereign caught movement out of the corner of his eye and looked up. He recognized Glen's height, body shape, features, and hair color. In less than a second his brain had identified the visitor as a grown-up Glendennon Catch. Before he knew what he was doing he was out of his chair, advancing to greet Glen warmly like a returning hero. His smile had begun to form before he'd fully processed that the man standing in the office resembled Glen in many ways, but was missing the spark that had defined the kid Rev had known years before.

Rev was not given to overly demonstrative expressions of emotional connection. He was the sort of guy who could fight his way out of hel, but struggled with giving praise when it was due. Still, when Rev took in the look of the kid, it stopped him in his tracks.

He worked to keep the smile in place while he stuck out his hand. "Welcome home, Catch."

Glen tried a reciprocal smile, but it didn't make it to his eyes. "Home. Yeah," he said with a hollowness that bothered Rev to his core.

"I hope you're ready to go to work because we could use your help tonight."

"Tonight. Sure."

"I'd planned to give you a couple of days to settle in, but something came up. We've got a flu making the rounds. Fennimore is filling in for Elora on B Team because she's ridiculously pregnant with twins."

"Twins," he repeated.

"Yeah. Then Fennimore came down with the flu. We quarantined him in the infirmary, of course, but once something like that gets a foothold, it's hard to control. I said I'd slide into Fennimore's spot until he's on his feet because, well, we need boots on the street more than ever. Just found out an hour ago that Harvest is down for the count also."

Illness was taken seriously at Jefferson Unit. Their job

was too critical to allow sickness to spread around the premises. After all, who would hunt for vampire and try to keep the city semi-safe if all the slayers were in bed with tissues and a fever? The infirmary staff would make Sin as comfortable as possible while wearing masks and gloves and keeping him isolated.

"Harvest?"

"Hmm? Oh. I guess he hadn't been here long before you left. Sinclair Harvest. Assigned to K Team."

"I didn't know there was a K Team."

"Oh. Yeah. Well. You know Hawking and how he likes to name things. It's the youngest team in the history of Black Swan. So Hawking dubbed them K Team for 'kids'. Before I could dial that back and rescue their dignity, it had stuck like glue. As it turned out, the members of K Team weren't prickly about it. I guess they're kind of proud about being the youngest knights to ever patrol without the supervision of more seasoned veterans. Still, I suspect there'll come a time when they won't want to be known as 'kids'."

"So this Harvest fella has the flu?"

"He does. Which means that, if you didn't take his place, we'd be down a team tonight."

"I slept some on the plane. I can do it."

"Good man."

"Anybody on the team I know?"

Rev smiled. "You know all of them. Falcon. Wakenmann. Chorzak." Glen managed a ghost of a smile and nodded. "Report here. Nine o'clock."

"Yes, sir. Where would you like me to bed down?"

"Oh, sorry. Got it right here." Rev took a card from on top of his desk. "343." Glen took the card and turned to go, but Rev's voice stopped him. "Good to have you back."

Glen didn't fully turn around. "Thank you, sir."

REV SAT DOWN in his chair and somehow felt heavier than before.

What Glen didn't know was that he'd been sent to Jefferson Unit for psychiatric evaluation. His last two Sovereigns had noted growing evidence of depression in his file. Rev hadn't planned to put him to work at all, but the need had arisen and he decided to take a chance that Glen could manage two or three nights of patrol.

That and it was a good way to not alert him that he'd been brought back for observation. Glen thought it was just another random transfer and that sooner or later it was bound to happen.

After seeing him in person, Rev had to agree that the man he'd just seen was not the same Glendennon Catch he'd known before. And the new Glen was not an improvement.

Chapter Three

MONQ WAS RUNNING low on vampire specimens. He liked to keep three or four on tap for experimental purposes. He wasn't cruel about it, always kept it in mind that they had once been human and had no choice about being infected. He kept them for a month and dispatched them in the most humane way possible. Subsequently the cells where they'd been held were disinfected by specialists in biohazard gear to be sure all traces of the virus were gone.

Whenever he was in need of restocking, he sent a memo to the Sovereign who, in turn, would notify the knights in rotation to capture rather than kill, when possible. Armed with tranq guns, knights would sedate, secure the vampire's fangs with duct tape, secure his hands behind him with a zip strip, then call for pickup and wait for the van.

Monq was poised to begin a new series of experiments based on a theory that had come to him while having tea one afternoon. All his best ideas came to him over a cup of Earl Grey while staring into his faux fireplace, which consisted of an elaborately carved mantel, salvaged from one of the homes of the robber barons from the early twentieth century, a marble surround, and a video fire where actual fire would normally be. People thought it was quirky, but that was the least of his concerns. If he couldn't have a wood fire, or even a gas fire, in Jefferson Unit, he'd make do with a virtual representation.

His latest idea had to do with the 'real' vampire who had made themselves known a few years earlier. Since the real vampire had unintentionally played a part in Loti Dimension's predicament, Monq had played the guilt card effectively and enlisted their help in combatting the constant threat to humanity or, in this case, helping to find a permanent cure.

Jean Etienne had agreed to donate some of his blood to see what would happen if small amounts were given to carriers of the vampire virus. He'd agreed to come on call when Monq was ready to begin. Given that they were embarking on new trials, Monq hoped the knights could procure more than the usual number of vampire for his experiments.

Chapter Four

A QUARTER HOUR before he was due to go on patrol, Falcon got a text to head to the Sovereign's office. Wakey and Spaz were already waiting in the outer office when he arrived.

"What's up?" he asked the two of them, lifting his chin as he approached.

"Not sure," said Wakenmann, "but I think Sin is sick. Last night he said he was feeling hot and barfy."

Rev's door opened and he motioned for them to come into his office. "Evening, gentlemen."

"Evening, sir," replied Kellan Chorzak, aka Spaz.

Rev walked around his desk and sat in his big rolling chair. "No point in sitting down. You won't be here that long. Your fourth has the flu. He's in quarantine."

"We going out as three, then?" Chorzak asked. Sinclair Harvest was his partner.

Rev gave him a visual 'duh'. "Of course not. You're getting a floater. Somebody you know. Glendennon Catch."

That news temporarily pierced through Falcon's worry and he joined the other two in grinning at that, just as Glen walked in.

Being nearest the door, Falcon was first to give a welcome. He stuck out his hand. “Good to see you, man.” His smile faltered as he took Glen in. “You look a little road weary.”

“Yeah.” Glen almost smiled in return. “You could say that.”

“So here you are back where you started,” Wakey said, shaking Glen’s hand.

“Yeah,” Glen repeated.

Falcon and Wakey shared a glance.

“You’re partnered up with Chorzak,” Rev told Glen as he turned his attention to his computer screen.

Chorzak nodded at Glen.

“Looks like you got the big dog seat at dinner,” Glen said. Chorzak was chuckling and shaking Glen’s hand when Rev said, “Leave the door open on your way out.”

As they climbed on board the whister, Glen was thinking that joining a team made up of people he knew was a first for him. That realization had him almost wishing he could summon enough feeling to have an opinion about it.

Glen had been partnered with every kind of personality imaginable. He’d patrolled with guys who might as well have been mute and he’d patrolled with guys who loved the sound of their own voices. Chorzak was definitely on the talkative end, which wasn’t the least surprising. He’d never had any trouble expressing himself.

That was okay with Glen. Given the two choices, he’d pick a talker every time. It helped pass the hours and didn’t put any burden on him to talk.

By midnight supper he felt like he was caught up on

everything and everyone associated with Jefferson Unit. All except for the one person he was curious about. He didn't want to be curious about what had become of Rosie. In fact, he gave himself a mental slap every time his mind tried to wander there. So far as he was concerned, the bitch could roast in hel.

K Team stopped for midnight supper at Five Guys Burgers on 8th and 42nd. It was no accident that they were in that location. The Port Authority Bus Terminal B stayed open twenty-four hours. To vampire that equaled all night diner.

Unlike New York pedestrians, Black Swan knights always took the long route. They broke into partnered pairs and covered a section of a district, walking the same direction, but a block apart. Whenever they came to an alley, they would turn into it and walk its length, meeting then passing in the middle. That way they kept the team close together while thoroughly, methodically covering that night's duty assignment.

Falcon and Wakey stood at the head of an alley on 42nd waiting for Glen and Spaz to walk around to 41st.

As Glen and Spaz approached the 41st street alley where Falcon and Wakey were waiting at the other end, they ran into B Team, at least part of B Team. The Sovereign was filling in for Fennimore who'd been filling in for the Lady Laiken.

When Rev had shown up at the whisterport on the roof and climbed on board, Storm, Kay, and Ram stared at him like he'd lost his mind.

Rev had slapped the back of the pilot's seat and said,

"Let's go." To the three quarters of B Team present, he'd simply said, "Fennimore's got the flu."

"You think you remember how it's done? Sir?" Ram had asked, smirking.

"Muscle memory, Hawking. And wipe that smirk off your face. I'm your partner for the night."

"This should be fun." Ram's sarcasm could be heard even in his whisper.

"You got the memo," Rev had said to the three of them. "Monq wants specimens. So capture over kill if you can."

Storm and Kay glanced at each other and then seemed to find the nightscape especially interesting. Saying 'capture over kill' sounded easy, but adding anything to an already improbable task of ridding the world of vampire without being bitten, scratched, or scraped? Not their favorite thing. And it wasn't like they were in their early twenties with nothing to worry about but their own hides. They both had wives who'd have a hard time getting past the loss of husbands.

It took Storm a minute to realize it was Glen standing in front of him. First, it was night time. Second, he would have expected that, after all the years of unanswered voicemails, if Glen was coming to Jefferson Unit, he'd do Storm the courtesy of mentioning it. All the feelings swirling around that history made for an awkward reunion, if it could be called that. Glen offered his hand to Storm, but didn't hold eye contact for longer than a millisecond. He couldn't. Too much about Storm reminded him of Rosie.

Seemingly oblivious to Glen's standoffish behavior, Ram behaved like it was old home week.

"Good to have you back, wereboy. Elora will be ecstatic. Well, no' ecstatic like when I'm givin' her what she wants most, but you know what I mean. Did you hear we have twins on the way?" Glen nodded. "Aye." Ram laughed. "Hawking sperm was too much for one egg to handle without clonin' itself."

"That's not exactly how twins are made," Glen began before he realized he didn't want to have that conversation. Correcting such a gross error was just reflex.

Ram put his hand on Glen's shoulder and gave him an affectionate shake. His laughter was so infectious, it even coaxed a grudging smile out of Glen. "So you're finally where you belong. On the Kids Team."

Glen looked up at Chorzak who was tall enough to look eye to eye with Kay. "Looks like the safest place to be."

Storm looked over at Spaz. "Seen anything interesting tonight?"

"Other than the steam coming off my pastrami?" Chorzak shook his head. "Nah. It's quiet. We better get back on beat. Don't want to worry Kris an…"

Rammel slammed his palm into Chorzak's chest with enough force to stop speech mid word then turned his ear toward the alley that Glen and Chorzak were supposed to be covering. All six men went stone still. Ram had an Order-wide reputation for kidding around, but not in the field. He'd seen too much to be less than deadly serious about patrolling.

"Shite," he said. "Look alive." Ram was moving toward the alley at a run, reaching into his jacket to pull his tranq gun with one hand and a stake with the other. Four of the other men were behind for a few seconds, then Rammel was looking at the back of a knight who was younger and faster. Glen had overtaken him and was sprinting toward the mouth of the alley.

WHEN FALCON AND Wakey calculated that they'd given the other half of their team enough time to reach the opposite end of the alley, they proceeded slowly, giving their eyes time to adjust to the dim light. They didn't have a clear view to the other end because the back door lights were either out or missing, but they trusted that Spaz and Glen were close.

Falcon saw it first. He stopped Wakenmann silently by putting his arm out to block his partner's forward progress.

According to standard procedure, Wakey automatically took one side of the alley, back angled toward the wall, keeping to the cover of shadows, while Falcon mirrored his movements on the other side. They crept forward in sync, each knowing exactly where the other was until they were within four yards of the dark figures they were stalking.

There appeared to be a victim on the ground with the hideous, but familiar pose of a vampire crouching over it. It wasn't their first staking. They'd seen this before. Only something was off.

The victim was not a young woman, but a man. And

the figure of the vampire feeding was small with decidedly female curves. Female vampire were so rare that many knights finished entire careers and retired without ever seeing one. Certainly Falcon and Wakey hadn't expected to come across something so exotic.

Falcon looked across the alley at Wakey, but his face was in the shadows so Falcon couldn't get a read on whether or not Wakenmann could confirm the sighting.

When Falcon turned his attention back to the vampire, something about the way it moved caused his breath to catch. With the vampire's heightened sensory perception, just that tiny intake of air was enough to alert it to their presence. The vamp's head jerked back and around so that her face was framed clearly in the blue back door light behind her. When she bared her bloody fangs and hissed at Falcon, his blood ran cold.

Even with caramel-colored eyes gone pale ice blue and blood smeared all around her mouth, there was no mistaking that she had been, until recently, the young woman named Genevieve Bonheur. Part of Falcon's mind was correctly processing identification of the vampire, but another part was steadfastly refusing to accept that fate for her.

Seeing that the vampire was about to flee, Wakenmann raised the tranq gun he'd been issued for capture and leveled it at the vampire's upper body.

Falcon was in such shock, he'd forgotten all about the capture order. All his mind was able to grasp in that moment was that there was a gun aimed at Genevieve. *His* Genevieve.

"Nooooooo!" Falcon shouted as he launched himself through the air at Wakey to misdirect the shot.

Wakenmann was so surprised and distracted that his attention was diverted from the vampire to his partner. He had only enough time to say, "What the…!" before Falcon plowed into him sending his body back into the brick wall behind him with bruising force.

"It's Gen!"

Wakey had never heard Falcon sound either panicked or anguished, but he knew it when he heard it. His eyes jerked back toward the spot where she'd been a moment before. "You're wrong. It's not her. It *can't* be her."

"It was," said Falcon.

Wakey's jaw clenched as his face hardened. "I have to go get her, Kris."

He looked into Wakey's eyes for a minute, his knight's oath replaying in his head on a loop. He nodded. "Capture. Don't kill."

Wakenmann lowered his chin and said firmly, "If possible."

He didn't wait for a response from Falcon. He took off toward the other end of the alley, but by that time, they heard voices calling their names.

WHEN GLEN REACHED the head of the alley and turned in, he had no less than three seconds to confirm that the figure running toward him, regardless of gender, was vampire. He raised his tranq gun and fired. The dart went straight into her heart, immediately releasing a sedative powerful enough to take her down in less than two full steps, especially since it had been calibrated for a much larger body than hers.

She stopped, looked at him with wide crazed eyes, then looked at the dart in her chest. She took hold of it to pull it free, but the chemicals were already running through her bloodstream.

The vampire crumpled into a heap that mimicked death. Everyone present recognized that she had been the J.U. Operations Manager.

"Great Paddy," Ram said softly, almost reverently.

Storm looked up to see Falcon running toward them. When he realized that the kid wasn't slowing down, Storm stepped in front of the vampire's body.

"Get out of the way!" cried Falcon.

Storm deftly moved to the side, turned, stepped behind Falcon and gripped him in a wrestling hold so that he couldn't move. "Hold on. We need to secure the nails and fangs."

"Don't talk about her like that!" Falcon raged, using all his youthful strength to try and get away from Storm's hold on him.

"Okay," Storm said. "I won't talk about her that way. Just calm down while we make the situation secure."

Storm looked at Wakenmann who seemed to be in almost as much agony as Falcon. Clearly he couldn't stand witnessing the emotional dismantling of the guy who'd been his partner for much longer than he'd been officially called that.

Rev had stepped away a few paces and made two calls. First was to the clean up van to come pick up Monq's research subject. Second was to his wife to tell her that the woman she'd worked next to every day for six years wouldn't be coming back to work. Or even to humanity.

Ten minutes later the unmarked white van backed into the alley. The clean up crew had experience with safely securing transports bound for Monq's labs. They'd done it many times. They had a specialized gurney with restraints strong enough to hold any vampire and additional sedative if there was a traffic jam in the tunnel. They'd figured out that it was safer to just secure the vampire in the van designed for that purpose where they'd be able to drive into sublevel access at J.U. rather than try to manage loading on and off a whister and two elevators.

After carefully duct taping her mouth closed and just as carefully covering her hands with big thick gloves, the crew hoisted her into the van and restrained her on a specially-made gurney that could be wheeled right into the cell that had been custom designed by Monq to hold a vampire.

When they started to close up, Falcon grabbed hold of the door nearest him. "I want to ride with her."

The driver looked at Rev as if to ask what to do. Wakenmann stepped in front of Falcon, made sure that he was looking him in the eye and almost whispered, "Kris. That's not her."

Falcon searched Wakey's eyes as he tried to make himself say, "I know", but the words couldn't get past the giant lump clogging his throat. All he could force past a clenched jaw and vocal cords thickened with pain was, "Going."

Glen didn't know anything about Falcon and his attachment to Genevieve Bonheur, but he'd had enough experience with love gone south to know that look. He felt sorry for the poor bastard, but that was as much empathy as he could afford to drain from the meager well of emotion left in his heart.

Rev started to say, "I don't..." but he didn't get any further into that sentence before Wakey yelled, "HE'S GOING! OKAY?!?"

Normally speaking to a Sovereign in an argumentative way, particularly with raised voice, would not be tolerated and especially not by that particular Sovereign. But in recent years Rev Farthing had come to know that there was an emotional side to life that was just as powerful as duty and honor. Married life had also given him some insight into the wisdom of picking your battles.

The Sovereign cleared his throat and decided dignity would be saved all around. "I was going to say that I don't see any reason why not."

Wakenmann's shoulders relaxed and he had the good sense to look contrite. "Sorry, sir. Begging your pardon. I got carried away."

Rev simply nodded and left it at that.

Seven knights watched the van pull away and stood silent for a minute after it had gone.

Rev was first to speak. "Catch. We're a man down. I'm going to head back with Chorzak and Wakenmann. You take my place on B Team."

Glen nodded. He was used to being odd man out in a game too much like musical chairs. He sighed as B Team watched the three men walk away. He was thinking that there had been a time when, if he'd been told he was going to get to patrol with the legendary B Team for a night, he'd have thought he'd won the Black Swan lottery. As a matter of fact, it was Engel Storm who had impressed Glen so much, as a teenager, that Glen had decided he would cast his lot for knighthood, even though, after his time in Edinburgh at headquarters, he could have had just about any job he'd wanted within the organization.

No doubt there'd been some hero worship on his part and a desire to emulate Sir Storm to the best of his ability. But a whole lot of sludge had flowed under the bridge since then. Some of it gory. Some of it nasty. But all of it had taken up residence in Glen's heart and mind, and left him feeling always the outsider. Always alone.

After what seemed like a respectful amount of time, Storm ambled away. Kay went with him.

Ram's sharp eyes took Glen in and seemed to appraise his mood. "Okay, partner. Looks like we're on the other side of the street." Glen made no response other than to fall in beside Ram. "Maybe we can salvage some of this misbegotten evenin'. Tell me where your travels have taken ye and what you've been up to."

Ram didn't miss the fact that Glen almost winced at that question. Apparently Glen would rather be boiled in oil than talk about how he'd spent the past five years.

"Believe me," he said, "hearing about my life wouldn't salvage your evening. I've got a much better idea. You tell me about you and Elora. Is Blackie still alive? Helm must be big."

Ram angled his chin upward so that he was looking down his nose at Glen. He knew Glen was deflecting, but figured the kid had a right to his privacy.

"Oh, aye. Blackie would be growlin' if he heard you suggest that he might be beyond his prime. Helm is a firecracker. Got it from his mother." Glen had to snort at that. "What? I was no' a difficult child." Glen looked at him sideways. "Well, I may have been a bit of trouble, but do no' be tellin' Helm that."

"Okay."

"Good."

"He's going to find out about your childhood, you know."

"Well, maybe that can be delayed until I can explain."

"Right."

CHAPTER FIVE

WHEN ROSIE HAD left the land of the Exiled, she simply wasn't in a frame of mind to go home. She needed to find something to make her feel useful and she had. She'd located dozens of dimensions where humans had played around with genetic engineering and, in every case, they'd created a species superior to themselves while clinging to the notion of their own superiority. Almost all treated the hybrids badly, restricting their freedoms and viewing them as lower classes to be exploited.

At times it had required a lot of self-discipline to keep from using her special abilities to right wrongs, especially when the wrongs were directed against hybrids. But she'd made a promise to herself that she would not do anything an ordinary elemental, like her grandfather, could do. She handed out print collateral, organized meetings, and used every means of persuasion available to her to appeal to sympathy and sense of fair play.

She would organize a group, populate it with true believers, arm them with enough print collateral and righteous fire to last for half a century, then move on to the next such situation.

Occasionally she thought about visiting Newland to

see what had become of the Exiled, but she couldn't face the aftermath of what had happened there. So she kept moving and tried to keep her thoughts focused on the days ahead. Her grief had run its course from open wound to scabs, to scars, and finally to dull ache. She'd gone through the process alone without family or friends or home. Her purpose had kept her going and been everything to her. But her heart had finally spoken and told her that it was time to go home and reconnect with her parents and the friends who had been like family to her.

She went to the villa first, but found no one there. There were several alternate places where she could look, but she decided to begin with the most likely, Jefferson Unit.

She stepped out of the passes into the Hub and stood still so that she could simply drink in the familiar sights and sounds. In some ways J.U. was more home to her than the Sonoma villa. It was comforting. So much so that she closed her eyes and allowed herself a moment of internal peace.

She smiled, recalling her baby laughter as she danced across the polished tile floor. She remembered how the people at the Atrium Café had practically adopted her. That smile was replaced with a pang of regret when she remembered Glen leading her across the room by the hand, patiently explaining that he would get into a lot of trouble with her parents if she disappeared.

Getting Glen into trouble hadn't been on her agenda. She remembered being small enough to straddle her mother's hip and clapping her hands when Glen would arrive. All those memories and more came back in a rush as she stood watching people pass on their way to work or school or recreation.

She was standing off to the side near a cluster of people when she heard someone behind her say that the Operations Manager had been infected by the vampire virus and had been brought in that very night. Rosie was alarmed. She knew Farnsworth and hoped that wasn't who they were talking about.

She was still lingering in the Hub near the elevator when it opened. Glen stepped off, but clearly didn't recognize her. He looked right through her as if she wasn't there and never broke stride on his way to the bar.

Her lungs had stopped working, more because of how awful he looked than anything else. Oh, he was still a heartbreaker, filled out with more muscle and an unmistakable confidence in the way he moved. That attractiveness wasn't going to change at any age. What was different was that the life in his eyes that made him Glen was absent. The animation was gone. If she'd had to describe what she saw, she might have said that he looked like a bad copy of himself.

After a few seconds of staring after him, Rosie got on an elevator that would take her to the floor where her parents' apartment had been the last time she'd been there. She was prepared for the possibility that they weren't there. She'd be the first one in any crowd to acknowledge that things change.

Chapter Six

FALCON SAT ON the cement floor outside the cell where the vampire who had once been Genevieve Bonheur was being held. She was far too new a vampire to be able to think, much less speak. She simply sat on the cot that was built into the wall and looked at Falcon like she was starving and he was food.

When word reached the Sovereign's office that Falcon refused to move from that spot, Rev pulled K Team from that night's rotation and called Monq.

"You need to get a handle on Falcon."

"By that I assume you mean an evaluation on his state of mind."

"Call it what you will. Just fix him. I need him on the street."

"I'm not going to dignify that with a response. I have final say when it comes to readiness."

"Whatever. You might as well do an evaluation on Glendennon Catch while you're at it."

"Oh? I didn't know he was here. What's the problem?"

"There've been rumors that he's not fit to hunt. Psychologically speaking."

"I see. Does he know that he's to be evaluated?"

"He does not."

"Alright."

"Tonight."

"What about tonight?"

"I need it done tonight."

"You want rush service on a psych eval? That's going some, even for you."

"What's that supposed to mean?"

"It means there've been rumors, for years, that you want things *your* way and the timing is always *now*."

"What's wrong with that?"

Monq sighed and tapped his retractable pencil on his desk. "Nothing. Your position probably stipulates that the successful candidate for Sovereign has similar personality traits."

"Damn straight."

"Although Catch was able to keep the ship running without so much bluster."

"I do not bluster."

"You never do anything else."

"Do you want your funding recommendation renewed at the end of the fiscal year?"

Monq laughed. "My funding has nothing to do with you and we both know it, but never mind. Regarding Catch, it's already six o'clock."

"I'll tell him you're expecting him for dinner in your library. Seven okay?"

"Naturally. It's not as if I have anything else to do."

"Sarcasm doesn't suit you. He likes lamb."

After a noteworthy pause, Monq said, "You remember

what he likes to eat? Hmmm."

"Don't start with that 'hmmm' business and don't go reading anything into that. He did my job for a while and I got to know him. That's all there is to it."

"If you say so."

"I do."

"Okay."

"Seven o'clock."

"You want to give me some more detail about the nature of complaints regarding his performance?"

"Disengaged intellectually and emotionally. Possible depression."

Monq sighed again. "That's a shame. I'll do what I can."

"Can't ask for more."

Rev ended the call and yelled for his assistant. He had interoffice communications at his fingertips, but found that yelling was just as effective and a *lot* more satisfying. The admin appeared at his door almost instantly.

"Yes, sir?"

"Find Sir Catch and tell him I said he's expected in Dr. Monq's library for dinner at seven o'clock."

"Yes, sir."

Chapter Seven

Day One – Psych Eval

"Come in," Monq replied to the knock on his door and glanced at his watch. Seven o'clock exactly. There was nothing like Black Swan training to instill punctuality.

With a slight hesitation Glen opened the door and walked in. Monq hadn't seen him since he'd been back. The years had made him more handsome in some ways. He'd filled out and carried more muscle. His jawline and cheekbones were more prominent. Some would say chiseled. The boy that Monq had known was gone and in his place was a man with a hard edge and the world-weary expression of an old man whose life hadn't gone well.

Glen confirmed that Monq's office was unchanged since the last time he'd been there. Same warm sage green color scheme designed to relax people into telling all. Same combination of oddities on the walls and shelves. When he brought his gaze back to Monq, his posture and demeanor broadcasted suspicion. "What's this about?"

Monq chuckled. "Right to the point. Sit down. Let's eat and say hello. It's been a long time."

Glen eyed the chair with the same suspicion he'd

aimed at Monq. After a brief internal struggle, it seemed he'd decided to be polite, up to a point. "Yeah. What's this about?"

Glen turned at the sound of a knock on the door.

"Dinner," a wait staffer announced as he wheeled the cart into the study. Looking at Monq, he said, "Would you like it set out on the table, sir?"

"Certainly," Monq answered.

Glen stood watching while the server, whom he did not recognize, covered Monq's cleared library table with a tablecloth, set out linen napkins, silverware, covered dishes, condiments, glasses of iced water, wine goblets, and a bottle of pinot noir.

"Shall I open the wine, sir?"

Monq nodded and said, "Yes," while trying not to seem impatient.

"Would you like the door closed, sir?"

"Yes. Yes." Monq waved.

When they were once again left alone in the room, Glen was still standing. Monq motioned toward the table. "Have dinner with me for old times' sake. You can say as much or as little as you please."

Glen raised an eyebrow, but relented and took a seat across from Monq next to his video fireplace. After all, he'd been ordered to report and didn't really have a choice in the matter. He lifted the stainless steel cover off the plate in front of him. "Lamb," he said. "That's my favorite."

"I know. That means you have friends here who care about you." Monq pulled out the padded leather chair across from him and sat down.

Glen raised his eyes to meet Monq's, but remained distrustful. Monq noticed that he swallowed before saying, "I did have friends here. Once."

The way he said it made it sound like he no longer believed that to be true.

As a man, Monq wanted to ask why Glen thought those friendships had dissolved, but as a psychiatrist, he knew that wasn't the way to proceed.

"Let's just catch up. Tell me about yourself. What's happened since I last saw you?"

Glen barked out a laugh that was startling. Even though the effect was to make Glen look more mean than jovial, there was a hint of the boy Monq had known. The part of his heritage that was a quarter werewolf was evident in the way his eyes flashed and the contrast of white teeth against tanned skin.

Glen looked into his goblet like it was a crystal ball before taking a drink of red wine. "Nothing worth mentioning."

"Well, that can't be true. I mean, wasn't your first assignment to fill in as Z Team's fourth and try to redeem them? There has to be several hours' worth of stories there alone."

Glen cut off a bite of lamb and began to chew. "It would bore you to tears."

"I doubt that. I'm not easily bored." When Glen added nothing more, Monq said, "That was rough business out there with K Team."

Glen hesitated. "Yeah. It was. Poor son-of-a-bitch."

"You mean Falcon?"

"Yes." Glen looked over at Monq like he was dim. "I mean Falcon."

"He must have cared a great deal for Mademoiselle Bonheur."

Glen shrugged. "Apparently."

"I heard the Storm girl is here. Weren't you close with her years ago?"

Monq made a mental note of everything he saw. Glen tensed, stopped chewing and sat back, looking guarded. "I knew her." He did his best to sound ambivalent.

"Hmmm. Well. Tell me about your time with Z Team."

Glen raised an eyebrow while he took another drink of wine. He found that deflecting always worked. People would always rather talk about themselves. "You said you want to catch up. So you start. What have you been up to?" It would have been a better question if Glen had made it sound like there was any genuine interest supporting the query.

Monq noted the tactic and decided to play along. He couldn't expect to get what he was unwilling to give.

"Well," he began, "I know you can imagine my disappointment when the vampire virus surged back stronger than ever, because you've had to deal with the consequences in the field. Since then, I've been highly motivated to find something else that works. As you can imagine, I'm sure.

"Eventually we found a cure for cancer. So I'm operating on the theory that, if I just stay after it, I'm bound to come across something that works. Fortunately for me, and I mean that sincerely, I'm well-funded.

"Right now I'm embarking on a new set of trials that will introduce little bits of real vampire blood to our captives. My hope is that, in the right dosage, it might kill the virus. Or, if not that, stabilize the minds of the victims so that they can think like humans. If we could achieve that result, we could probably create a synthetic diet that would suffice. Of course they would have to be quarantined from the general population because they would still be a danger, but we might be able to curtail the continual spread of the disease.

"It's too early to start talking about either result, but I'm hopeful."

Glen gave every sign of paying attention, even appearing to care about what was being said. Moreover, he seemed to relax within minutes after the topic of discussion shifted away from him. Monq decided the matter was too deep seated to rush. So he would be content with gaining trust.

"The Frenchies going along with this?"

"Yes. Jean Etienne is on board."

"If you give the vampire you're holding immortal blood..." he paused and looked at the wine in his goblet, "you're not afraid it might make them immortal? What if it made them immortal and that was the *only* change?"

"Out of the frying pan, into the fire?"

"We'd have virus vamps who couldn't be killed."

Monq sighed deeply. "I admit it's a risk although we're going to try to mitigate that possibility by beginning with amounts too tiny to have a lasting effect."

"You can't know that. Introducing immortal blood? You have no idea what the effect will be."

"That's the burden of risk, isn't it? You think it's worth the gamble? Or not?"

"Who cares what I think?"

"I do. I wouldn't have asked you otherwise. It wasn't a patronizing question."

"It wasn't? So, in other words, my answer will have some effect on how you proceed?" Monq frowned at that. "Yeah." Glen chuckled. "That's what I thought."

Glen finished his lamb and pushed back from the table.

"Dessert?" Monq asked.

"No sugar, doc." Glen's hand went straight to his rock-hard abs as if to demonstrate the physical rigors expected of a field-active Black Swan knight. "Well," he stood up, "thanks for dinner and, ah, 'catching up'. See ya."

Monq watched Glen leave without saying a word. He called the kitchen to come pick up the dinner setup and then headed over to Area Thirteen, where the vampire were kept.

Chapter Eight

MONQ NODDED AT members of his staff on the way past and found Kristoph Falcon sitting on the floor outside the cell of the captive vampire.

He sat down on the floor next to Falcon, which was neither easy nor pleasant for someone his age. The floor was hard and, regardless of the fact that the sublevel was heated, it was cold to the touch. He immediately felt the chill seep through his pants where his body came in contact with the cement and wondered if it would aggravate the advancing arthritis.

"Sir Falcon," he said. He hoped that the use of the formal title would bring Falcon into the moment so that Monq could get an accurate reading on his state of mind.

Falcon's eyes appeared to clear. As he turned his head to the side and looked at Monq, he gritted his teeth. "You're not going to kill her. I'll kill you first."

"I see," Monq replied with a detached professional calm that gave no hint his life had just been threatened. "Have no fear. The vampire is not in any danger at present." He looked at the vampire, whose unwavering gaze was unnerving, then turned his attention back to Falcon. "Is that why you're here? You're afraid she'll be killed if you aren't watching?"

"Isn't that what you do when you're finished with the ones you keep down here? Isn't that what we do? Every day? We kill them. Right?"

"We do, but this one is different, special in several ways. For one thing a female is very rare, as you know. I've never had a chance to study one for clues as to *why* they are rare. Up to now we've had nothing but speculation. For another thing, this vampire used to be a person we all knew. And liked." That got Falcon's attention. "We're going to try to find a way to bring her back."

"You're lying."

"I'm not. Why would I?"

"To get me to leave."

"I admit that I'd like to see you have something to eat and get some rest. Will you not take my word that she's not in danger?"

"No. I won't take your word. If you want me to eat and sleep, then bring me some food and a bed. I'm not leaving here."

That evening Monq had made two attempts at getting knights to trust him and he was batting zero for two. He wondered if he was losing his touch.

"If there's really no way I can change your mind about that then so be it. You can stay on one condition. You don't interfere with our experiments. If you do not abide by my condition, I will not hesitate to have you removed. Understood?"

Falcon looked at Monq like he was really seeing him for the first time and nodded.

Monq had a moment's trouble getting his knees to agree to help him stand. He'd gone stiff sitting on the floor for even that short time. He ambled away leaving Falcon exactly like he found him.

HALF AN HOUR later Kris Falcon heard wheel noise growing louder. He couldn't have been more surprised to see a cart laden with a four course meal being pushed by the Area Thirteen guard on duty, who'd accepted it from kitchen staff. That was closely followed by a hospital bed, with two pillows and big thick blankets, being delivered by two of Monq's staff who'd gotten the bed from the infirmary.

With a grateful look at the people delivering his requests, he said, "Thank you."

AFTER ORDERING FOOD and bedding for Falcon, Monq had dialed the Sovereign.

"Yeah," Rev said.

"Falcon and Catch are off rotation until further notice."

"Are you shitting me?!?"

"I beg your pardon. Could I speak to the Sovereign? The one who has an absolute no-common-language policy?"

"Don't talk to me about language. If you crawled up out of the ground now and then maybe you'd know we're at war with an all new and improved vampire virus."

Monq bristled at that and was on the verge of depleting his own well of patience. "I'm more aware than most.

I'm the guy who's trying to find a new cure. Remember?"

"I remember. What I'm saying is that I *cannot* be down two knights. I need them."

"I sympathize, but it can't be helped. These two are not fit for duty at the moment."

"What the blazes am I supposed to do?"

"How should I know? Call up Z Team!"

"This place is already in enough of a shambles without turning those fuckwads loose on J.U. Again."

"You know, I don't want to beat a dead point, but this u-turn you've done on colorful language is a big change. Are you sure you're okay?"

"I'm careful about what I say around the kids."

"No judgment. Just an observation. Why don't you call up B Team?"

"When was the last time you poked your head up out of your hole? B TEAM IS ALREADY IN SERVICE! Except for Elora. She's pregnant. Fennimore was standing in for her, but he has the flu so I stood in for him last night. And I feel guilty all the time about sending those guys out on the street because every one of them is too damn old. They want to be retired, concentrating on growing grapes or puppies or horses as the case may be. And they *should* be!"

"I'm hearing that you're under a lot of stress and that it's coupled with guilt. Would you like to come down and talk about it?"

"What?! NO!"

"Well, door's always open. You could call up Dr. Renaux and get her husband to fill in."

After a pause, Rev said, "That's a possibility. Although

it wouldn't make my step-daughter-in-law any fonder of me. Also, they're in the Amazon right now, days away from an airstrip. Infirmary says Harvest should be good to go in another two days, which means he'll be back on the street before Nightsong could even get here."

"You almost make me glad I've got my problems instead of yours. I'll keep you posted on Catch and Falcon."

"Yeah. Do that," he grumbled.

WAKENMANN SHOWED UP just as Falcon was finishing dinner and said, "Hey." His gaze went straight to the vampire in the glass-fronted cell. Few things were more unsettling than seeing a vampire in captivity, but the way she was focused on Falcon was so disturbing it was hard to look away.

"Hi," Falcon said. "What do you want?"

"Is that any way to talk to your best friend?"

Falcon sighed. "Okay. How about this? I need a john break. Will you watch her while I go?"

"Watch her?"

"Yeah."

"What exactly am I watching for?" Wakey glanced at the cell then tilted his head to the side when he asked, "What do you think she's going to do?"

"It's not what she's going to do, farts-for-brains. It's what they might do *to* her if I'm not here."

"What do you think they might do if you're not here?"

"Just watch her. Okay? Make sure nobody comes near her with…"

"A green-wood-bullet pistol, for instance?"

"Yeah."

Wakey quietly appraised his friend for a few seconds. "Okay. I'll be here."

Falcon relaxed visibly. "Thanks, man. It was getting hard to hold."

"Enough info, all right? Just go."

Falcon started away, but turned back with a scowl on his face. "You wouldn't break your word. Thinking you were doing me a favor or something. Would you?"

Wakey gaped with his mouth open. "You going paranoid on me? *I'm* the one who hit my head when you slammed me into that wall. No! I'm not going to tell you one thing and do another. It's me you're talking to."

Falcon attempted a small smile. "Yeah. Sorry."

"Go."

Wakenmann took Falcon's perch on the side of the hospital bed to wait for his friend to return. The vampire shifted the focus of her attention to Wakey. He started whistling, "Row, Row, Row Your Boat" to distract himself, but distraction was difficult because her gaze was strangely compelling. He felt like one of those prey animals that are supposedly hypnotized by snakes, and suspected that the vampire would be the subject of night terrors for years to come.

On arrival she'd been cleaned up and changed into plain blue scrubs. So at least he didn't have to look at the thing with the bloodstains and smears she'd been wearing when they'd first come upon her in the alley.

He understood why Falcon was worried that someone would kill it while he was gone to the bathroom. All

Wakenmann's instincts as a vampire hunter told him to do it himself. Perhaps that was why Falcon was worried about leaving it unprotected. It was easier for Wakenmann to try and think of the creature as 'it' because it was disturbing to bestow personhood on a vampire. But it was just as disturbing to see the soulless shell of a person whom he'd known housing a vampire. He'd liked Genevieve, but she was no longer home.

"Hey," he said to the poor creature inside the holding cell. "Don't you have something else to look at?"

If it registered at all in the vampire's brain that he'd spoken, she hid it well.

Chapter Nine

Day Two – Psych Eval

THE NEXT MORNING Glen reported to the Sovereign's office as requested. Rev's door was closed when he arrived, but the duty admin rose and showed him in right away. Rev didn't even look away from his monitor. Without a greeting or any semblance of pleasantry, he said, "Catch, you're off rotation until further notice."

Lines formed between Glen's brows. "Off rotation? Why?"

"You need some down time."

"Who says?"

Glen felt panic rise in his chest. Off rotation? Without vampire hunting, what did he have to hold onto? Nothing. He'd be afloat on a raft in a sea of emptiness.

That tone got Rev's full attention. He looked up from the monitor and said evenly, "Because you and I have history, I'm going to pretend you did not just use that tone with me or question my order. The fact that you did only firms up my thinking that you're in need of down time. Bottom line. When Monq clears you to return to duty, you're back. Not before."

A muscle in his jaw rippled visibly. "Monq."

"Get on his schedule. The sooner you get things sorted, the sooner you'll be back on the roster. And I *need* you back on that roster."

"I know you do." Under his breath, he said, "Everybody needs me on their roster."

"What was that?" The Sovereign was getting that severe expression that meant Glen had pushed his luck and overstayed his welcome.

"Nothing. Sir."

Glen stalked out of the office and fumed, nostrils flaring, all the way to Monq's complex, which consisted of offices, labs, quarters for himself and some of the staff and, of course, the vampire specimens. Glen went straight to Monq's office and happened to find him there. He stormed in and stood in front of Monq's desk, shifting from foot to foot like he couldn't stand to be inside his own body a moment longer.

"What did you tell the Sovereign about me?"

Monq looked up from whatever task he was addressing and managed to sound semi-cheerful. "Glen." He glanced at the door Glen had left standing open. "Come in."

"What did you tell the Sovereign to get me pulled from duty?"

Monq sat back, looking unperturbed. "That you've been overworked."

"That's BULLSHIT!" Glen shouted.

Then he proceeded to punctuate that declaration by picking up a priceless Chinese vase and smashing it against the nearest mahogany bookshelf. While Glen went about dismantling much of the office, Monq sat back in his chair and watched, looking as dispassionate as if the hunter was bacteria on a slide.

By the time Glen was finished with his spree of destruction, three-quarters of the books were off the shelves. One chair was broken beyond repair. A ficus tree was shredded and leafless. And numerous curiosities with value known only to Monq had been rendered trash.

Hearing the racket, Monq's staff had come to the door looking alarmed and wide-eyed. Monq had held up his hand to stay them. After a couple of minutes they had backed away and gone about their business assured by faith that, if *anybody* on Earth knew what he was doing, it must be Thelonious Monq.

Glen stood panting, in a half crouch, looking at Monq like he was waiting for a reaction.

"Dinner here again tonight. Seven o'clock," was all Monq said.

In response, Glen picked up the heavy pot that had held the ficus tree and, with a frustrated snarl amplified by werewolf vocal cords, threw it against the flat screen monitor that projected Monq's illusion of a fireplace. The glass fractured into an ugly web of shards as dirt spilled out of the cracked pot and onto the carpet. Monq's office looked like a horde of barbarians had swept through. It didn't seem possible that one guy could have done so much damage in less than ten minutes. Glen stared at his handiwork for a couple of seconds before walking out without a backward glance toward Monq.

SIX HOURS LATER Glen arrived at Monq's door. At precisely seven o'clock. The door was open. Monq was behind his desk. Glen stood at the threshold and looked around the room without entering.

Everything was in its place. Books were on the shelves. A cheerful video fire flickered from a shiny black monitor built into the wall underneath the fireplace mantel. There was even a new ficus tree in an identical pot, although it did appear to be somewhat larger and fluffier than the one Glen had destroyed.

Monq didn't look up. He simply said, "Come in. Dinner will be here in a few minutes. I felt like Swedish meatballs with egg noodles. Hope that's okay with you."

Glen stared at Monq for a few beats. "I'm sorry about, uh…"

"Dinner," the server announced as he neared the door with a rolling cart.

Glen stepped into the room and out of the way. He watched the man prepare the table for dinner, as he had the night before.

When the server had finished setting out dinner and opening a bottle of pinot noir, he said to Monq, "Is that satisfactory, sir?"

"Yes," said Monq. "Thank you. Please close the door on your way out."

The man nodded, pushed the cart to the other side of the door then closed it behind him.

Monq rose and walked around his desk. "Let's eat," he said with a smile.

Glen seemed confused by Monq's nonchalant manner.

He'd expected a right good railing. Instead Monq was behaving as if nothing unusual had happened earlier in the day.

Glen sat down looking chastised even though he hadn't been. "I was saying that I'm sorry about..."

"That's not necessary, Catch. It was of little consequence. Except for the eleventh century Bergere chair. Apparently Farnsworth had some trouble running one down and, when she found it, the upholstery was hideous. No matter. She got an antiques restorer to put a rush on replacement and it should be here tomorrow.

"You do, however, owe me a story for my trouble. Let's begin with your first assignment, shall we? Z team, I think it was."

Glen slumped back in his chair as Monq dived into his salad.

Staring at his plate without making a move toward a fork, Glen said, "Z Team." His eyes glazed over like he was having an out-of-body experience. "They sent us to Shanghai." He raised his eyes to meet Monq's. "You ever seen an Asian vampire?"

Monq shook his head. "Can't say that I have."

"Well, it's even more eerie because the ice pale eyes are so out of place on their faces." Monq noticed the rapid twitching of the tablecloth hem, which meant that, out of sight under the table, Glen's knee was juddering fast. It was an obvious indicator of stress and nerves and one that Glen would have taken care to hide if he'd realized the movement of the tablecloth hem was giving him away.

"Go on."

Glen's attention had wandered to the bookshelves, but his gaze jerked back at the sound of Monq's voice.

"Shanghai," Glen said dispassionately. "It's a wild place."

"Do you speak Mandarin?"

"I do now." He shrugged. "Limited. No Westerner who learns it as an adult is ever going to speak it well."

Monq nodded. "Probably not. So you were with Z Team in Shanghai and you were, what? Twenty years old?"

"Yeah. About that. Not old enough to be taken seriously by those guys. Not that they take anyone or anything seriously but themselves." He gave a slight headshake to the bookcase that had drawn his attention. "Anyway. Shanghai was wild and so were they. Nightsong had left the team, gotten married and had a new job that boiled down to being his wife's bodyguard." Glen laughed at that. "I understand that it's a job he takes *very* seriously."

"I'll bet. I got to know his wife a little. So who else was on the team?"

"Torn Finngarick. Of course."

"Of course."

"Gunnar was still active then. And they'd gotten a new guy besides me, only he came on the usual way somebody makes Z Team. Fuckup of phenomenal magnitude. Stephrelle Bridesmore. Never did learn Chinese worth a shit." Glen's eyes flicked to Monq and away. "Sorry."

"Stop apologizing. Continue."

"Well, Torn and Gun had already, I guess you'd say, bonded with Bridesmore. It made sense. He was just like them. Oozing attitude. All tatted up. Belligerent to the extreme. Hostile if you rubbed him the wrong way and, believe me, that was *not* hard to do. He didn't mind being called Steph, but would turn mean as a snake if somebody called him Stephie."

"Sounds like you found that out the hard way."

"Nah. It wasn't me. Some other fool in the unit." Glen picked up his water glass and took a drink. "The short and sweet is this. Steph belonged there. I didn't. End of story."

Monq chuckled. "I have a feeling there's much more to the story than that. These meatballs are perfection. You should give them a try." He made a yummie sound that was barely on the manly side of silly. "And the noodles are buttery. They make them fresh in the kitchen. Did you know that?" He nodded and laughed. "I wouldn't be surprised if they didn't have a milk cow and churn the butter that went into these little delights. Nothing's too good for Black Swan knights. You know what I mean?" Glen sneered at that. "And the rest of us including myself, a simple scientist, get to be the incidental beneficiaries of your good fortune."

Glen snorted out a derisive huff. "My good fortune? If you think it's good fortune to be a Black Swan knight, you should try it yourself. Want to trade places for a couple of weeks?"

Monq put his fork down and looked serious. "No. I wouldn't. You're not the first knight to come through my door looking the worse for wear."

Glen maintained eye contact with Monq for only a couple of seconds before he broke it off and pretended to be interested in looking around the room again. After a thorough sweep of the surroundings, his eyes came to rest on the plate in front of him, but still he didn't make a move to try the meatballs.

Undeterred, Monq continued prodding. "So you'd just arrived in Shanghai. And you were partnered with Bridesmore?"

"Yeah. Torn and Gunnar had been together a long time. Steph's a good guy in his way, but he never saw me as his equal. He never once called me by my name. Just Rookie. Even that was seldom. He had an adverse reaction to conversation of pretty much any kind."

"Quiet?"

Glen's responding smile was bitter. "Understatement. Severe." Looking at his plate again, the fake smile fell away. He suddenly sat up, reached for a fork, pulled the salad plate in front of him, speared a forkful of greens and stuffed it into his mouth. "So patrolling was kind of weird," he said absently, like he'd almost forgotten he wasn't supposed to have an appetite or be receptive to conversation.

"In what way?"

"Well, like I said, the district that draws leeches because that's where the night life is. It's buzzing with clubs and bars and neon lights. Place is full of rich expats from all over looking for a good time and sometimes their idea of a good time is, let's say, unusual. Sometimes it's what you might call dark.

"Some of the bars are so packed you can't move around. A vampire could be sucking somebody dry right next to clueless people drinking Manhattans and screaming in each other's ears, trying to be heard over the noise."

Monq raised his eyebrows causing lines to form on his forehead. "You saw that? Or you're just saying that could happen?"

Glen gave Monq a smile that didn't reach his eyes. "Yes. I saw it happen. Vamp looked right at me while he was killing somebody. Almost like he knew what I was and that I couldn't touch him in the middle of a crowd like that. Maybe I'm crazy, but it felt like a taunting. When he finished with the victim, he started pushing through the crowd in the other direction. We followed, or tried to, practically throwing people out of our way, but we lost him somewhere before we got to the back door. I wanted... no, I *needed* to talk about how frustrating that was. Steph just shrugged and walked off. If it bothered him, he did a spectacular job of covering it up. Like I said, talking wasn't his thing."

"What about other people at the unit?"

Glen set the salad plate aside and pushed the noodles around like he was deciding which would be the lucky winner. He forked three, put them in his mouth, and said, "There were some good guys. Some I might have become friends with if I'd been there long enough. A big part of the reason why knights are close to team members is because that's who you spend most of your time with."

"Makes sense. So did you discuss it with Torn and Gunnar?"

"I told them what happened when we met up. They just said 'happens'. One word. End of discussion."

"Sounds like they'd developed some emotional calluses. How long had you been active when that incident occurred?"

"Three days." Glen cut a Swedish meatball in half. "Emotional calluses. Clever, doc. You should be a writer." He took a bite. "I guess that's right though. They'd seen and done all this stuff at that point. They were closer to the end of their career than the beginning. But it was new to me. The ugliness. When I left here I was thinking I was charging off on this noble mission. Save the world." He mocked himself in a quixotic way, laughed and shook his head. "Stupid. Young and stupid and completely without emotional calluses, which, as it turns out, are crucial to the job. Well, except…"

Monq thought it best to ignore the fact that a sentence was left open-ended. "You don't think you've been on a noble mission to save the world."

Glen sighed and looked at the fake fire while he ate more noodles. "I get it. You want me to open my soul so you can dig around and find a way to decommission me."

"Nothing could be further from the truth, Sir Catch. I want to help restore your peace of mind so that you can continue serving The Order in the capacity of your choice."

Glen looked at Monq and held eye contact that time, assessing Monq for credulity. "That the truth?"

"Gods' own truth. Whatever you tell me remains between the two of us. *Only* the two of us and I will take it to my death. And, by the way, this office is a judgment-free zone."

Monq could tell that Glen was using his people-reading skills to evaluate his answer.

"Judgment-free, huh." Glen seemed to be considering that as he ate the last chunk of meatball.

Monq waited, knowing that the next sentence Glen uttered would be his implied consent for treatment or a rejection that would be almost impossible to break through.

When Glen looked up again, he said, "Okay. Here it is. Sometimes I think I'm the one that needs saving. Not the world."

Monq smiled. "Oh. Is that all?"

Glen laughed. To an observer it might have seemed like a simple, ordinary everyday thing. But to Monq, it was a thrilling signal of hope. It meant that Glen, the brilliant, affable kid with a universe of potential, the one everybody loved, was still in there, waiting for someone or something to bring him back and give him a kickstart out of his stall. A reason to start living again.

"By the way," Monq set his napkin beside his plate, "are you in touch with family?"

"Thought you read my file, doc. I don't have any family to be in touch with."

"Your file was, ah, vague on the subject." He waited for Glen to add something. After a few seconds of silence, he said, "Some other time then."

Chapter Ten

When the fourth vampire specimen was delivered to the cell prepared for him, Monq called Jean Etienne. Well, he called Baka and asked that a message be relayed the next time he was in touch with the immortals.

The delay between the initiation of that request and receipt of the message could have been days or even weeks, but the immortals were in Paris working with the Black Swan teams when Monq reached Baka. Within half an hour of hanging up the phone with the ex-vampire, Jean Etienne was standing in front of Monq's desk.

Jean Etienne was one of the original vampire created by the god-like brat, Heralda. He was thousands of years old, but appeared to be in his early thirties.

Like all the immortals he was beautiful. Beauty was part of the design that assisted vampire with easy sustenance. The first step in the process of feeding was to cause the blood donor to feel drawn to the vampire and at ease with being alone with them. The second was to take a small enough amount of blood that it wouldn't be missed. Except in rare cases of unusual brain chemistry, humans reached such a state of ecstasy that they forgot their encounters with vampire altogether. The effect was much like a petit mal seizure. By the time victims regained full control of their faculties puncture wounds were healed by the properties of immortal saliva.

Now and then a drop or two of blood might escape and be left on clothing as evidence, but humans were good at passing such things off as little mysteries then forgetting all about it. Or explaining it away with something as reasonably logical as a minor nose bleed.

On the rare occasions when humans remembered involuntarily nurturing a vampire, they quickly learned that their stories were fodder for ridicule or even serious concern for their sanity.

Jean Etienne's version of beauty presented itself as dark brown locks that fell haphazardly around his face and blue eyes that were almost as pale as humans-turned-vampire. He was medium height and build which made blood withdrawal physically convenient.

Most of Jean Etienne's peers, meaning those as old as he, had taken mates having found that time passing slowly is better lived with love. Some of them had reproduced, which may or may not have been part of Heralda's plan. Jean Etienne had considered the option, but had never crossed paths with a female worthy of the ultimate in long-term commitment.

For the past few hundred years, he'd been working as a vampire version of a nanny, babysitting adolescent males who, though hundreds of years old themselves, were as immature as human sixteen-year-olds requiring constant supervision. Although he believed the responsibility of working with the Black Swan knights had been good for them and given them a purpose beyond hedonism.

The occupation had originally relieved some of the boredom. Millennia can become monotonous, after all. But for the past fifty years or so Jean Etienne had begun to feel like he'd integrated all the personal value that particular service had to offer.

No doubt there would be panic amongst several sets of parents when he turned in his notice. He had the sort of quiet patience that could only come from knowing that he wasn't running out of time. He'd grown fond of the boys, of course, but they were not his *children*. They were his *charges*. And there was a difference.

At first their antics were amusing, but too much of anything wears thin. Jean Etienne was old enough to remember when Epicurous had suggested moderation in all things during the heyday of Greek culture.

He was skeptical about Monq's experiment, but felt compelled by honor to agree because they were not making much headway cleaning up the mess that the vampire virus had made in Loti Dimension. He was prepared, should it become necessary, to reveal the means by which so-called immortals could be killed. He would not enable the insanity produced by the vampire virus to become a menacing madness of eternal duration.

With vampire eyes Jean Etienne could see the aging that had changed Monq in the past seven years since they'd first met. A part of him thought it was sad that the entire life of a human would be no more than the length of a good nap. Another part of him envied them their short lives and the sense of urgency that motivated them to seek life at its fullest.

"Oh. There you are," said Monq. "Thank you for coming. This won't take long." Monq rose and gestured toward the door. "Right this way."

"Can I see them?" Jean Etienne spoke very good English, but with a definite French accent.

"Who? Oh. The vampire?" Monq looked curious. "You can, of course, but why would you want to?"

"I will need to monitor developments closely. Please don't take offense, but there is the possibility that results could create a situation outside your ability to manage."

"In that case, I should be grateful that you're offering more than just blood."

"Yes. Well. I'd like to see what the, um, specimens look like, act like, before the initial infusion of my blood."

"I like a methodical approach, myself. Follow me."

Jean Etienne looked over the facilities as he walked behind Monq. He scanned every office and lab as they passed. Of course, Monq's staff mirrored the vampire's curiosity. Some of them had seen Jean Etienne because they'd been in residence for some years, but many had been hired or transferred in since the French vampire were a common sight around J.U.

Last stop on the research level was the cluster of enclosures that housed vampire of the infected variety unique to Loti Dimension.

When Jean Etienne saw Falcon, sitting on the side of a hospital bed pushed against the wall, staring at one of the cells, he silently turned to Monq for an explanation.

"The knight on the bed is Sir Kristoph Falcon. He was

friends with the vampire that is currently preoccupying his time and attention."

Jean Etienne followed Falcon's gaze and said, "A female? I thought the virus infects only males."

"It's a rare occurrence, but we have records of several such anomalies."

Looking back at Falcon, he said, "Why is he sitting there like a gargoyle?"

"I'm right here and I can hear, you know." To Monq, Falcon said, "Is that him?"

Monq ignored Falcon and spoke to Jean Etienne. "Falcon was too young to have seen you when you were here years ago. He was a student then. The short of it is that he's afraid we'll kill her if he leaves or looks away. He's refusing to give up his self-imposed post unless one of his close friends is watching her."

Jean Etienne looked from Falcon to the infected vampire.

"Her name is Genevieve. Genevieve Bonheur," said Falcon with the proper accent.

"French," said Jean Etienne.

"Yes," Monq confirmed. "She was transferred from the unit in Paris. Been with us for six years and had been promoted to head of Operations."

"I see." With more empathy than one would expect from a vampire, Jean Etienne said, "That must have been difficult for all of you. I'll start with this one."

"I'll need to sedate her."

Jean Etienne looked at Monq and then laughed out loud. "Why?"

"Well..." Monq spluttered, "so you won't be harmed, of course." After a second, Monq said, "I suppose that was a silly thing to say. You can't be harmed, can you?"

"Not by a faux vampire."

"What are you going to do?"

Jean Etienne looked at Monq like he was senile. "I'm going to give her blood. As we agreed."

"You mean...?" Monq's expression vacillated between astounded and horrified. "You're not going to let her..."

"Bite me? Yes. I am. What did you think? That I was going to allow you to fill little syringes? With immortal blood?" Jean Etienne looked genuinely entertained by Monq's naivete. "Indeed no. I was not, as you say, born yesterday."

"You think I would use your blood for nefarious purposes?"

"Perhaps not you. Perhaps someone who works for you. The prospect of living forever could cause ordinarily honest people to act out of the ordinary."

Monq scowled. "As much as I'd like to argue, I see your point. And I hadn't thought of that. So you're going to allow each of these four vampire to, ah..."

"Bite me. Yes. I am. And we're going to begin with her."

Monq looked dubious, but he was more beggar than chooser in that situation. "What do you need from us? The environment is sterile."

"It matters not. I'm not subject to mal effects of bacteria. Likewise, I'm not carrying anything with deleterious effects."

"What about your clothing?"

"By the time the subject's body might react to such things, she will have properties flowing through her veins that would render her immune."

Monq looked uncertain.

Falcon jumped down off the bed and stood in front of Monq. "You are *not* considering letting this… guy in there with her!"

"This 'guy', as you call him, is her only chance, Falcon. Are you so sleep-deprived you don't know that?"

He stood in front of the opening. "No. That's final."

"Falcon," Monq began, but Jean Etienne held up a hand to stop Monq from trying to reason.

Jean Etienne caught Falcon's eye and hypnotized him almost instantly. When Falcon went to sleep, Jean Etienne caught him and lifted him onto the bed as if his large muscled body weighed no more than a baby.

"Perhaps he needed a little sleep. Yes?" Monq simply stared at Jean Etienne. "Do not be concerned. He will awake feeling refreshed and…"

"Relaxed. I know. I've recited that line hundreds of times," said Monq as he looked at the vampire who used to be the J.U. Operations Manager. "You're sure this is the best way?"

"I will control the amount. Tiny increments. As agreed."

"Okay." He shrugged. "It's your…" Monq caught himself mid-sentence, deciding that it would be stupid to say *it's your funeral* to an immortal. "Whatever you say," he finished. "I'll let you in." Monq walked toward the control pad and looked back at the vampire, who was studying him with an amused expression. Monq dropped his hand. "I don't suppose you need me to let you in."

Jean Etienne began shaking his head on the outside of the enclosure and finished on the inside.

The vampire possessing the body of Genevieve Bonheur rushed him in a fury of fangs and pupils dilating to make the pale blue eyes look even more disturbing. But before she reached him, he held up his hand and froze her in place.

He switched from English to French and said quietly, as one would to calm a wild animal, "I will not hurt you, mademoiselle. Nor will I allow you to hurt anyone else. You will drink from me until I tell you to stop then you will return to your cot and sleep for a while. Do you understand?"

Apparently Jean Etienne was able to pierce through the guise of psychosis and reach cognitive function. She nodded her head slightly, though she looked confused by her own actions.

Jean Etienne opened his shirt, baring his hairless chest. He took Genevieve's hand in his and used the once-manicured nail on her index finger to open the vein in his neck.

"Drink," he said. She looked hungrily at the rivulet of blood. Jean Etienne gently pulled her face toward his neck. Her tongue flicked out and touched the scarlet liquid. After lapping eagerly for a few seconds, she bit down.

Jean Etienne knew she'd already taken more than he'd intended. "Stop." He felt her desire to resist, but her mind wasn't strong enough to overpower his will. "Stop." He pulled her away gently but firmly, and then said, "Sleep."

She turned, crawled onto the bed that was bolted to the wall, lay down as obediently as a sleepy child, and closed her eyes so that she looked peaceful as a picture in repose.

Jean Etienne appeared in the hallway again. "Next," he said.

Monq watched as Jean Etienne fed the other three vampire though he noted he allowed the males to drink only from his wrists and not his neck.

When all four had received their first "treatment", Jean Etienne's clothing looked like he'd been to a massacre.

"Do you have some spare clothing?" he asked Monq. I'll be staying until the subjects awaken to monitor the results of the first test.

"Of course. I'll be right back."

Monq stepped a few yards away and instructed one of his lab assistants to procure men's clothing in a size large. When he returned, he asked, "How long do you expect them to sleep?"

Jean Etienne lifted a shoulder. "Perhaps four, perhaps five hours. Impossible to say conclusively since this has not been done before. But I will be here."

"I see. What can I do to be hospitable and make you comfortable in the meantime?"

Jean Etienne pursed his lips. "TV?"

"We don't have a cable feed in this section of the building, but I can bring you a device with television programs and movies loaded."

Jean Etienne smiled. "That will be fine."

"Would you like anything to, um, eat or drink?"

Jean Etienne smiled. "Just a chair so that I can sit in the hall and keep an eye on the subjects."

"Of course."

When Monq's assistant arrived with soft khaki pants and a flannel shirt, men's large, he told the assistant to get maintenance to bring one of the cushy overstuffed club chairs down from the bar and put it in the hallway. The assistant turned around and left, mumbling something about the hallway turning into a lounge.

Chapter Eleven

Day Three – Psych Eval

"Yeah. Sao Paulo," Glen said between mouthfuls of prime rib, end cut, well done, a tiny bit charred on the outside. "But that wasn't nearly as bad as Marrakech." Glen blinked rapidly like he was surprised he'd said that. "This is confidential. Right?"

"Nothing has changed since last night and the night before, Sir Catch. What you say goes no further than these old ears. What is it that needs to be privileged about a reference to Morocco?"

Glen took in a breath that caused his chest to heave visibly and let it out. "It's just not like any other unit. Half the knights there are jumped up on something. On any given day you'll find a few tweaking, and if you don't think that's a recipe for disaster… A trained knight in that condition?"

Monq had been a professional at listening for so long he rarely had to school his features, but that revelation caused him to work at looking passively detached. He was shocked that such a thing could be going on in an installation of Black Swan, but would have bet The Order's bank that if Glen said it, it was true.

While Monq was trying to sort his thoughts, Glen continued, "I didn't know whether to be more afraid of the leeches or being accidentally shot or staked by another knight hallucinating. It's nothing like this." Glen waved to indicate Jefferson Unit. "It's the unwashed crotch of the world and people who are sent there by The Order act like they fit right in. They have whores coming in and out of the unit." He laughed and shook his head. "It's not even considered a security compromise."

Monq couldn't help looking a little unsettled as he reached for his wine. "Do you know how many posts you've been assigned to? Altogether?"

Glen cocked his head slightly, thinking. "I'd have to make a list."

"I see. Tell me, why did you choose to be a floater?"

Glen stopped eating long enough to gape at Monq. "Choose?" The bitterness in his chuckle was unmistakable. "You're kidding, right? Who would choose that?"

"I looked at your file. You've had eleven assignments since your induction. Hardly time to put your full weight down in any one place." Glen continued eating, pretending to be blasé about what Monq was saying. "What about girlfriends?"

Glen shook his head. "Girls? Yes. Girlfriends. No."

"Didn't you used to be close to the Storm girl?"

Glen stopped chewing and, judging from the look on his face, Monq perceived that he'd hit a nerve.

"Long time ago, doc."

"Hmmm. And no family, you say?"

"Again. You read my file. You know there's no family."

"Tell me how you feel about that."

"I don't feel anything about that. There's nothing to feel. Some people have families. Some don't." When Monq appeared to be waiting for Glen to continue, he took a sip of wine and added, "I was put in foster care before I was old enough to have any other memories. I thought there was something wrong with me until I was recruited by Black Swan." He shrugged. "You know, because I can make sounds that aren't completely, ah, human. That's when I learned that there's some werewolf mixed in. I was told likely one quarter. That would be one of four grandparents, none of which ever turned up asking about me. To my knowledge."

"Did you try to find your parents?"

"No."

"You weren't curious?" Monq read the hesitation on Glen's face. "Oh. It's not that you weren't curious. You were afraid to learn that they had never regretted giving you up."

Glen nodded, looking like the idea had haunted him most of his life.

"Tell me something. If you could have anything from life, what would it be?"

Glen smirked, but didn't hesitate. "A do-over. And don't ask me what that means because it's personal and I'm not going to..."

Before he finished the sentence, the screaming began.

"What the...?" Monq was out the door surprisingly quickly for someone his age.

The sound was coming from the part of the labs where vampire specimens were contained. Glen was right behind Monq. When they reached the enclosures, the air was filled with a macabre duet of screams coming from two of the male vampire. The headless corpse of the third was lying on the floor of his cell.

Monq looked at Falcon, who'd been awakened from his vampire-induced coma. He looked decidedly rattled.

"What happened?" Monq asked him.

"The biter started screaming and throwing himself against the walls." Falcon looked at the remaining two males. "Like those two are doing now. That fucking Frenchy disappeared, then reappeared inside the cell. He ripped the guy's head off and vanished with it."

Just as Falcon finished relaying his eye witness report, Jean Etienne appeared in the cell of one of the two other vampire. As Falcon had reported, Jean Etienne forcibly removed the head of the specimen who seemed desperate to get out of his skin and vanished with the head while the rest of the corpse slumped to the ground. Monq, Catch, and Falcon watched in morbid fascination, meaning that they wouldn't have been able to look away no matter how hard they might have tried, as the process was repeated.

Jean Etienne reappeared in the hallway next to them. When the immortal looked at Genevieve, all eyes followed his gaze. The psychotic expression she'd worn since she'd awakened in the lab had been replaced by an expressive intelligence that looked remarkably like that of the Operations Manager prior to infection.

They stared at her for a few seconds before Jean

Etienne said to Monq. "The only conclusion I can offer up to this point is that the experiment was largely unsuccessful." Glen was thinking that was the understatement of the century. "Whether or not this is something worth pursuing seems doubtful. However..."

Jean Etienne looked down at his clothing, soaked in blood. "I'd like a shower and more clothes. Then I will look in on the subject who appears lucid."

Monq couldn't recall having ever, before in his life, been speechless. He attempted to clear his throat, but failed at even that, making a sound that was part gargle and part choking. With a concentrated effort, he composed himself enough to say, "You can use the shower in my quarters. I'll send for more clothes." Monq pointed at one of the assistants who'd been drawn to the scene because of the ruckus. "Marissa, please show our guest the way." To one of the white coats standing by, he said, "Bertron, please bring another change of clothes. What you brought before will do. You can leave them outside the door to my private bath."

Bertron nodded and left as quickly and quietly as a trained butler.

Falcon hadn't looked away from Genevieve since he'd awakened. When Jean Etienne was gone, he said, "She's different. You can see she looks like herself. I want to talk to her."

"Let's let Jean Etienne evaluate her condition first."

"Why? It's not like he *knows* her."

"Just indulge me. Shall I review our agreement? You can stay so long as you don't interfere."

Looking at the scene of carnage that had become of three-quarters of that part of the lab, Glen said to Monq, "You're not going to be high on the maintenance crew's popularity chart. I'm thinking we're done for tonight."

As he walked away, Monq croaked, "Dinner tomorrow night at seven."

Glen paused, looked back over his shoulder and shook his head. "Only at Jefferson Unit."

WHEN JEAN ETIENNE returned looking clean, wearing jeans and a dark navy Henley, he walked toward the enclosure where Genevieve was being held. He arrived just as she had risen from the cot and approached the glass wall separating her from Monq and Falcon. She no longer looked rabid. More than anything she seemed confused. She had just opened her mouth to say something when Jean Etienne's approach drew her attention.

His pace didn't slow when he reached the barrier between the hallway and the cell. He more or less blinked out and then was on the other side.

Genevieve did not appear alarmed. Personnel who are easily alarmed are not candidates for being hired by Black Swan.

"What am I doing here?" she asked Jean Etienne in English.

He answered in French, which was understood by both Monq and Falcon, because he thought using her native language would help put her at ease.

"Unfortunately you were infected by the vampire virus," he said.

She took a step back as the recognition of that truth sprang into her consciousness. She brought a hand to her mouth as her eyes filled with tears almost instantly.

Falcon said to Monq, "He shouldn't be the one talking to her. She needs the familiarity of somebody she knows."

"Quiet," Monq said without looking at Falcon. "Let him handle it. We could be looking at a miracle and, as a scientist, I don't bandy that word about indiscriminately."

Falcon chuffed.

"I remember," Genevieve practically whispered as big tears rolled down her face. "So that means that I..." Her eyes jerked to Monq, whom she could see looking on from the other side of the glass, then moved to Falcon and lingered there for a few beats.

"You exhibited all the symptoms. Yes," Jean Etienne continued.

"Then how...?" She looked down at the scrubs she'd been dressed in after having been brought into the lab, then ran her hands over her body as if she was checking for wounds. "How is it that I feel... all right?"

Before Jean Etienne could answer she took in a big gulp of air. "I didn't hurt anyone, did I? Please tell me I didn't hurt anyone."

"What's important for the moment is how *you* are feeling. Do you know who I am?" She shook her head. "We've never met. I'm Jean Etienne. I'm a vampire. A, ah, real one. I've been working with Black Swan to find a cure for this virus that plagues your dimension."

Genevieve was clearly wrestling with a desire to restore her dignity. "Yes. I know about you."

While it was clear that Jean Etienne was studying her current state, he was also deftly managing a difficult situation with kindness, the sort of kindness that isn't transmitted by words, but by expression and intonation.

She looked over at Monq and Falcon again before returning her attention to Jean Etienne.

"You have ingested some of my blood. It appears that you've been restored to yourself. Perhaps temporarily. Perhaps permanently. It's too early to know. That's why we must carefully observe you for changes, however small, in the coming hours and days."

"I see," she said, making every effort not to sound plaintive. "No. I don't see really. When you say I'm restored to myself, you mean I'm not going to want… blood. Is that what you mean?"

"No. I mean your personality has been restored. But I don't want to be dishonest. More than likely your biology has been permanently changed."

Genevieve stared at Jean Etienne as if he were a devil come to take her soul to the nether realms. "You mean the next time I'm hungry it will be for…" She couldn't quite manage to say the word out loud.

"For blood. Yes." She looked so distraught and horrified that Jean Etienne wanted to say something to soothe her. "It isn't bad, you know."

"Oh, gods." Genevieve clutched at her stomach and all but stumbled back to sit on the cot.

Seeing that his effort had not had the desired effect, Jean Etienne looked at Monq as if for help.

"We do not know for certain what you will want or

when you will want it. This is new to all of us. You're the first person ever to be exposed to the virus and drink immortal blood."

Incredulity had replaced disgust when she looked up at him. "I'm an experiment."

"Well…"

"I am! An experiment!"

Jean Etienne looked at Monq. "Well…"

"What's the goal of the experiment?"

Jean Etienne scowled. "I think perhaps the goal has changed?" He looked at Monq. "Because the result was unexpected."

"Unexpected in what way?" Jean Etienne hesitated. "TELL ME!"

"There were four of you when the experiment began. The other three had to be…" he glanced at Monq again, "euthanized."

"Euthanized?" She looked even more horrified.

Jean Etienne sat down at the other end of the cot. "This is a shock for you. Yes?"

In English, she said, "You think?" She then reverted to French. "What is the goal of this experiment now?"

Jean Etienne looked at her. "The goal is to keep you alive."

"So that I can stay in here for the rest of my life and be a lab rat? No thanks."

"What do you mean. 'no thanks'?"

"I mean no. I do not accept this option. Just '*euthanize*' me now."

"I'm certain those are not the only two options."

"Really? What's the third?"

Jean Etienne looked at Monq, who had no answer for that. "We'll figure something out."

Genevieve scooted to the rear of the cot so that she was sitting with her back to the wall. "Why were the others euthanized?" she asked quietly.

"They were also given a small amount of my blood. We had hoped there might be properties that would create a curative effect."

"What happened?"

"They were not able to tolerate it."

"But I did."

Jean Etienne nodded. "Yes. So far."

"And why do you think that is?"

"I have no conclusive answer."

"Fine. Speculate."

"You know that human females rarely survive exposure to the vampire virus?"

"I'd never thought much about it."

"It's quite rare. I imagine that whatever enabled your system to integrate the virus and survive has also enabled you to benefit from this experiment."

"Benefit," she repeated to no one in particular. She looked out toward the hallway beyond her glass partition. "Why is there a hospital bed in the hallway?"

"The young hunter refused to leave. He was afraid you'd be harmed. He believes he's looking after you. Protecting you. So they brought him a bed."

"Oh, gods," she said for the second time and brought her knees up as if to shelter her body from more information.

"I need to ask you a few questions."

"Go ahead," she said quietly.

"What are you feeling right now? Do you feel hot or cold?" She shook her head. "Hungry or thirsty?" She shook her head. "Do you need to relieve yourself?" She looked around the room and saw that there was no toilet facility with the possible exception of a drain in the middle of the floor. "I suppose it's a good thing I don't."

He nodded and continued. "Do you feel ill at ease?"

She glared at him. "I'm a prisoner in an experiment that can't end well for me. It means I'm either dead or worse. OF COURSE I'M ILL AT EASE." He held up his hands. "Idiot," she muttered.

At that Jean Etienne had the thought that she had probably been a magnificent woman. He would have smiled except for the fact that he knew she'd think it sadistic, given the circumstances.

"So what's next?"

"We wait."

"That's it?" she asked.

"Yes."

"So. You're going to wait in here? With me?"

"Would you rather I wait outside?"

"I don't care what you do."

"In that case I'll wait in here."

"Whatever."

"All things considered, you are handling this very well. It can't be easy to go shopping then wake up in a lab."

"Feeling sorry for me?"

"Yes," he said honestly.

She sighed. "Well, stop it or I'll start feeling sorry for myself."

"You don't feel sorry for yourself?"

"If I do, it's none of your business."

"Are you sleepy?"

"No. I'm not sleepy. Look. Let me make this easier for both of us. I don't feel anything except sad. Physically I feel disturbingly good."

"Why do you say disturbingly?"

"Because I've just found out that I'm a vampire. My days for feeling okay are over."

"Feeling good is a natural state of being for vampire. I mean real vampire, like myself."

"As opposed to the fake vampire that my employer is sworn to hunt down and kill?"

"Yes. As opposed to that."

"Look. If you're going to hang around, why don't you think of something else to talk about? The least you could do is try to distract me."

"Yes. I could do that. I have movies on a... thing."

After a pause of a few seconds, Genevieve said in a tone of casual conversation, "So. You're immortal?"

Jean Etienne turned toward her and gave her a grin that was blinding in its beauty. "That has yet to be established. What we do know is that I've been around for longer than the oldest history you've studied. And I'm still here."

Falcon grabbed Monq by the shoulder of his lab coat. "He's flirting with her!" he hissed. Whereas Falcon had always cherished Genevieve's French accent and thought it was unbelievably sexy and adorable, he found the same accent supremely irritating on Jean Etienne.

"It would… seem that way," said Monq.

Falcon narrowed his eyes. "And what's the reason why *I* can't talk to her now?"

Monq gave Falcon's hand holding a fistful of clothing a pointed look. "I know you care about her, but there are bigger things at stake. If you want to stay and observe, you can so long as you do not interfere in *any* way. Though I think it would be best for you to take a break. Go upstairs. Have dinner with your friends. Have a drink with your friends. Shoot some pool. Play video games. Do something besides sitting here in this hallway staring at the vampire. You can see that she's not in danger. So there's no reason for you to feel like you need to be here every second."

Falcon looked at Genevieve carrying on a conversation with Jean Etienne. "She's not in danger? How do you know that?"

Monq softened his tone and expression. "We may not have gotten the result we were hoping for. But it's not all bad either. A few hours ago she was lost, with no hope of ever being Mademoiselle Bonheur again. Now she is carrying on a conversation as easily as if she was hosting a dinner party. Well, except for the anxiety over what's going to happen next."

Falcon stared at Monq for a few beats before saying, "Okay. At least tell me this. What are the markers you're looking for that would give me yes for an answer?"

"Regarding talking to the subject?"

“Don’t call her that.”

Monq pursed his lips. “Twenty-four hours without incident.”

Falcon looked at his watch. “All right. I’m going to go to my place. Check email. Take a jacuzzi. Have dinner with my team. Then I’ll be back. You’d better not let Blood Pudding get out of line with her.”

“Blood Pudding? Oh. I get it. Very funny. No. No one will be *‘getting out of line’* with her.”

Chapter Twelve

Day Four – Psych Eval

"You called?" Elora knocked on the door to Monq's office.

"Yes, my dear. Come in and sit down. Oh my," he said, looking at the impossibility of her protruding abdomen. "What can I get you?"

"Hot chocolate."

"Of course. I knew that."

"Should have," she said as she more or less fell backward into the burgundy velvet club chair. "I hope you have a forklift down here because it might take that to get me back up."

Monq ordered cocoa for Elora, tea for himself, and put the house phone back in its cradle. "Don't worry. We'll think of something." He sat down in the matching chair facing hers next to the fire video.

"If this is about you wanting to deliver the babies, I already told you no five times and no means no, doc."

"It's not about that. Although…"

"No."

He sighed. "It's about Glen. Have you seen him since he's been back?"

"I had to hear it from my husband. Strange he hasn't called. We used to be close."

"That's what I thought. And speaking of close, wasn't he dating the Storm girl at one time?"

"Yes." She looked Monq over. "Not enough to do down here? You need some juicy gossip? 'Cause there's lots that's juicier *and* more recent."

Before he'd thought about what was coming out of his mouth, he'd said, "Like what?" Elora parted her lips to answer, but he put his hand up to stop her. "Never mind. Stop confusing the issue."

"How can I be confusing the issue? I don't know what the issue is."

"Glen."

"What about him?"

"Just like you said. You don't find it noteworthy that he didn't let you know he's back at Jefferson Unit?"

Elora grew serious and sat up as straight as twins pressing into thighs would allow. "Is something wrong with Glen?"

"Elora, this is *not* gossip. Juicy or otherwise."

"I understand. What's wrong?"

"He's very different from the boy you knew and not in a good way. We need to get to the bottom of what's happened. That's why I'm asking about the Storm girl."

"Rosie."

"Yes. Rosie."

"You know she was named Elora Rose, after a grand-mother and me."

"I might have heard that. I don't remember. Anyway

I'd like to have a conversation with her."

"What about? Listen, Monq, you'd better go easy on her. I don't know all the details about what she's been through, but she's changed, too. She's… I don't know… sad. Or sadder."

"I'm a professional, Mrs. Hawking."

She narrowed her eyes. "That's no way to get a favor. It's Lady Laiken. Not Mrs. Hawking. And you know it!"

Monq waved his hand dismissively as he always did when the subject of her name arose. "Could you arrange a meeting? Ask her to have breakfast with me tomorrow morning?"

"I'll ask, but I'm not going to pressure her."

"Of course not. Just tell her that her insights might be helpful."

"She's out on the Courtpark throwing frisbee for my dog right now. Come help me up."

"Your cocoa isn't here yet."

"Some other time. Help me out of this chair."

Monq walked to the door and called two assistants. "Help the lady out of the chair, would you please?"

In the end, Elora pretty much got herself up. It seemed her weight was beyond the capacity of research assistants.

She got off the elevator at the Hub and began to waddle toward the Solarium. She hadn't seen Glen in over five years and he'd changed a lot physically, but she still knew that the man facing away, looking out onto the Courtpark through the Solarium windows was her former dogwalker. He was watching Rosie and Blackie out on the field. He felt Elora's approach even before she came into his peripheral vision, but didn't react visibly.

"I remember when you used to be the one throwing frisbee for Blackie."

Glen simply sighed. He didn't turn to face her, but glanced at her out of the corner of his eye. "So. Got more on the way?"

Elora's hand automatically went to her protruding belly. "What makes you think that? Oh, this? Had a burrito for lunch. This is just gas." Glen's mouth turned up. "Ha! Got you to smile." Her gaze wandered back to the field. "You should go say hello to Blackie. He'd love it."

Glen turned away. "Some other time. Good to see you, Lady Laiken."

"Same here, Sir Catch," she said as he kept walking.

Glen felt bad about giving Elora the brush off. She'd always been wonderful to him. She was the one who took him along to the Edinburgh unit where he'd had the time of his life discussing everything from dimensional ladder theory to the most effective way to move ghosts along on their journey. Not to mention fae girls.

The problem was that he knew Elora well enough to know that, if he encouraged interaction, it would only be a short time before she'd start asking questions he didn't want to answer. Or couldn't answer. Questions like, what's wrong with you?

He'd changed and didn't want the Lady Laiken, whom he had admired on so many levels, to know that it wasn't for the better. Not that she didn't already know that, given the way he was behaving.

Rosie had changed, too. He could tell, even from a

distance, that she moved differently. He wondered what she'd been doing for the past five years and hated himself for wondering. It was a moot point. Because he never intended to ask or to stand around listening while somebody told him.

MONQ MADE A point of checking on Genevieve and Jean Etienne every hour or so. He didn't announce his arrival. Just observed and quietly eavesdropped on the conversation for a few minutes at a time.

"So you never sleep?" She was asking.

"Not for the past few hundred years. Young ones sleep. I don't know why."

"You can procreate."

"Oh yes. Happily."

"So vampire childbirth isn't painful?"

He cocked his head. "I don't know. I suppose it could be. I wasn't thinking in those terms."

"Of course not. Like most men you were only thinking in terms of the pleasurable friction that precedes the procreation."

"Guilty." Once again he gave her the smile that Monq hadn't known Jean Etienne possessed.

Monq had never seen the immortal vampire look anything other than pissed. Perpetually pissed in perpetuity. When he chuckled at that thought, Genevieve and Jean Etienne looked up. "How's it going?"

"All is well," said Jean Etienne.

"Need anything?"

Jean Etienne looked at Genevieve. "Do you need anything?"

"The key code?" she asked.

Jean Etienne said, "We'll let you know."

"When you said the other, ah, experiments didn't tolerate your blood, what happened to them?"

"They became supermanic."

She took in a deep breath. "So. Is that what we're waiting for? To see if I go nuts?"

"Partly."

"What's the other part?"

"We need to know if the results we're seeing will last and, if so, what you may need in the way of," he paused, "maintenance."

"Blood."

"Yes."

"What's the best case scenario?"

"I'm not a writer of fiction."

"That's a ridiculous answer, unworthy of someone who is sooooooo old."

His lips twitched. "The best case scenario is that the vampire virus has been completely cleansed from your system."

"In which case I will be human again. I can go back to work and never set foot outside Jefferson Unit again as long as I live."

Jean Etienne frowned. "That would not be a best case. That would be a tragedy. It is a very big world and humans have precious little time in which to experience it."

"Blah. Blah Blah."

"What does that mean?"

"It means immortals shouldn't spout off about what humans should and shouldn't do or feel."

"Very well."

"Unbelievably, you are pouting." She laughed out loud. "I'm the one whose entire life is in crisis here, in the balance really, and *you're* going to pout because I said it's not your place to lecture on what I should do with my remaining time if I became a real girl again."

"Let's change the subject."

"Go ahead."

"You're being difficult."

"Better than being an ass's rump."

"You're taking your predicament out on me. I'm not the one who bit you, mademoiselle."

Jean Etienne was sorry he'd said it as soon as tears sprang to Genevieve's eyes.

"I know you're not. Sorry. I'm not in a good place."

"Of course you're not. How could you be? I'm an insensitive lout."

"No. You've been kind to keep me company while we're waiting to learn my fate. How long will that take, by the way?"

"We're explorers. We have no idea what will or will not be next. We simply have to live through it one minute at a time."

"You mean I simply have to live through it one minute at a time."

"No. I meant *we*." Genevieve looked at Jean Etienne with a mixture of surprise and gratitude. "I will see this through no matter what comes next. I will not leave you."

Jean Etienne looked away. He hadn't thought through making such an open-ended commitment, wasn't prepared for the ramifications, and was quite surprised at himself. It had just sort of popped out, but once it was spoken, he couldn't say he regretted it. The girl was a multilayered puzzle of contradictions, need, orneriness, and delight.

Genevieve swiped at the tears on her face, hating that she looked so vulnerable. "Thank you," she said.

Her eyes hadn't returned to the warm brown they had been before the infection, but they were no longer the pale ice blue of virus-carriers. For the time being, their color had resolved to an exotic caramel. Jean Etienne could also see that properties in his blood had caused a metamorphosis in her appearance. She was gradually beginning to exhibit the flawlessness of immortals. Her skin was taking on the poreless and even look of youthful perfection. Her flesh and muscle were taking on tone similar to that of a twenty-year-old.

Jean Etienne would say that, by looks alone, it would be hard to tell that she was not an immortal.

FALCON RETURNED TO the hospital bed in the hallway late that night. He'd thought about sleeping in his own bed, but the pull to keep watch over Genevieve was stronger. He was sitting there, watching Genevieve and Jean Etienne when Wakey showed up.

Wakey had been coming three or four times a day to relieve Falcon. Sometimes he'd stayed to talk about everything and nothing. Just to keep his friend company.

On that occasion, neither said anything. They sat without speaking, listening to the conversation taking place in the cell.

"Do you have family?" she asked Jean Etienne.

"No. I'm one of the originals."

"I don't know what that means."

"It means I didn't come into the world the usual way. I was created as I am."

"Oh." Her mind groped about for what she might say in response to that and came up with nothing. "But you said you make families. Do you have a wife?"

He smiled. "We do *make* families, but I've not found someone who makes me feel inclined to be half of a pair."

She nodded. "Me either."

Falcon's mouth pressed together as he thought about the fact that it was hard to find the right someone when you wouldn't even accept a dinner invitation.

"Do you have a, what do you call it?"

"Boyfriend?"

"Yes. That's it. Do you have a boyfriend?"

"No. I did once. It didn't work out. So I decided to concentrate on my career here."

"And you were good at what you do?"

She shrugged. "I like to think so. They promoted me when my boss retired. I didn't really have a chance to implement all the changes I'd planned." She said it sadly.

"If you weren't going to spend your life working for The Order, and you could do anything, what would you want to do?"

"If I could do anything?"

"Yes."

"I'd like to be a singer in a cabaret."

"Can you sing?"

"No," she shook her head and laughed.

He laughed with her.

Wakey whispered to Falcon. "I'm going. Get some sleep."

Falcon nodded.

Chapter Thirteen

Day Five – Psych Eval

Elora ushered Rosie to Monq's corner table in the Mess at nine-thirty. Things were quiet at that time. Students and instructors had already eaten and begun their day. Knights weren't up yet.

"Thelonius Monq, this is Elora Rose Storm." Rosie beamed at Elora as she always did when Elora insisted on announcing her birth certificate name. "Otherwise known as Rosie."

Monq had risen to greet them. "How do you do?" he asked Rosie who took his hand. "Please join us," he said to Elora.

"Okay," she answered.

Monq and Rosie sat facing each other with Elora in between.

"I understand you're recently back from travels," he said to Rosie.

"Yes. That's true. Not much has changed," she said in an effort at pleasantries.

"Well, yes and no. The surroundings don't change much, but people do. That's actually why I asked you to breakfast."

"Oh?"

The waitperson appeared. "What can I get you?" he asked cheerfully.

"Bacon, lettuce, and tomato sandwich on wheat toast," said Rosie. "And a fruit cup, extra red grapes."

"Plain bagel with peanut butter on the side and a cranberry juice," said Elora.

"Ooh," said Rosie. "I'll have cranberry juice, too."

The man looked at Monq. "I'll have that skillet thing you make, but substitute broccoli for the asparagus spear tips, use chopped chicken breast instead of beef, and bearnaise instead of Hollandaise. Also, cut the potatoes in half and poach the eggs for two and a half minutes. I'll have that twenty-five percent Kona blend coffee with the Bailey's hazelnut creamer and two pieces of rye toasted on one side only. Butter on the side. Not on the toast."

The server took it in stride as if that was not an unusual breakfast request for Monq. "Juice?" he asked.

"Yes. Thank you, Ronald. Grapefruit if you please. But put four tablespoons of sugar in it and shake well."

"Of course."

Rosie gave Elora a what-have-you-gotten-me-into look, which inspired a chuckle.

"Something funny?" Monq asked. "What did I miss?"

"If you don't think your breakfast order was funny, you're missing a check in with reality."

"Over the top?" he asked.

"Completely," she said.

"I'll work on it."

"Or just save yourself the embarrassment of being eccentric. Stay in and make your own."

"First, I'm not embarrassed and, second, why would I do for myself what I can have others do for me?" He turned to Rosie. "So, may I call you Rosie?"

"Yes," she answered.

"Good. Call me Monq."

"All right."

After an acceptable period of small talk, Monq dived into the reason for the breakfast meeting. "I understand you've been away for about five years."

"That's right."

"Coincidentally, Glendennon Catch has been away for about that same length of time. I understand you know him?"

Rosie took on a posture that looked slightly guarded. "*Knew* him," she clarified.

"So you're not still friends."

"It seems that would be safe to say."

"I see. That's a shame. Just between the two of us," he looked at Elora, "or I guess I should say the three of us, I wonder if you could help me with some background on Sir Catch."

"Why?"

"Well, this is a sensitive and tricky business. I have ethical and professional boundaries in play here."

"Is there something wrong with Glen?" Rosie asked, looking more than casually concerned.

"Nothing serious. I believe he may be experiencing a form of post traumatic stress."

"That doesn't sound *not* serious to me."

"I believe a few minor adjustments will make all the difference. Right now he seems to be closed off to the people who care about him. At the same time his anger is volatile, an outward expression of an inner conflict."

Rosie scowled. "What happened?"

"Getting to the bottom of that. Slowly. You can help," he looked between the two of them, "both of you, by giving me some insight as to who he was before he became active duty."

"Just ask what you want to know," said Elora.

"You knew him first, right?" Monq asked her.

Elora looked at Rosie. "Yes. I knew him for some time before Rosie was born."

"Give me something I wouldn't find in his file. Fill in between the lines, if you will."

"My impressions?" Elora asked.

"Exactly," Monq replied, pleased that she seemed to have caught the subtext of what he was after.

"Well, he was one of my trainees. He hit it off with my dog and began dogsitting for me. When Ram and I were sent to Edinburgh on temporary assignment, right after the wedding, I took Glen with me to take care of Blackie when I couldn't be around." She chuckled. "Well, he ended up making quite an impression at Headquarters. Stood all those dusty old professor-types on their ears." She looked at Monq. "He's one smart kid, you know. And by that I don't mean smart, I mean off-the-charts brilliant."

Monq nodded. "Go on."

"Well, he dated a lot, but no one in The Order. First,

he was too young and, second, as you know, work place entanglements are discouraged." Rosie snorted and looked at Elora's belly pointedly. Elora made little clockwise circular movements on her abdomen and smiled before she continued. "Not that the personnel wouldn't have jumped at the chance. I heard a girl in archives, who didn't know I was in the stacks, refer to him as a walking phallic symbol."

Monq giggled. "I can see that." Elora and Rosie both stopped and gave him a speculative look. "What? I'm not blind!"

"Hmmm. Well, I hated hearing him objectified in that way. I felt offended on his behalf."

"Because women are always objectifying your husband?" Rosie asked.

"They are?" Elora narrowed her eyes. "I'm taking names. Make a list."

"Hold on," said Monq. "If there's any psychoanalysis to be done at this breakfast, I'll be the one doing it."

Elora sighed. "Where's breakfast? I'm hungry."

"Eating for three? I see him coming this way now," said Monq.

They waited until after their orders had been set in front of them and Ronald had left.

"I'll tell you this though," Elora began. "Glen's mind was full of possibilites about what he might do with his life. He had so many talents… He could have done anything." She sighed while she spread peanut butter on her bagel. "And everything excited him. It was a joy to watch. But something happened right around the time

Helm was born. I'm not sure what it was, but all of a sudden Glen had decided he was going to be a knight and that was that. There was no more talk about options after that."

"Interesting," Monq said while he made sure the bite of skillet breakfast he was about to eat had sufficient bernaise sauce on it.

"What about you, Rosie?"

Rosie stopped eating like she'd been caught redhanded doing something wrong. "What about me?"

"What can you tell me about Sir Catch?"

She set her fork down and sat up. "Look. I'm not sure I feel comfortable giving Glen's shrink *insights* into my relationship with him. It feels like it might be a betrayal."

"Might you tell me something incriminating?"

"Incriminating? Well, no. Not *incriminating* per se. But personal."

"Loyalty is one of humanity's loftiest expressions of higher self, my dear. Admirable and commendable. Let me assure you that my motives are born entirely in the interest of restoring him to the person that people once described as affable and easygoing as well as sharp and quick. He lost his way. The Sovereign has asked me to help him find it. He's back here at Jefferson Unit because concerns were logged by the last three Sovereigns at his duty assignments."

Monq observed the line that formed between Rosie's brows and the fact that she might have paled a little. "Concerns?" she said. "That's impossible. Glen is the most solid, grounded person in the world."

Monq raised his chin as he studied Rosie. "By all reports, he was. At one time."

"Oh gods," she said.

"It seems to me that you still care about him. I'm happy to see that he still has people on his side. He's probably going to need that."

Rosie looked at the napkin in her lap for a minute or so before making a decision to share.

"My parents say that 'Glen' was the first word I spoke." She looked up and smiled just a little. "I have a memory of wiggling, trying to get my mother to put me down so that I could go to Glen. I think I idolized him a little bit and loved him a lot. I don't know why. It was like I was born thinking he was the best thing that ever happened to two-legged creatures. I grew up really fast. Did you know that?"

Monq glanced at Elora. "I've heard that."

"Well, after I hit puberty, the fact that Glen was dating girls was driving me insane. It was confusing to me because I was sure I was supposed to be *the* girl and he just thought of me as the kid he was babysitting. Eventually my mother and her friend," her eyes flicked to Elora, "invited the two of us to have dinner with them. They'd cooked up a sort of matchmaking thing.

"Well, it worked. That night Glen and I were officially dating. I think I was about a year old and telling him we were exclusive or he was in big trouble. Once he gave in to the idea of a romantic relationship with me, he was okay with the exclusivity. As it turned out, he liked me a lot, too."

Monq and Elora watched a deep blush creep up Rosie's neck and color her face. She didn't share what she was thinking, but they could guess it was outside the parameters of what Monq needed to know.

"I was so proud of him when he became temporary Sovereign. Then I panicked when he was inducted. I told him that he wouldn't accept an active duty position, as a knight, if he loved me. I told him he couldn't have that particular job and me and I gave him a deadline to choose."

Elora frowned. "I never knew this. Litha didn't tell me."

Rosie raised her head. "She was probably ashamed of me. She should have been. I wasn't expressing love for Glen. What I was expressing was my own selfishness. I was way too inexperienced with life to understand love."

Monq and Elora remained quiet when she stopped talking, absorbing the implications of what had been said. At length Monq said, "So he didn't acquiesce and you…"

"Disappeared. Just like I said I would. I didn't even tell my parents where I'd gone." Elora looked away. "Now I understand that it was cruel to do that to him. It's the biggest regret of my life. So far."

"Thank you, Rosie," Monq said. "This has been more helpful than you know." Monq looked at the face of his phone. "I'm needed in the lab. Rosie, I have another couple of questions. Could we pick this up again tonight over dinner? I need to stay close by the experiment underway, but if you would be so kind as to join me in my offices?"

Rosie glanced at Elora. "Uh, sure. I guess."

"Excellent. Seven o'clock."

MONQ HAD INVENTED a reason to leave breakfast. There had been no message, urgent or otherwise. But something about Glen's case had been niggling at him and he knew what it was. When he reached his office, he closed the door and connected to the Black Swan archives, recently made available via a satellite that The Order owned and controlled.

He typed in the search term 'floaters' and began reading. By lunch time he was satisfied that he'd found a crack in Black Swan procedure that, in the case of Glendennon Catch, had become more like a black hole than a crack.

Around three, Monq strolled into Rev's office without an appointment. The admin began to rise, but Monq stayed him with a raised hand. "Don't bother to get up. I'll see myself in."

"But, sir…"

Rev's attention jerked toward the door when it opened without a knock because, first, that wasn't acceptable, second, everyone knew that, and, third, it simply didn't happen because of the first two things.

"Sovereign," said Monq, "we need to talk." Monq closed the door behind him and sat down in the chair in front of the massive desk that was as imposing as the personality who sat behind it.

Rev looked at his screen. "I don't see you listed on my schedule."

"I didn't see Glendennon Catch listed on my schedule

when you *insisted* I take that on."

"Is this about Catch?" Rev scowled.

"The immediacy is certainly about Sir Catch although there is a larger issue to be taken under serious consideration."

Rev looked at his watch. "Five minutes."

"That will do for a start. What do you know about floaters?"

"I don't have time for games."

"All right. I assume you know that they're temps who fill team vacancies and are then reassigned to do the same elsewhere when the vacancy is filled."

"Four minutes," said Rev.

"I read Sol's file today."

"Sol's file?"

Monq nodded. "Well. The part of his service that was spent as an active duty knight. He was assigned a partner right out of training, Miles Copper. Spent eight years with that same partner. Both survived. Copper retired to a chicken ranch, if I recall. Wanted to raise a family in Nevada. Sol became a career Swan."

"Point?"

"Knights with permanent partners form deep bonds with each other. They rely on each other for backup, of course. But experiencing near-constant combat stress, they rely on each other for companionship and emotional support as well. They know they can count on each other and many report that they wouldn't hesitate to die for their partners."

"You're not telling me anything I don't already know."

"What if, instead of having one partner for eight years, Sol had been assigned to a part of the world where he'd never been, to be temporary partner to a knight who wasn't completely over the loss of his own partner and was resentful toward Sol for taking the place of the departed. What if Sol never stayed in any one place long enough to make real friends, form real attachments, or even feel like he could count on his teammates."

Monq had Rev's complete attention and he was beginning to look disturbed by what he was hearing.

"Did you know that the longest any one knight has ever served as a floater, before Glen, is two years?" Rev shook his head. "Well, it's a fact. That's as long as they can take it. You know how long Glen lasted?"

Rev cleared his throat. "Five years."

"That's right. From what I gather, it's indicative of a dedication to The Order and a personal strength of will that is extraordinary, even for a knight. He deserves to be decorated for that service, which has left him so broken psychologically. It seems his own strength of character has been his undoing. Other knights quit before they were drawn into a psychological quagmire that sucked them under."

He definitely had Rev's full attention. "Furthermore, The Order is going to have to find another way to handle temporary vacancies. We're destroying good knights. Stress without a shared bond and the belief that you're not in it alone creates too much strain on the personality, like a rubber band pulled until it breaks."

"I didn't know."

"Now you do."

Rev sat back and sighed. "What do you need from me?"

"For starters, make sure that when, if, I can put the kid back together again, he gets a permanent job in a place where there are people who care about him."

Rev sucked in a big breath and nodded. "Okay."

"And make sure this doesn't happen to any more knights. They're not disposable."

Monq got up and left without another word leaving Rev to mourn the loss of potential and think about the knights who could have been utilized so much better if they'd been paying more attention.

ROSIE HAD AGREED to meet her mother for tea. Litha was working in Edinburgh that day, but it was less trouble for Rosie to travel from New Jersey to Scotia than it would be for most people to get in their cars and drive for five minutes. Because of the time difference, tea in Edinburgh was an hour after breakfast at Jefferson Unit. Rosie wasn't especially hungry, but she couldn't turn down half a scone with clotted cream.

Litha had walked down to the Balmoral Hotel and was waiting in the lobby. There was really nothing more that she wanted in the world than time with her daughter. So when she saw Rosie outside the front door, she beamed like it was Yule morning.

The doorman had jumped and given up a little squeak when she suddenly appeared next to him. "Sorry," he said. "I do no' know why, but I did no' see you there."

She smiled politely. “Snuck up on you.”

“Aye. Ye did,” he said as he opened the door for her with an embarrassed smile.

Rosie put on her best face for Litha. She crossed the rich carpet to receive a big hug and bigger kiss on the cheek complete with an, “Mmmmmmwhah.” There’s nothing in the universe more satisfying than maternal adoration.

After they’d been seated in high back chairs in the Palm Court, Litha said, “I’m conflicted. It’s so wonderful to have you close after so long apart. Your father is beyond thrilled to have you home again, but it gives me no pleasure to see you sad.”

Rosie smiled brightly. “What makes you think I’m sad?”

“It’s a good act and I give you points for effort, but I’m your mother.”

“What does that mean?”

“You’ll see. Someday.”

“Well, that’s not helping communication *today*.”

“This is the important thing. What would make you happy, my darling? No. Wait. Let me rephrase that question. If you could have anything from life, what would it be?”

“I know I’ve been gone too long if our conversation has been reduced to party games.”

“It’s no game. It’s a legitimate question and one that everyone alive should be asking themselves on a regular basis.”

“What if I said I wanted to play professional football

and be a defensive lineman?"

Litha gave that laugh that Rosie loved, the one that started deep in her mother's chest and sounded like her whole body was committed to the act. "You don't want to play football. Although, if you did, I'd be very worried for players on the opposing team."

Rosie couldn't help but smile. "Well, you're right. I don't." The waiter poured tea. "Want to bang heads with monsters whose necks are thicker than their waists, that is."

All the training in the universe couldn't have kept the waiter's eyes from flicking toward Rosie after that statement. Rosie noticed, even though it was just a millisecond and said, "Care to join us?"

"Rosie!"

"Sorry, miss," said the waiter as his face turned scarlet.

When he was gone, Litha said, "Rosie, what has gotten into you? You weren't raised to be rude."

"No. But when I worked at a, um, tavern, I learned that wait staff are supposed to be deaf and blind to conversation when it's not directed at them."

"Not to take anything away from that policy, but that's a bad excuse."

"You're right. Do you want me to apologize to him?"

"Do what you think is right."

"Okay."

"So back to my question. What you'd want from life if it could be anything?"

"You're not going to let that go, huh?"

"Not a chance."

Rosie looked around at the lavish setting steeped in the history of people of means. "I like working. I'm not saying it's not nice to take Blackie out for a frisbee toss or have tea with you, but I need to feel useful."

Litha smiled. "I was hoping you might say something like that. We might be able to help each other out."

Rosie looked skeptical. "This sounds like one of those schemes that you cook up with Auntie Elora."

Litha shook her head. "Nope. This is *all* me. See, here's the thing. I've been wanting to take a break from tracking." Rosie realized her mother suddenly looked nervous. "We, uh, your dad and I want to have more children."

Rosie laughed out loud. "Well, I couldn't be that awful, if you're deliberately going for it again."

Litha's look changed to serious. "You're the furthest thing from awful, Rosie. You're the best thing that ever happened to us." Rosie felt an unbidden pressure behind her eyes and knew that she had that reddish pre-tears look. "If we were lucky enough to have another child just like you, we'd be over the moon."

"Mom." Rosie's breath hitched. She wasn't accustomed to being told she was loved and she really wasn't accustomed to being told she was cherished.

"The only thing stopping me is that I provide a service to The Order that is uniquely valuable. There's only one other person I know of who can do what I can do."

"You want me to track for The Order."

"It's not bad work, you know. Not usually. I've had some interesting times." She chuckled. "There was this ghost in Venice who didn't want to be tracked…"

The waiter arrived with a choice of tea treats. Rosie looked up into his face and said, "Please forgive me if I made you uncomfortable earlier. I've been spending time with rough company."

The waiter looked first shocked, then embarrassed. "Not at all, miss."

"So what do you think?" said Litha.

"I wouldn't be taking over for you permanently, right? Just filling in for a while?"

"Absolutely! Come down to Headquarters with me. There's something I want to show you."

Litha didn't give Rosie a choice about walking arm in arm. As they strolled, she pointed out the museum and told Rosie about the Hall of Heroes, that Uncle Ram had a portrait hanging there, and that she'd always thought it was a travesty that there wasn't also one of Storm, because no one deserved it more.

Litha took Rosie down to her private room and told her the history of the artefacts. Rosie was immediately drawn to the dragon and to her mother's scrying mirror.

"Can I touch?" she asked.

"Of course. Only you," said Litha. "The thing is, there are times when I need this elaborate paraphernalia to do the job. But I suspect you won't." Litha pulled the crystal pendant from its hiding place underneath her blouse. "I have a feeling this is all you'll ever need. Your grandfather gave me this and, while you're working as tracker, it's yours. Don't lose it. It means a lot to me."

"If I couldn't keep track of my mother's prize possession, I wouldn't be much of a tracker, would I?"

"True. Let's go speak to Simon although I think bringing you on board will simply be a formality." She stopped and looked at Rosie. "You were born here, you know. Right here in this building."

Rosie laughed. "Yeah. I know, Mom."

AS LITHA PREDICTED, Simon was pleased to have Rosie fill in for her mother's leave of absence.

"You were born here, you know," he said, smiling at Rosie.

"Yes." She nodded. "I've heard that."

"Well, you may find the job comes with interesting situations. Your mother has had to get out her creative hat now and again."

"She'll be so good that you won't want to see me come back," Litha said.

"Well, I doubt that. You've become something of a legend."

"That's nice of you to say, Simon."

"Just a simple truth. So, Rosie, when will you be starting?"

Rosie looked at Litha. "I guess that's up to her. And Dad," she snickered.

Litha tried to give Rosie a look of reproach, but couldn't hide her smile. "I'll make sure she's familiar with policies and procedures, where there's wiggle room and where there's not." Litha shrugged. "Then she's on her own. It's not the kind of thing you can apprentice for, especially not when you were born with more mastery than the master."

"Well, then, welcome to Black Swan, Elora Rose Storm. We'll want to issue you a new phone and I want to be sure you have my twenty-four hour number. Never know when you might need it."

"Yes, sir. Thank you."

"It's we who are thanking you. Both of you. Who would have guessed there might be someone in the world who could stand in for Litha?"

Simon shook his head, but smiled, clearly pleased with the arrangement. Litha's pride in her child was shining so bright it almost looked like there was a spotlight above her. Rosie, unaccustomed to so much concentrated adoration, felt a hint of shyness and ducked her head.

GLEN ARRIVED AT Monq's door at precisely seven. He didn't bother to knock because he knew he was expected.

"Hey, doc. What's for dinner?" Before Monq could answer Glen's eyes had drifted to the table set up in front of the video fire. "Three people? Who else is…?"

There was a soft knock on the open door.

Glen turned to see Rosie standing there, looking just as uncertain as she was unbelievably beautiful. He pinned Monq with a look that should have caused him to explode into millions of tiny bits.

"You. Did. Not," he said slowly and distinctly, each word dripping with outrage.

"I did," Monq said casually as he rose from his chair. Looking at Rosie, he said, "Come in, my dear. We're having sea bass with pasta primavera and Alfredo sauce."

He gestured toward the table, but after Glen's reaction

Rosie didn't exactly feel welcome and didn't move from the doorway. Looking at Glen she said, "I saw you a few nights ago. In the Hub. You walked right by, but I guess you didn't see me."

His dark eyes flashed at her for less than a blink as he sneered. "I saw you."

"Oh," she said in a quiet voice. She searched his face as he looked away and couldn't find anything that resembled the boy who'd loved her except for facial features. In addition to the physical changes, he had a hard edge that broadcasted bitterness.

Monq decided he'd better establish himself as an arbiter or things were going to deteriorate quickly. "I understand you two used to know each other."

Glen smirked and looked away, shaking his head. "No. Not really. I thought I knew her. Turned out not."

Rosie was just beginning to understand the depth of the hurt she'd delivered to her first love. She'd been too selfish, too immature, and too shortsighted to grasp the consequences of her rash behavior. Now that she'd come face to face with the results, it looked like it was far too late to do anything about it. The damage wasn't just done and over. It had reinfected itself again and again and festered past the point of repair.

She stood there staring at Glen, wondering if an apology would help or make things worse. Looking at the way he was clenching his jaw, she decided things couldn't get any worse.

"I'm sorry," she said.

Glen's gaze jerked up to her eyes. He could see she was

sincere and, if anything, it made him hate her more. At least it made him angrier.

"Oh, good. Dinner is here," Monq exclaimed cheerfully.

All the while dinner was being set out Glen and Rosie continued to look at each other, but nothing changed. He was resolute in his rage. She was genuine in her contrition, silently willing him to accept that.

When the waiter was gone, Monq persuaded them to sit down at the table set for three.

"I don't know how you see this playing out, old man." said Glen to Monq.

"There's no reason to be disrespectful to Mr. Monq," Rosie chastised.

"Dr. Monq," Monq corrected.

Judging by Glen's reaction, he didn't appreciate being chastised about manners, especially by Rosie. "I don't know how you see this playing out, *Dr. Monq*, but no good can come from it."

By that time Rosie was beginning to feel a little less sorry. "Oh? And why is that?" she asked.

"Because, wunderkind, you can't change the past with a couple of words like *'sorry'*."

"I know that, Glen. But apologizing is a start."

"Really?" He bit out the word. "A start toward what?"

"It's a start toward forgiveness and maybe, eventually, being friends again."

He startled both Monq and Rosie by laughing out loud. "FRIENDS!?! Friends don't give each other ultimatums and then disappear. FOR YEARS!"

Rosie sighed. "You're right. It was dumb. And thoughtless. And if I could take it back..."

"Well, you can't." Glen fumed as he shoved a huge forkful of pasta into his mouth knowing that Rosie would think his table manners were hiding in the same closet as his ability to be civil.

"Rosie, why don't you tell us what you've been doing since you last saw Glen."

"I'm not particularly interested in what she's been doing," Glen said, looking anywhere but at Rosie.

"Well," she said to Monq, "I can tell you what *he's* been doing. He's been mastering the art of being an ass. You've changed, Glen."

"I..." Monq started.

Glen cut him off. "I've changed? You know what your problem is, Elora Rose? You *haven't* changed. You're still the same self-involved brat who thinks all she needs to do is prance back in here... Oh, look at me, I'm practically royalty. Black Swan's precious little princess is sorry she made a mess."

"You're making this harder than it needs to be," she said quietly.

"Yeah? And who gets to decide that? You? You get to decide *everything*, don't you?"

"I made a mistake, Glen. A big one. But what you've made is a gigantic fucking mess of yourself."

"You don't know anything about me, little girl."

Rosie stood up so suddenly it knocked her chair over. She threw her napkin down and her own eyes sparked with anger. "I know you're the one releasing the hogs of war."

Glen sat back and crossed his arms, then gave her a smile that broke her and tugged at her heart strings at the same time. "That's *dogs* of war," he said with a smugness that made her want to smush his smarmy face.

"Forget what I said about being sorry. All I really want from you is to stay away from me." As punctuation, on the way out of the room, she grabbed a pillow from Monq's settee and threw it at Glen, who simply caught it in the air and laughed.

"Fine by me."

"Loser. Do you even have any friends?" It as a parting shot that she couldn't have known hit way too close to home. But she decided to add one last thing on her way out the door. "AND I DON'T PRANCE!"

Glen's taunting laughter melted into a seething anger that had him breathing hard. "Bitch," he fired back, but she was gone.

Monq said, "Well, that went better than I expected."

Glen stood, glowering at Monq, then raised his dinner plate to shoulder height.

Monq managed to say, "Please! Not the fireplace again!"

Glen huffed. "How's this?" He raised one bent leg and broke the plate over his own thigh.

As he stormed out of the room Monq said, "Dinner at seven tomorrow night. Don't be late."

Glen gave him the finger without turning around.

Monq sighed and looked at the broken plate and ruined food on the new carpet. He was thinking he was glad he'd opted for Alfredo sauce instead of marinara.

FALCON HAD NO good reason to be relieved from duty. Genevieve's condition was stable. Nothing had changed. So he'd been on patrol for two nights in a row.

When he returned after the second night, he showered, had something to eat and went straight to the lab. Monq was standing in the hallway talking to Jean Etienne. Genevieve was in the cell alone and appeared to be sleeping.

"Is she okay?" Falcon asked Monq.

"There's been no change except that this is the first time she's slept since taking Jean Etienne's blood. Needing less sleep is apparently one of the side effects."

"Where is this going?"

Monq looked troubled. "What do you mean?"

"I mean is she cured? Or is she going to have a shadow forever?" He looked at Jean Etienne when he said it.

"I'm not a shadow."

"Then what are you?"

"I'm the host of the blood that is keeping the virus from destroying her. If you love her, why does this anger you?"

"Because you're not just a blood donor. And I don't like what I'm seeing."

Jean Etienne caught the subtext. "Yes. I care about her."

"Don't you think you're too old for her?" Falcon could have kicked himself for saying something so stupid. Of course Jean Etienne was too old for Genevieve. He was too old to date the Sphinx.

"What if she required regular doses of my blood to survive? What would you want for her?"

"Maybe she doesn't want to live forever."

"I couldn't guarantee that she'll live forever. We're not really immortal. It's just, what do you call it? Shorthand, for outliving record-keeping. We can be killed." He smiled. "No. I will not tell you how. But until we are deliberately snuffed from existence, we age very slowly. At least as compared to you. If Genevieve needs to go with me to live, she will probably stop aging and appear as she does now until she dies."

Falcon's internal process was more a war than a conflict. It was bloody and horrific. He'd looked at his dilemma from all sides round and couldn't find his way to a desirable outcome. Simply put, he didn't want Genevieve to die, but he didn't want her to go with Jean Etienne either. Seeing that no resolution would be reached at that moment standing in the hall, he jumped onto the hospital bed that was made fresh for him daily and pulled the blanket up to his chin.

CHAPTER FOURTEEN

THE FIRST THING Falcon did when he woke was to look at his watch. It was two o'clock in the afternoon.

He heard the familiar murmur of Jean Etienne talking to Genevieve. He turned his head on the pillow in time to see Genevieve's fangs extend just before she latched onto Jean Etienne's neck. His mind grappled with trying to make sense of seeing his Genevieve as a vampire. It was quiet enough that he could make out soft lapping and sucking sounds accompanied by moans of pleasure from beyond the cell barrier. Jean Etienne's eyes had closed, but it was impossible to tell if that was from pleasure or pain.

Falcon watched silently without moving until he heard footsteps approaching. He moved his head enough to see that it was Monq.

"Enough," Jean Etienne said firmly.

There was a little bit of a struggle before he pulled Genevieve away.

Jean Etienne glanced over at Monq and held up a finger to signal that he should wait a minute.

Falcon sat up and rubbed his eyes.

"How long have you been awake?" asked Monq.

"Long enough to see the… thing."

Monq nodded just as Jean Etienne appeared in the hallway next to them.

"What happened?"

Jean Etienne shrugged. "She got hungry. I gave her what she needed. I think your experiment is done, at least for now."

Monq looked at Genevieve. "What will happen to her?"

Jean Etienne looked at Monq like he was daft. "She's coming with me, of course."

"No," said Falcon, shaking his head. "She's not. You can leave some of your blood if that's what she needs, but she's not going anywhere with you."

"Why not?" asked Jean Etienne. "I like her."

"You like her," Falcon repeated drily. "That's not enough. Not *nearly* enough for someone like her."

"Yes. It is." Genevieve had risen and walked toward the barrier. She was standing just on the inside of the glass, looking out at Falcon.

"Gen, you don't know him or what he's really like."

"I know enough, Sir Falcon. Gods know I didn't ask for this, but this is what I've got and Jean Etienne, well, I like him, too."

Falcon was shaking his head. "No."

"I'm sorry this has caused you pain," said Jean Etienne, "but the decision has been made. By the two of us."

Falcon looked at Genevieve. "So you're committing to spending forever with this creep?"

When she laughed, Falcon realized how much her

looks had changed. Her hair seemed to have brighter highlights. Her skin was glowing. And the caramel-colored eyes would haunt him for the rest of his life. She almost looked like an airbrushed pinup version of herself. In short, she was eerily flawless.

"I guess 'creep' is in the eye that beholds. No?" She shook her head. "I've been flattered by the attention you've given me, the beautiful flowers. I was never right for you. But someone is. Someone will treasure your capacity to woo and desire you above all others."

"Open the door," he said to Monq.

Monq looked at Jean Ėtienne who shook his head. "She's not ready for that. In time, she will gain control over her appetites, but at present, it would be foolish to risk putting a human within her reach."

Monq looked at Falcon with pity. "Sorry. We can't take the chance."

"So you're just going to let him walk out of here with her."

"We're not going to walk," said Jean Etienne, "but that's the general idea. The choice is hers and she's made it."

Falcon turned to Monq. "She's going to be completely dependent on him for *everything*. Do you realize that? And she won't even be able to ask for help if it goes south. She's one of our own. You can't let him just disappear with her."

Falcon made points that caused Monq to look uncertain. He turned back to say that perhaps he should let headquarters make the final decsion, but it was a moot point. Without having made a whisper of a sound, the two vampire, old and new, had vanished.

Falcon whirled and threw his fist at the wall behind him with such force that Monq thought he heard a crack.

The young knight walked away without another word. He took the elevator to the fourth floor, got off and climbed the stairs the rest of the way to the rooftop whisterport. At that time of day there was no one around. Most of the knights would be having breakfast. It would be hours before whister maintenance and pilots showed up to check over the transport equipment and get it ready for the coming night.

Flying a whister is like driving a car with a stick shift. Learning takes some effort, but once the process is programmed into muscle memory, you don't forget how to do it.

Kris checked the fuel tank, went through the checklist, turned the engine over and lifted off.

He had no jacket, no belongings, just sixty dollars in his pocket and the clothes he'd slept in. He hadn't even brushed his teeth.

He wasn't especially close with his family. They'd always been completely involved with the oldest son and, though they would never have admitted it, they thought of Falcon as the throw-away. He'd become a virtual son of Black Swan when he was fourteen. His friends were Black Swan. His history was Black Swan.

He had no idea where he would go or what he would do. He only knew that he had to get away.

He set the whister down on one of the Manhattan whisterports. He wasn't worried about the whister being stolen. First, whister pilots were not a dime a dozen. Second, it was impossible to access the roof without a body scan that registered the unmistakable uniqueness of an individual.

He'd been careful to leave his phone on the pilot seat. Black Swan phones had extremely sophisticated tracking that couldn't be disabled. They'd be able to quickly locate the whister. But not him.

Chapter Fifteen

Day Six – Psych Eval

FALCON'S DEPARTURE WASN'T confirmed until after the whister maintenance tech came on to check the birds over and make sure they were ready for evening duty. Black Swan was meticulously careful about equipment. They spent a lot of time, money, and effort to train knights and they were determined not to lose any to accidents that could have been avoided with a little more attention to detail and one more review of the checklist.

The tech went straight to the rooftop office and dialed the Sovereign's phone on the in-house system.

The admin on duty answered. "Sovereign's office."

"This is Wilson. Let me speak to the man," he said with the roughness of a long-time cigar smoker.

"He doesn't like to be disturbed when he's working on the duty roster. I'll ask him to return your call."

"No. You won't. You'll put me through right now."

The admin hesitated, but decided the more prudent choice would be erring on the side of caution.

"Just a minute," he said.

"What is it?" Rev answered with a gruffness that matched Wilson's, if not in gravelly tone, in attitude.

"We're missing a whister."

"I know I heard that wrong. Say again."

"You heard right. Got two out of three topside."

Rev didn't bother to say goodbye. He hung up while he was rising from the chair. He knew it wasn't going to take Sherlock Holmes to figure out who had absconded with a three million dollar machine. There were exactly four pilots in residence at Jefferson Unit.

Rev came to a standstill in his outer office before he even reached the hallway when he remembered. There were only four *professional* pilots. But there were two other people who could fly whisters. Falcon and Wakenmann.

He turned back to his admin. "Get Falcon on the phone."

"Yes, sir." After brief clicking of the keys, Rev heard through the speakers that Falcon's phone went straight to voicemail.

"Try Wakenmann."

"Yes, sir." Again brief clicking, but Wakenmann picked up right away.

"Wakenmann," was all he said.

"I'll take it in my office," Rev said.

The admin nodded. "Hold for the Sovereign."

Rev closed the door, picked up his phone, and pushed the lit button. "When was the last time you saw Falcon?"

"This morning when we came in. Why?"

"Can you think of any reason why he would borrow a whister without permission?"

"Fuck!" said Wakey.

"Beg pardon?"

"Can I get back to you on that? Sir?"

"Quickly, Sir Wakenmann."

"Definitely."

Wakey ran down the hallway to the elevators. When he didn't get one right away, he pushed through the door that led to the stairwell and descended to Monq's sublevel taking the stairs three at a time. He was out of breath by the time he reached the cell where Genevieve had been held.

Except for Falcon's freshly made hospital bed, the place was empty.

Wakey scrubbed his hand down his face then jogged back to Monq's office. The door was open and Monq was in front of his computer.

"Seen Falcon?"

Monq looked up. "No. Why?"

"Do you know what AWOL means?"

Monq scowled. "Conjecture? Or fact?"

"How many people do you know around here who can fly a whister?"

"Dagnabbit! I should have anticipated something like this."

"Yeah," Wakey nodded. "You should have. I'm not a shrink and I saw it coming."

Monq looked serious. "Does Rev know?"

Wakey raised his eyebrows. "Oh. Yeah."

Monq got up. "I'll take it from here."

"What does that mean?"

"I'm not sure. I'll figure it out on the way upstairs."

"I'm coming."

"If you want, but the Sovereign's not likely to be in a good mood."

"Think not?" Wakey said sarcastically.

When Monq wasn't moving fast enough for Wakey, he said, "You need me to carry you?"

"I'm a scientist. Not a slave to treadmills."

"Never would have guessed. About that last part, I mean."

"So go on ahead of me if you're in that big a hurry for a meeting with Farthing in head-rolling mode."

Wakey rethought his perspective. "You're right. Slow is good."

"This is not slow!"

"You want to argue that right now?"

Monq paused before replying. "Not in the least."

WHEN MONQ AND Wakey walked into Rev's office, he held up his hand.

"If you're here to confirm that Falcon has left the premises without leave and with one of The Order's extremely valuable mechanical assets, you're too late. I'm already ahead of you. We tracked his phone to the TS whisterport. He apparently left it there, because it hasn't moved in four hours.

"If, on the other hand, you're here to give some insight as to why a decorated knight would not only go AWOL but steal a whister in the process, then I'm listening." Wakenmann looked at Monq, who looked at Wakenmann. "Cat got both your tongues?"

Wakenmann cleared his throat. “Well, he’s been off his game.”

“Yes,” said Monq. “He’s been upset ever since Mademoiselle Bonheur was brought in.”

“I know that. Did something in particular happen to precipitate *this* rash response?”

“Ah, yes, well, she left with Jean Etienne.”

Rev’s eyebrows drew down so far that his eyes were almost obscured from view. “When did this happen?”

“Earlier today.”

“And no one thought to inform me?” When no answer was forthcoming, he added, “Are you under the impression that the post I occupy is a figurehead?”

“Of course not,” Monq said, while Wakenmann vigorously shook his head no. “I didn’t think the report required immediacy.”

“Seems you were wrong about that,” Rev said each word as if it was deliberated individually. Monq nodded. “What is his state of mind?”

Monq glanced at Wakenmann before saying, “He’s off his game.”

Rev’s lips pressed into a thin line. “And is that your professional psychiatric opinion, Dr. Monq?”

“Well, sort of. I’d say he’s somewhere between off-kilter and…”

“AWOL?”

“I suppose that’s as good a description as any.”

“Did you know that in the entire history of The Order this is only the third time a knight has given himself permission to take leave?”

"No. I didn't know that," said Monq.

"I'm mentioning it to illustrate the serious nature of this course of action."

"I understand."

"And that you should have anticipated that there could be a problem." Monq nodded. "Do you agree?"

"Yes."

Rev looked at Wakenmann. "This is the first time that Falcon has left without permission *as a knight*, but it's not the first time he's been away without leave, is it?"

Wakey's brow knitted slightly as he tried to figure out where the Sovereign was going with that question. "No, sir."

"The first time you were with him, weren't you?"

"I was. Sir."

"If I remember correctly, the two of you stowed away on a whister. Is that right?"

"Yes, sir."

"What was it that was so attractive that the two of you were willing to take such a risk?"

Wakenmann dropped his head for a moment, willing his superior to withdraw the question. When it seemed unlikely that wishful thinking would work, he forced himself to answer. "Strippers. Sir." It's not that he was ashamed… exactly. It's just that it's not the sort of thing one confesses to a Sovereign. Especially not when the Sovereign has a reputation for being on the side of tight laced.

Rev had to exercise considerable self-control to stop himself from smiling. To school his features into submission he gave himself a stern internal lecture about the fact that there was nothing amusing about Falcon abandoning his duty. When a knight like Falcon reacted so drastically, it meant that something was desperately wrong.

"Well, Sir Wakenmann. You're his partner. Is it safe to assume you're also his best friend?"

"That would be a safe assumption, sir."

"Then you may have some insight as to where he would go? And why?"

"I can tell you why. I think. But no idea about where."

"All right. Tell me what you think you know."

Wakey's gaze flicked to Monq.

"Kris didn't just have a thing for the Operations Manager. Over the years it has become more like an obsession. We, ah, his friends, were always trying to get him to look around for somebody who would return his, um, interest. It's not like he never attracted female attention. Just the opposite. Of the four of us, he'd be most likely to experience a..."

Wakenmann caught himself before he finished that sentence and seemed momentarily frozen, thinking how he could finish the thought without crossing a line into offensive territory.

"A what, Sir Wakenmann?"

Wakenmann blushed a bright red. "A, um, choice of feminine companionship without making much effort."

"I assume that's not what you were going to say. Dr. Monq and I both appreciate your being considerate of our sensibilities."

"Yes, sir."

"You were saying that Falcon was obsessed with Mademoiselle Bonheur?"

"Yeah. Not in a creepy stalker way. He just wouldn't accept that she was never going to warm up to the idea of, ah, dating him. I mean, after six years it was pretty clear that she just wasn't interested. At least it was clear to us. Obviously not to him. He seemed to think that one day he'd take her flowers and she'd say yes to dinner."

"I see."

"So she left with that vampire, I guess?" Wakenmann looked at Monq, who nodded. "It must have been hard to take. Really hard. I know he wasn't himself when he took the whister. Please take the circumstances into consideration. To Kris, it's, well, I think it's probably worse than if she died."

Rev steepled his fingers and pursed his lips. "You're a good friend. I'm not angry, if that's your worry. I'm concerned for your partner. I agree that he's been thrown off balance. I also agree it's more than likely temporary. Regardless, we've got to get him back. If he wants to leave the knighthood, there's a process and, like everybody else, he needs to follow the rules."

"Yes, sir."

"Thank you for your insight, Sir Wakenmann."

It was a dismissal, but Wakey wasn't ready to be dismissed. "One question before I go, sir?"

"Can we, I mean K Team, have leave to go search for him?"

"Thank you for the offer. I'm sure you're anxious about him. But no. I have someone in mind."

Wakenmann looked beyond disappointed. It was clear he was itching to hit the streets to look for Falcon and that he hoped he'd be the one to find him. He scowled, but said, "Yes, sir."

Wakenmann left and closed the door behind him.

"I'm putting Fennimore on K Team and sending Catch out with the tracker. When we get Falcon back, you will need to be prepared to evalutate whether or not his career is salvageable."

Monq's interest had definitely engaged. "You're sending Glen out with Litha? That could be just what the doctor ordered. A change of scenery, something to do, but with a calming feminine presence – someone he knows and trusts."

"Yes to all of that except Litha isn't the tracker."

"No?"

"She's on leave. Her daughter is filling in for her for a while."

Monq looked away before saying, "Oh boy."

"What?"

After a brief internal struggle, Monq concluded that putting the two of them together on a mission would force a confrontation that gave every appearance of being unfinished business. It was a gamble. If it went well, it could be a better choice than years of therapy. If it went wrong, Monq would be in even hotter water with the Sovereign. He'd never thought of himself as a thrower of dice, but decided the potential for resolution between the two young people was worth the risk.

"Nothing."

"Very well. Close the door on your way out."

Monq left quietly. For once.

GLEN REPORTED TO the Sovereign's office as requested.

"Come in," Rev said.

Glen stepped through the open doorway and stood in front of the Sovereign's desk. "I got a call that you wanted to see me?"

"Indeed, Sir Catch. I need you on a run down. Falcon is away without leave. I need you to find him and bring him back here."

Rev opened a drawer and withdrew a plastic zip baggy containing three sedative syringes dosed for a human, but sized to fit in a tranq pistol.

Glen reached out to accept the proferred bag, but did so with a frown.

"Is there a problem?" Rev asked.

"Speaking freely, sir?"

"Go for it."

"Well, I'm not sure I understand why you're suggesting that I hunt down a knight, sedate him, and drag him back here against his will. When did we become prisoners of The Order?"

"Dr. Monq and I have reason to be concerned for Falcon's state of mind."

"The last time I was in this office you were concerned about *my* state of mind. Does that mean I'm not free to leave if I want?"

Rev stopped multitasking and looked at Glen. "You're not asking because you're considering giving up your commission."

"No, sir. It just doesn't feel right. The idea of tranquing a knight, especially not one who practically became a legend when he was still a kid. A trainee."

"That's exactly why we're sending you after him. We need to get him back here and help him heal. He's valuable *to* us, but he's also valued *by* us." He looked Glen over thoughtfully before saying, "You up for this, Catch? If not, I can get somebody…"

"I am. When do I go?" He put the baggy in the inside pocket of his jacket.

"You're going to be working with the new tracker. She'll decide. Here she comes now."

Rev motioned someone inside. Glen turned toward the door in time to see Rosie stepping inside, looking wary.

"*This* is your new tracker?" Glen laughed bitterly while he looked at the carpet and shook his head. "Of course she is."

Rosie looked at Rev. "I'm working with him?"

Rev looked between Glen and Rosie. "Is there a problem?"

They turned to him and said, "No!" emphatically and in unison.

Glen walked toward the door without glancing at her again. "Let me know when you're ready to go."

IT TOOK GLEN less than three minutes to get to Monq's office.

"Did you arrange to get me stuck on a mission with

Rosie?"

Monq chuckled, shaking his head. "No. I know it's easy to mistake me for a god, but the arrangement was made entirely by fate."

"What's so funny?"

"Just curious how things work out sometimes. You'd almost think there really was an unseen intelligence at work trying to create opportunities for people to sort things through."

"Since when do scientists believe in fate?"

"I'm a scientist *AND* magician. Not to mention philosopher, inventor, and physician. If pressed, you'd have to call me a renaissance man."

"What I would *have* to call you would earn me a week in the stockade."

Monq giggled. "You can say what you want in here without repercussions. Even if your comments about me take a derogatory turn. You should know that by now. Call me what you want." Glen sat down and clammed up. "What? No schoolyard rejoinders?" Glen sat back, pulled his arms over his chest, and glowered. "Very well. Tell me about the assignment."

Glen's knee began to judder. He looked around the room for a few seconds like he was deciding whether to continue pouting. "You know Falcon's AWOL?"

"Yes. I do know that."

"The Sovereign wants me to go get him." Glen stopped and looked at Monq. "Or, since you're a magician, maybe you could just pull him out of a hat."

Monq nodded. "I could, but where would be either the

fun or the lesson in that for you? And how does that involve the Storm girl?"

"Will you stop calling her that!?!"

"All right. What would you like me to call her?"

"Rosie. That's what *everybody* calls her."

"Really? Why does everybody call her that?"

"It was a grandmother's nickname. The one Deliverance was, um, in love with."

Monq removed his glasses and began to clean them. "That's deeply personal trivia. I wonder if she knows you remember such details."

"Who knows what she knows? Who cares what she knows? What I need *you* to know is that her name is Rosie. Calling her 'the Storm girl' sounds stupid."

"Very well. From here on Rosie is Rosie." Glen wished his little victory didn't feel so empty. "But before we leave this subject behind, why does it matter so much to you that I call her Rosie?"

Glen's eyes glinted. "Oh no you don't."

"You're right. I have work to do. We'll talk about it at dinner tonight. Seven o'clock. Don't be late."

Monq turned back to his work. When he looked up again, Glen was gone.

Chapter Sixteen

GLEN NEVER MADE it to dinner. An hour after he left Monq's office he got a text from Rosie.

ROSIE: ***Ready to go.***

GLEN: ***Where do you want to meet?***

"How about here?" she asked after she appeared right in front of him where he stood in the kitchen of his temporary quarters.

Out of reflex, he jumped. It had been a long time since he'd been in the practice of expecting Rosie's surprise arrivals.

"Crap, Rosie. What are you doing? This is my private space."

"What's so private about it?"

"What's so private is that I'm not expecting people to just pop in, literally, unannounced. I could have been undressed or engaged in something really private."

She raised her chin and looked around. "It wouldn't be anything I haven't seen before."

"The fact that you can defy physics doesn't give you a right to go anywhere you please."

"It does when I'm on a mission. I'm on company time

right now."

Glen sighed because he knew there was no point in arguing. "You have the handcuffs?"

Rosie laughed. "The purple fuzzy ones? I'd forgotten all about those. No. They belong to my mother. You got a rubber band?"

Glen shook his head. "Just rubbers."

"Funny."

"It wasn't meant to be." She made a face he didn't recognize. "I can get a rubber band from Farnsworth."

"Okay. While we're at it, I need to get into Falcon's place. Since I don't know him, I need something of his."

Glen snorted. "Like a dog? You need to sniff his shorts?"

"When did you get to be so vulgar?"

"Vulgar." He shook his head. "That wasn't even close. I've seen *real* vulgarity."

"Good for you. I'm sure someone somewhere would like to hear about it."

She took hold of his shirt sleeve and before he could register that he might be dizzy, they were standing in the Operations Office.

"You did not take me through the passes without securing me!" he said. "You could have lost me!"

"Please. I'm not going to lose you going from one floor at J.U. to another."

Glen glared at her.

"Can I help you?" Farnsworth asked.

They both looked at her like they'd forgotten why they were there.

"You got handcuffs?" Glen asked.

Farnsworth cleared her throat. "Well, that's not usually the sort of thing I arrange..."

"No. No. No," Glen said. "They're for making sure she doesn't lose me. Losing people in the passes may run in her family and I don't want to be the next victim. I have a feeling she wouldn't search as hard for me."

Rosie glowered.

"You know," Farnsworth looked around, "after the aliens were here, I think we did requisition some in case we were ever put in the position of needing to secure prisoners. Just a minute."

She picked up the in-house phone. "Do you have any handcuffs down there?" She paused. "Hysterical. No. I'm serious. I'm sending Sir Catch and Ms. Storm right now. Give them what they need." She paused, said, "Uh-huh," then hung up.

"You know where armory is, I assume?"

Glen gave her a look that said, "Duh," as clearly as if it had been spoken. Since he had served as temporary Sovereign of J.U., he knew every inch of the facility. "Thank you, Ms. Far... I mean, Mrs. Farthing."

She smiled prettily. "You're welcome. You kids have fun."

Glen gaped at her. "We're not having fun. We're on a mission."

"There's no reason why you can't work *and* have fun."

Glen could think of plenty of reasons why he couldn't have fun with Rosie. He could scarcely tolerate the idea of working with her. But rather than go into that with

Farnsworth, he simply nodded and walked away.

He made a point of going through the door first. He didn't want to give Rosie even the tiniest courtesy or gesture of respect. As far as he was concerned she'd ruined his life and was continuing to do so.

When he stopped outside in the hall, she almost ran into him. He turned around and, while he looked down at her, she was trying to remember if he'd been that tall the last time they'd stood so close together.

"Why don't you get the Sovereign's admin to let you into Falcon's apartment while I go get handcuffs?" Glen said.

"Okay," she said. "Do you want to meet back here?"

"Here would be fine," Glen said evenly through clenched teeth.

She let out a huff of breath and disappeared, shaking her head.

Fifteen minutes later Glen was standing in the same spot where he'd agreed to meet Rosie thinking that just a mere two days before he would have laughed at anyone who might have suggested that he would voluntarily allow himself to be handcuffed to her. If the circumstances that had brought about that turn of events was due to fate, as Monq had suggested, then fate had a wry sense of humor.

He jumped when Rosie appeared beside him, but refused to give her the satisfaction of saying anything about it.

"So. Where is he?" Glen asked.

"Still in New York."

"Did you take something that belongs to him?"

She shook her head. "Didn't need to. I got a sense of him." She looked at the handcuffs he was holding. "So get dressed. Did you bring a barf bag?"

She was referring to the fact that he used to get nauseous in the passes.

"Just make it fast. And try to bring us out somewhere where we won't be noticed either for poofing into existence or for being handcuffed together."

She eyed him. "I will try to be careful. In the spirit of give and take, you need to lose the authoritative tone. I don't work for you personally."

"You don't work for me personally. The thought of that is too preposterous for imagination. But I'm the knight in charge of this run down. You're the tracker. We're not a team. You're assisting me."

"Oh really?"

"We don't have time to massage your ego, Missy."

"Missy!?!"

Glen snapped a handcuff onto his left wrist and held it dangling in the air until she took it and attached the other half to her right wrist.

She grinned, knowing he was going to hate the next two minutes. "And away we go," she said cheerfully.

They emerged from the passes at 6th and Houston. Glen looked green enough that Rosie felt too sorry for him to taunt him about it.

"You got the key?"

He unzipped a small outer pocket of his jacket, withdrew the key and handed it to her as he leaned back against a brick wall. While she unlocked the cuffs, he said,

"We're taking a whister back."

"We'd have to do that anyway, Glen. Falcon is human. One hundred percent."

"Yeah. Forgot."

"Hey. There's a Chipotle. If we don't spot him right away, let's get a chicken burrito."

Glen barely suppressed gagging. "You didn't eat before we left?"

"I guess I was focused on the job."

"Speaking of that, why is Litha taking a leave?"

"I guess they want to give me siblings."

Glen nodded. "Well, you've got some big shoes to fill. She's got quite a reputation."

"Trying to make me doubt myself on the first day of a new job? That's not nice."

"Just sayin'."

"Whatever." She pulled the crystal necklace from inside her shirt.

"What's that?"

"Secret weapon."

"Seriously."

"Why do you question everything I say? It belonged to my mother. It was a gift from Deliverance."

"Demon magic? You're using demon magic!"

He was beginning to irritate her.

"Glen! How do you think my mother's shoes got so big?"

"All right. Settle down." He looked around. "Why are we here?"

"He's around here somewhere."

"Around here somewhere," Glen repeated. "That's a big help."

"Look. I'm not supposed to do your job for you. I'm supposed to get you within striking distance. And I have."

"What are you talking about? I can't *'strike'* what I can't see."

"You've never done this before, have you?"

"What does that have to do with it?"

"For that matter, why did they pick *you* for this job? Why aren't you with a team?"

Glen pressed his lips together. "Let's just get through this. Okay?"

Rosie studied Glen's reaction and the fact that he'd tensed in response to a question that should have been innocent chit chat. Among Order personnel, that was.

"Okay. I think he's over that way."

"You can't pinpoint where he is."

"There could be as much as a five minute delay. Or so."

"Five minutes? Great. You could put Falcon down anywhere in Manhattan and he could get far away in five minutes."

Rosie shrugged. "Is what it is and that's better than any alternative that The Order knows of."

Glen crossed his arms in front of him and said, "Which way?"

"I think he's over there," she said.

Glen looked in the direction where she was pointing. It was the Film Forum, which was a mostly foreign film venue for Greenwich Village movie buffs.

"*Deux Amis*," he said. "A French movie. Yeah. That's it."

His long legs started eating up the distance as he strode toward the theater.

She hurried to catch up. "What? No 'good job, tracker'?"

Ignoring her, he kept walking past the row of bicycles chained up outside. It appeared that ticket sales were inside. He pulled open the door and let it close behind him, leaving Rosie standing on the sidewalk. She huffed, but followed him in. When she caught up, he was standing in front of the cashier saying, "Deux Amis. Deux s'il vous plaît."

"Wow. That popcorn smells good," she said. Glen acted as if she hadn't spoken. When he stepped away with the tickets, Rosie caught him by the arm and said under her breath, "What if he's in there, Glen? Are you going to tranq him in the middle of a movie theater? Then what? Carry him out and hope that either nobody notices or nobody cares enough to say anything?"

"I see your point." Glen stood there juddering his fingers against his thigh for a minute. Then he started moving toward the entrance to the movie in progress.

"What are you going to do?" she said.

He stopped long enough to say, "I'm going to ask questions first and shoot later. I'm going to tell him that I've been sent to bring him back and ask him to come with us."

Rosie cocked her head. "That's so perfectly reasonable that I'm kind of impressed."

Glen gave her a smile that was pure meanness. “The last thing I’m trying to do here is impress you, Elora Rose.”

“Okay. That’s it. That was the last time I’m going to try to be nice to you. That was it. Right there.”

“Good. Because you trying to be nice to me feels all kinds of false and sort of makes my skin crawl.”

“Not going to dignify that by responding.”

Another mean smile. “You just did,” he said as he let the door close in her face.

Rosie followed him inside. She glanced at the screen while waiting for her eyes to adjust to the darkness. Glen was standing in the back, scanning the theater. It wasn’t full by any means, which made it easier to spot Falcon sitting in the middle, about ten rows back from the front.

Glen pointed. Rosie nodded. She went down the left aisle. He went down the right. Falcon was the only moviegoer sitting in that row, which made it convenient for his pursuers. Rosie sat down on Falcon’s left side at the same time Glen sat down on his right.

Falcon’s gaze remained steadfastly locked on the screen as he continued eating popcorn as if they weren’t there. When Rosie couldn’t stand it a minute longer, she reached over and snatched a handful from his bucket.

Falcon looked at her. “Get your own,” was all he said before returning his attention to the show.

“Kris,” Glen said. “They sent me after you. You’re not in trouble, but if you need to take some leave time, there’s a process. Come back to J.U. so we can straighten this out. Then you can take a leave of absence if you want.”

Falcon shook his head no.

"Why not?" Glen asked.

"I don't want to be there right now. I'll go back when I'm ready."

"Yeah. Well, here's the thing. The Sovereign wants you back now. I don't have to tell you what that means. It means you don't have a choice. And neither do I."

Falcon looked Glen in the face. "You ever ask yourself why you're doing this job?"

Glen stared back for a couple of beats before answering honestly. "Every damn day."

From the other side of Falcon Rosie heard that exchange and something about it made her chest ache. She'd always thought that Glen loved his job more than anything. She'd always imagined that things had turned out the way he'd wanted. But what if they hadn't?

Falcon nodded. "Go back and tell them you didn't find me. I'll come in when I'm ready."

"Believe it or not, I'd like to be able to do exactly that. But I can't."

Falcon barked out a laugh. "Why not? Because The Order has been so great to you?"

Glen searched Falcon's face in the darkness. "No. Because they have my vow."

Falcon looked away and sighed. Then he handed the popcorn to Rosie. She knew it was probably unprofessional to start stuffing her face with buttery salty little explosions of corn goodness, but after all, she was a fraction human. So she shoveled a handful into her mouth.

"Okay. Let's go," Falcon said.

They exited right and Rosie followed. When they reached the lobby, Glen gave Rosie a look that clearly conveyed what-the-hey-are-you-doing? As he took the bucket of popcorn out of her hand, he leaned into her and said, "We're working," through clenched teeth.

She grabbed the popcorn back and said, "I can work *and* eat popcorn. I'm only human."

He jerked the bucket out of her hands again and said, "You. Are. Not. Human."

"Well, you know what I mean."

"I don't, but that's neither here nor there," he said. Without taking his eyes away from hers, he turned the bucket upside down in the trash receptacle. She gaped as the remaining popcorn tumbled down, instantly becoming garbage. "But if you want to dumpster dive for kernels, I won't stop you."

He walked off as if he intended to never give her another thought. Rosie looked at the trash bin longingly for a second, but followed the two men out onto the street.

It was close to dark, which meant the whisters would be in use bringing knights into Manhattan for drop off. If they were lucky they would time it so they could catch a ride back right away and not give Falcon the chance to change his mind.

The closest whisterport was at Eighth and University and the shortest distance was as-the-crow-flies straight through Washington Square. Rosie could see that Glen was getting more anxious by the minute, but she was busy trying not to fall behind the long-legged pace of two knights in their prime. The streets were getting crowded as commuters spilled out of office buildings on their way to subways, or buses, or trains.

When they were halfway across Washington Square, Falcon turned to Rosie and said, “Isn’t that your dad over there?”

Rosie looked the way he’d pointed and craned her neck, searching for Storm, as did Glen. Then he turned back to Falcon saying, “I don’t see…”

Falcon was nowhere in sight.

Glen practically shouted, “SHIT!”

When it dawned on Rosie that they’d been tricked with a child’s tactic, she giggled.

Glen looked furious. “You think this is funny?”

“Well… kind of.” She was unapologetic.

“It’s not a game.”

Glen turned three hundred and sixty degrees hoping to catch sight of a disappearing target, but knew that catching up to Falcon a second time would be about a thousand times harder. He’d blown his chance for easy.

Angry features came to rest on Rosie. “Well, tracker. Looks like you’re up.”

She gave him a coquettish smile with a little curtsy and pulled on the chain that held the family scrying crystal. Glen watched as the crystal slowly defied gravity and pointed northeast.

Naturally, he thought. Falcon was heading in the direction of the theatre district and Times Square where tourists would be thick as thieves.

“If he’s going where I think he’s going, we can get

there first. Can you get me to 46th and Broadway? Do you know where it is?"

"I know where it is."

When Rosie didn't move, he said, "Well?"

"What about the handcuffs?"

"We don't have time for that." He looked down at her. "Just put your arm around my waist and I'll put my arm around yours. Hold tight and *don't lose me*!"

"Okay." Rosie felt a wave of familiar feeling when she slid her arm around Glen's waist. She might have been mad at him, but her body didn't seem to know or care about that.

Likewise, Glen's expression became hooded when he wrapped his arm around her. She thought she saw his nostrils flare slightly, like he might be taking in her scent. He was only a quarter werewolf, but that quarter was expressed in surprising ways. She remembered that sometimes, when they'd been together, she would forget about his mixed heritage and begin thinking of him as totally human. Then his chest would rumble with a growl or huff or other animal sound that would have been impossible for a human.

"You don't hate me enough to deliberately lose me. Do you?" he asked.

She looked up into his face, just inches away from hers. "I could never hate you, Glen. And I would never lose you."

She saw a flicker of something pass behind his eyes, but didn't wait to investigate. It wasn't the time or place to find out if the damage to their friendship was irreparable.

She moved them into the passes, but they were there for only a few seconds. They walked into reality in an alley just off Times Square, hidden by two large dumpsters, the kind that are borne aloft by trucks equipped with giant robot arms.

Glen let go of her immediately. "You see the Marriott Marquis over there?"

"Yes."

"There's a Starbucks on the street level at the pedestrian alley. Go wait for me there."

"What?"

"I can move faster without you."

"Oh yeah? Says the person who was sixteen blocks from here sixty seconds ago courtesy of none other than *me*."

"It's not a review of your job performance. He won't be looking for one person. He'll be looking for two. Or one person and a demon."

"Haven't you ever heard that four eyes are better than two?"

Glen ran a hand through his hair in exasperation. "No."

"I'll look while you're looking. If I see him, I'll call you. If I don't see him, I'll be at the Starbucks in an hour."

He looked dubious, but said, "Starbucks in an hour."

"If you can't get there, call." He nodded. "Say it. Say you'll call if you can't get there in an hour."

"What's the matter? Afraid I'll just disappear?"

"That's exactly what I'm afraid of."

"Feels awful, doesn't it?"

Rosie just stared. There was nothing to say. It was becoming clear that he wanted to lash out at her, make her understand that she had hurt him. Badly.

When they reached 7th, Glen turned left and Rosie turned right.

An hour later and emptyhanded, Glen walked up the alley next to Shubert's toward the Starbucks. He spotted Rosie from half a block away standing outside and looking around anxiously.

Before he could shore up the armor around his heart, he felt a tug, remembering how protective he'd felt when he babysat her as a child, and how proud he felt when she looked at him with an adoration that went well beyond mere affection. Of course his ego had been affected. He'd been equally fascinated with her, but with the added complication of guilt over having feelings for someone who was, technically, only a year old, someone he'd babysat and even rocked to sleep. The conflict and confusion was indescribable. There was no support group for young men who found themselves with his dilemma. Their relationship was as unique as she was.

He chastised himself for allowing his thoughts to go there. *Idiot.*

When she saw Glen approaching, relief showed on her face. He wondered if she was relieved because she was bored with the game and tired of waiting or if she was actually concerned for his well-being.

"You're back." She smiled.

"I'm back," he said drily.

"No luck?"

"Obviously."

"What's next?'

"You're the tracker. You're supposed to tell me what's next."

"Okay. I'm glad you asked. What's next is food. I can't go on without it."

"You can't go on?" Glen smirked, looking over her curves. "Falcon's popcorn didn't do it for you?"

She narrowed her eyes. "Don't you dare suggest that I could stand to go without dinner."

Truthfully, Glen thought Rosie's shape was feminine perfection, but he certainly didn't want her to know that he felt that way. So he said, "Okay," like he was avoiding an argument, knowing that it would leave her believing he thought she was too curvy. He'd learned when he was still a boy that the way to torture the opposite sex was to suggest that they could afford to lose a couple of pounds, whether it was true or not.

"You're not hungry?"

He shrugged and looked around. "I could eat. But let's make it fast."

"Fast food? Or eat food fast?"

"I'm an active duty knight. I don't eat 'fast food'." He looked to his right. "There's a closet-sized Italian place two blocks from here. And it's good."

"I like Italian," she said with an enthusiasm that pleased Glen, and the fact that he was pleased made him despise her even more.

"I know you do," he said without emotion.

She followed his lead to a hole-in-the-wall place called

Mama Rosa's. Her lips parted in surprise when he pulled the door open and waited for her to enter.

"Signore Glen!" A woman's voice called out as soon as they were inside.

"Buonasera, Mama Rosa," said Glen.

The woman's eyes went to Rosie. "A lady friend?" She looked askance at Glen. "Where have you been hiding her?"

"She's someone I work with. This is Elora Rose."

"Oh! Her name is Rose. I should have known. The most beautiful women in the world are named Rose, you know."

Glen smiled. "I suspected as much."

They followed Rosa to a booth near the back.

When they sat down, Glen refused menus. "Two samplers," he said.

"Wine?"

He shook his head. "Not tonight. We're working."

"Oh. What do you do?"

Glen seemed to have frozen at that question, but Rosie answered smoothly. "Private investigations, but it's very confidential. Please don't tell anyone or we'll have to stop coming here."

Rosa looked very serious. "Your secrets are my secrets." She looked around then leaned into the table and said quietly, "Italians are very good at knowing when to keep our mouths full of cannoli and free of talking."

Rosie smiled. "I see why Glen likes to come here."

Rosa beamed. "And the food is good, too."

When they were alone, Glen asked, "What's next,

tracker?"

"After samplers, whatever that is, I'll see what the crystal has to say."

"The crystal," he said drily.

"Do you have a problem with the crystal?"

"Well, it didn't exactly lead us straight to the target."

"Are you always so disagreeable now?"

"What do you mean by 'now'?"

"Now as in this calendar date. As opposed to how you used to be when I knew you before."

"I'm not that person anymore."

"Yeah. That's a shame. Because I much preferred *that* person."

"Really? So much so that you disappeared? For YEARS!?!"

A couple of heads turned at his raised voice.

When people resumed minding their own business, Rosie said, "That wasn't what I intended." She met Glen's gaze. "Like I told you before, I'm sorry."

Glen looked away. "Drop it."

"Okay. Where have you been? What have you been up to?"

A beautiful girl who could have been a decades-younger version of Rosa brought two glasses of water and a basket of breadsticks. She did a good job of pretending Rosie wasn't there and just as good a job of trying to capture Glen's attention.

"Hello, Glen," she said, putting her hand on his arm in a familiar way. "Nice to see you."

Glen responded with a smile that Rosie had all but

forgotten, but her heart remembered when he used to look at her like that.

"Rosalie. Nice to see you, too."

Glen felt a little bad about using Rosalie's infatuation to make Rosie sorry she'd lost him, but at the moment he wanted to make Rosie uncomfortable more than he cared about Rosalie's feelings.

Rosie looked between the two of them and said, "I'd like lemon in my water, please." The girl slowly dragged her eyes away from Glen and blinked at Rosie as if she couldn't imagine her being able to speak. "Sometime tonight," she added.

When the girl left, Glen said, "That was rude."

Rosie barked out a laugh. "I think you've lost the cred necessary to be able to render judgment on rudeness, Glen."

The swinging doors opened from the kitchen and a young waiter brought two gigantic platters of Italian variety.

"Wow," Rosie marveled. "This is enough food for everybody eating here tonight."

"It's also fast. It's fast food. And if we eat it fast, then we can get back to work before the trail goes cold." Rosie gave Glen a silent snort. "What?"

"Before the trail goes cold? How exactly is that going to happen? His footprints are going to fade from the impression they made in the cement?"

"*I mean* the more time he has to come up with a plan to disappear, the harder it will be to find him."

"Where do you think he's going to go?"

"He's not thinking straight. So who knows?"

"You do."

"What's that supposed to mean?"

"The minute you saw that theater you knew he was in there."

Glen's eyes sparked. "Because what was playing was a French film."

"So where do you think he's going to go?"

"France."

Rosie nodded. "Chances are."

"He's going to Paris because he knows Jean Etienne is there and where he finds Jean Etienne…"

"He'll find Genevieve. But why would he do that?"

"I gather he's both unstable *and* in love. Not that thinking you're in love isn't *always* a form of instability. He may still be thinking he can persuade the woman, or vampire, to be his."

"Wow. How would that work?"

Glen shook his head. "I don't want to think about it too hard. Maybe he has a death wish."

"Where did that come from?" Glen just shrugged. "So let's say he was going to Paris, it shouldn't be a problem to use the crystal and find him on a map, but how's he going to get there without a passport?"

"If knighthood teaches you anything, it's how to be resourceful. He might have a safety deposit box somewhere with money or credit cards and a second passport."

Rosie looked up at Glen with wide eyes. "Or he might be ballsy enough to walk right back into Jefferson Unit, get what he needs, and walk out again. He might have guessed that there's only a handful of people who know he's AWOL. There's us, Monq, the Sovereign, and the whister pilot who had to pick up the whister Falcon flew one way."

Glen's eyes were focused on Rosie. "He could get a ride back, walk down to his quarters, get his passport and whatever else he wants, then go back upstairs to the whisterport. If he never went downstairs, he could evade Rev and Monq. All he would have to do is manage to not run into Wakenmann and, since he knows K Team's schedule, that wouldn't be hard to do.

"As far as being ballsy… He and Wakenmann both walked into a firestorm when they were teenagers without blinking. I saw it on video. Ball size is not in question." Glen took out his phone. "I'm going to get the pilots' numbers. Can you write them down?"

"No pen."

"Put them in your phone."

"Okay.

Glen called the Sovereign's office on the off chance that somebody was still there. No answer. He called Rev's cell phone.

"Yeah?"

"Sorry to bother you after hours, Sovereign. I need direct numbers for all the pilots working tonight and nobody picked up in your office."

"Okay. Hang on."

Glen knew that Rev would have a portaputer with him at all times just as he had when he'd held the Sovereign's job. Rev came back on the line and read off three names and numbers, which Glen repeated to Rosie.

"Thanks," Glen said.

"Something I should know?" Rev asked.

"Nothing to report yet. We're working on a hunch."

"Okay."

"Oh, hey. One more thing. Which pilot picked up the whister that Falcon stole?"

"I prefer the term borrow. It was Morgan."

"Is he the only pilot who knows Falcon is off the reservation?"

"Yeah. This is not something we want broadcast on the nightly news."

"Got it. I'll report tomorrow." He ended the call and looked over at Rosie.

She handed over her phone. He glanced at the name and dialed. When the pilot picked up, he said, "James? This is Sir Catch."

"Evening," said James.

"You seen Sir Falcon tonight?"

"No."

"Okay. Call this number if you do. Do not mention this to anyone else and, if you do see him, do not alert Sir Falcon that you were asked about him."

"All right."

Glen hung up and went to the next name. "Foster? This is Sir Catch."

"Howdy do."

"You seen Sir Falcon tonight?"

"Yeah. Twice. I picked him up at midtown. Half an hour later I gave him a ride back. The teams were all out. So there was no reason not to go. Right?"

"Right. How long ago was that?"

"Set him down about forty-five minutes ago."

"Thanks. Keep this talk to yourself."

"Yes, sir."

Glen handed Rosie her phone. "Next move?"

"You think he's going to an airport?"

"Yep. Question is, which one?"

"You think he's going commercial?" Glen gave her a full teeth grin. "Okay. Private. So we need jet charter with international service."

As Glen typed on his phone, he glanced over at Rosie's chest then back to the screen in his hand. "Get that demon stone to tell us which direction."

Rosie pulled the crystal out and whispered a few unintelligible words. Glen watched the crystal defy gravity and move of its own accord. No matter how often he was exposed to the paranormal world, such things still amazed him.

"Well?" he asked.

"That way," she pointed.

"Are you sure? That's northeast."

"Positive."

Glen whistled. "He's dipping deep into the piggy bank. He backtracked to New Jersey, which was smart. If we're right about where he's going, he's headed for Teterboro. Gonna charter a private jet. Apparently he was mulling over what to do when we found him at the movies. I guess somewhere between there and Washington Square he decided he's going after her."

"What do you want to do?"

"Let's head back to J.U. We can get a few hours' sleep and still get there ahead of him. We can also let Baka know we're coming just in case Falcon gets there before we do."

Rosie's eyes were wide. "You're going to commit to the passes for that long? It'll take twenty minutes, Glen."

"That's the job, right? I'll manage."

"Macho, macho man." He made a face. "I'm not complaining. You've managed to be civil for," she looked at her watch, "five minutes."

"That wasn't my intention."

"Which just goes to show that you have to work at being a bad guy." Glen scowled at that. "You ever been to Paris?"

"Yeah. I worked there for a little while."

The way he said it left Rosie with the impression that he hadn't enjoyed his post there, but she knew she wouldn't get anywhere asking a personal question about how he'd spent his time.

"Did you see the sights?"

He laughed. "Only if we were passing them while chasing down a biter."

"Oh. That's a shame."

"Is it?"

"Yes. Of course. And the fact that you speak French so well…"

He dialed a number like she wasn't talking. "Two need a ride." Pause. "Yes." Pause. He looked at his watch. "Seven minutes."

Glen signed the check and scooted out of the booth. Conversation was over.

"Let's go."

Rosie hurried toward the door so she could go through first, and made a show of holding it open for Glen. As he passed her, he said, "Such a lady," in the most sarcastic way possible.

Out on the street the wind had picked up. Glen stuck both hands in the pockets of his jacket and pulled up the hood of the lightweight hoodie he'd worn underneath.

Rosie simply sent a thought to regulate her body temperature so that external circumstances were irrelevant.

By the time they reached the entrance to the building with the closest whisterport, Glen's teeth were chattering. Rosie, on the other hand, looked like she could be ordering an umbrella drink from a beach side bar, and it didn't escape Glen's notice.

"See," he said. "That's exactly why things never would have worked out between us. Everything comes too easy to you."

"So says the only person to ever come close to being named acting Sovereign of an elite Order facility at the age of NINETEEN! Most people would look at that and say that's impossible, that everything must be way too easy for that kid."

"I worked hard at stuff."

"So what? You worked hard and succeeded where almost everybody else in the world who worked just as hard would have failed. You need to face the fact that you have *innate* gifts, too. You don't get to take credit for how smart you are, or how likeable, or how good-look…"

He grinned. "What was that?"

She looked away feeling embarrassed in a way she didn't think was possible after all she'd been through the past few years. "Nothing you don't already know."

Rosie followed Glen into the elevator reserved for Order passengers. The one that would only operate with Order I.D.

On the ride up, he glanced over at her. "I was good at being Sovereign."

She looked straight ahead, but said, "I know you were."

Glen hated that his heart responded to Rosie's praise by swelling up and forcing him to take deeper breaths. She was old news. Old, old, old, old news. And she didn't mean anything to him. At all.

They waited for the whister in awkward silence and made the flight back to Jefferson Unit without speaking another word. When they stepped out onto the roof at J.U., Glen walked away without a goodbye or a last look.

Rosie stood there staring after him, wondering what had happened to make him so angry and distant, apart from her abandonment.

When the pilot passed her, he said, "Fighting, are you? Don't worry. The making up part makes it all worth it." He winked at Rosie.

"No. Um. We're not together like that."

The pilot smiled. "Right." Then he disappeared into the little building known as the crew hut leaving Rosie standing on the whisterport wondering if she really wanted the tracker job. For years she'd wondered if the day would come when she'd have to face Glen. She'd never expected that he'd just say, "No harm done," but she hadn't expected it to be so hard. She hadn't expected *him* to be so hard.

She wanted to explain that she'd just been a toddler throwing a fit. Like a child with a powerful sports car and no drivers' license, she'd had no business making love to a man with a woman's body. Hindsight is always perfect. Part of her felt like he had every right to his anger, but the other part felt like he was being unreasonable, holding her to a standard she hadn't been capable of reaching at that moment in time. She knew he might never be ready to open up enough to hear that, which meant it was likely she'd have to cut her losses, with regret, and live with having hurt someone she cared about.

Glen went straight to his guest apartment at Jefferson Unit feeling like he needed nothing more than to be alone and away from *her*. Hours spent with Rosie had been exhausting, an assault on all his senses and on all his defenses.

He turned on the lights, sat down on the sofa and looked around. It was as generic as any upscale hotel suite. Nice, but designed to look like it belonged to no one. He realized that it had been years since he'd last slept in a place that felt like home. He didn't "live" anywhere. He "stayed" in temporary quarters until the next transfer.

On that despondent thought he pulled out his phone and sent Rev a text update.

GLEN: ***We don't have him, but we think he's getting a charter out of Teterboro for Paris. We're going to nap for a few, then head there. Maybe you could brief Jean***

Etienne and tell him to expect us?

REV: ***Not what I'd hoped for.***

GLEN: ***We're handling it.***

Monq had asked Rev to keep him posted daily on Glen's activities. He wanted to monitor the situation closely because it could go either way. It could be beneficial or detrimental. Even someone with Monq's perceptive abilities couldn't make a prediction with a hundred percent accuracy.

REV: ***Check in with Monq before you go. That's an order.***

Glen sighed. The last thing he wanted to do was 'check in with Monq'. He scrolled to Monq's number.

GLEN: ***Rev said to check in with you.***

MONQ: ***My office. Fifteen minutes.***

GLEN: ***I've already had dinner.***

MONQ: ***It won't take that long.***

Glen looked at his watch, tossed the phone on the sofa beside him, and closed his eyes. Moments later he heard the phone buzzing. He picked it up and looked at the text.

MONQ: ***Where are you?***

Glen looked at his watch. It had been twenty-five minutes. He ran a hand through his hair.

GLEN: ***Sorry. I dozed off. Be there in two.***

True to his word, Glen was standing at the threshold

of Monq's office in two minutes.

"Come in," Monq said. "Close the door." Glen did as he was told, but didn't sit. "You know," Monq began, "the more you cooperate, the faster you'll be out of here."

"Meaning?"

"Meaning sit yourself down and sack the attitude long enough to tell me how you are."

"How I am?"

"The concept of asking how you are is foreign to you?"

Glen sat. "It's not a social call. I was ordered here."

"Well, that is true. But since you're here, how are you?"

"I. Am. Fine. Is that all?"

"No, it isn't. How is your pursuit of Sir Falcon going? I'm very concerned about his state of mind."

"We think he's chartered a jet to take him to Paris. That's not conclusive. Just a hunch."

"And you're going after him?"

Glen made a face. "Yes. In a couple of hours."

"Transportation via the Storm girl?" Glen dropped his chin and glared at Monq under his eyebrows. "Oh, that's right. You're sensitive about her name. Elora Rose, isn't it?"

"I'm not sensitive about her name. Yes. She can get us to Paris ahead of Falcon. And I'd rather take a beating."

"Why's that?"

"Nausea. It's brutal."

"Why didn't you say so? I have something for that."

Glen gaped. "You do?"

"Of course. It's a variation on common motion-sickness drugs. Wait here." Monq left, but returned in a few minutes with a small rectangular tin. The pills were as tiny as miniscule breath mints. "Let one of these melt on your tongue at least five minutes before you need to travel. It should last for eight hours or so."

Glen took the tin, opened it, and looked inside at the little pink tablets. "This is probably the best gift I've ever received."

"Demon travel is that bad, huh?"

"Oh, yeah. Thank you. So, on the matter of Falcon. I talked to him. He said he was coming in, then used a sucker trick to get away."

"You talked to him? How did he seem?"

"To be honest, he seemed perfectly okay. Since it looks like he could be hours away when apprehended, what's your proposal as to how to get him back here without injury?"

"If we need to mildly sedate him for the trip, we will."

"Gods." Glen looked away. "Doesn't seem right."

"You think he should be able to walk away whenever he wants to."

"Yes."

"I would agree if I was satisfied that he was fully himself and knew what he was doing. Unfortunately I feel certain that's not the case. You and I both know that, if he was in the right frame of mind, he would have accompanied you back here and gone through the process of discharge."

"Yeah. Maybe."

"So you think he'll go straight to Baka's unit looking

for Jean Etienne?"

"That's my guess."

"How are you getting along with the St… with Ms. Storm?"

Glen grinned, showing all his very white teeth and canines that were just a tiny bit more pointed than normal. "None of your business."

Monq chuckled. "If this assignment is too much for you, now is the time to say so."

Glen's humor died abruptly. "I've never ducked an assignment and I'm not going to start now. Working with… *Ms. Storm* is not a problem. Not for her. Not for me."

"Glad to hear it." Monq rose and opened his office door. "Thanks for stopping by. Let me know when you find Falcon, any hour of the day or night. Don't worry about the time change."

"Yeah. Easy for you to say."

Glen left Monq's office feeling a hundred pounds lighter. The dread of traveling the passes had weighed that heavily. His hand went to the little tin of pills just to reassure himself that he had them. He felt like he'd been armed with a magical object from myth, like a cup of immortality or a stone that makes its bearer invincible.

He went back to his temporary quarters and texted Rosie.

GLEN: ***ETD four hours.***

ROSIE: ***Okay.***

He set the alarm on his phone and stretched out on

the sofa. He didn't even bother to remove his jacket or his boots.

After Glen left, Monq made a call.

"Hello?"

"Mrs. Hawking."

There was a sigh on the other end of the call. "There's no point in correcting you. I'm not playing that game anymore. You enjoy bungling people's names. What do you want?"

"That's not especially friendly."

"That's because I know you're about to ask me to do something that I probably don't want to do."

"A cup of tea and a brief conversation."

"What is the 'brief conversation' concerning?"

"I'll tell you over tea."

"You are not delivering these babies."

"It's not about that."

"I can't trust you. You always think you're being crafty, but you're not. You're just being you and I know it."

"I have no idea what that means."

After a pause she said, "You'll have to come here. My husband is on patrol and I'm watching Helm."

"Five minutes."

"Okay. If I don't like what you have to say, I'm throwing you out."

"Hmmm."

"I mean it this time."

"Of course, my dear."

AS MONQ PASSED through Elora's open door, the tea kettle began to chug and toot. The kettle was housed in a red train engine. Most of the steam was forced out of the stack, but some of it was diverted to make the wheels spin. Ram had brought it home when Helm was still a toddler. While he still loved it, Helm was beginning to think that a boy such as himself should be too grown up for such things. So he rolled his eyes and made himself content with loving it secretly.

Elora carried the wooden box of tea bags to the table and opened it for Monq to make a selection. When they'd both poured tea and complemented it with sweeteners or cream or lemon, she said, "What's this about?"

"That crème brulee creamer is very nice, isn't it?"

"Yes. Thank you. What's this about?"

"Still concerned with Sir Catch."

"Go on."

"This is classified."

"I have clearance."

"I know, but I don't want it to get around to anyone who doesn't."

When Monq looked pointedly at Helm, Elora laughed out loud. "Helm, you have permission to play Dungeons and Demons while I talk to Dr. Monq."

Helm grinned at Monq and said, "Stay as long as you like," as if he was thirty. He grabbed a lemon poppy seed muffin on his way out of the room.

Elora called after him. "Do not let Blackie have any of that muffin." Lowering her voice, she said, "The room is secure."

"The Operations Manager is a vampire."

Elora looked serious. "That's a shame. I liked her."

"Yes. Well. So did Sir Falcon."

Elora took a sip of tea. "That part is common knowledge."

"He didn't take it well. Her becoming a vampire, I mean."

"Did he kill her?"

"No. No. He didn't kill her. He did everything in his power to protect her. Long story short. She left with Jean Etienne, who is going to keep her alive and in control by giving her his blood."

Elora's eyes went wide. "Immortal blood?"

"Yes, supposedly immortal. Anyway, Falcon didn't take it well. He left."

"You mean he left? As in, walked out?"

"Not exactly. He flew out. Took one of the whisters and left it in New York. Rev sent Glen to fetch him back so that I can evaluate his mental state."

"Okay."

"The Sovereign also put the new tracker on the case."

"The new tracker," she repeated. Then understanding dawned. "Oh. You mean…"

"Yes. The Storm girl. You knew her mother had taken a leave of absence."

"Yes. Of course."

"So they lost Falcon in New York. Now they think he's headed to Paris to find Jean Etienne."

"That," she nodded, "seems like a logical assumption. Are you getting to the part where this has something to do with me sometime soon?"

"Yes. Almost there."

"Go for it."

"Well, I was thinking Sir Catch and the Storm girl in Paris la ville des lumières... working together."

A smile slowly spread over Elora's face as understanding dawned. "You old devil. You want to play Cupid and you're here to get me to help with some crazy scheme."

"Precisely."

"Isn't this a little outside the parameters of psychiatry? Never mind. I don't care. I'm in! But I'm not really the one you need." Her eyes flew open with the realization that she was being manipulated. "Ohhhhhh. You already knew that. You want me to use my influence as Litha's friend to get her on board with your plan. Whatever it is." She could tell by the satisfied look on Monq's face that Litha was the ultimate target. "What is your plan anyway? Let me just preface this whole thing by saying that, whatever it is, if it backfires, there'll be a lot of people out for your head."

"Well, all the minor details haven't been ironed out, but I have a framework on which to hang a fully developed strategy."

"Strategy? If people are meant to be together, you don't need a strategy. All you need is a way to put them in the same place at the same time until the chemistry kicks in and bakes the cake."

Monq was nodding. "I know that. The problem is keeping them in the same place at the same time. First, Glen has concluded that he's never going to be happy and has settled into that role with all its accoutrements and satellites. Second, regarding Elora Rose, it's hard to pin down someone who can walk through walls, cross dimensions, vanish in an instant, etcetera, etcetera, etcetera."

"Hmmm."

Elora got up to restart the tea kettle then picked up her phone and dialed Litha.

"Hello?"

"What are you doing?"

"Playing twenty questions with you?"

"No. Really."

"I'm reading an ancient esoteric Sumerian text on demon young."

"Of all the things I imagined you might say, that wasn't one of them."

"What did you want me to say?"

"I wanted you to say, 'Nothing. What's up?'"

"Got it. Ask me again."

"What are you doing?"

"I'm not doing anything. What's up?"

"You're a terrible liar."

"Elora."

"Monq is here with something very interesting to discuss. Can you run over here?"

"Now?"

"Now."

Litha appeared in the kitchen next to the stove with her phone still held to her ear. "Yes."

Elora looked at her. "I will never get used to that if we are friends for a thousand years."

"That could happen. I don't know how long I'll live,

but it might be long enough to figure out how to extend your life."

"You can't do that."

"Why not?"

"It wouldn't be right to extend my life because I'm your friend and not offer the same thing to everybody. And if you offered it to everybody we'd have the rats in a bottle problem and populate the world beyond tolerance within a few years."

"There are lots of other dimensions with no population at all."

"That may be, but exponential is exponential."

"When I suggested that I might want you to live forever I'd temporarily forgotten how irritating you can be." She looked at Elora's stomach. "My gods. You are bigger than when I saw you this morning."

Elora chuckled. "Monq is here."

Litha looked behind her. "Hello."

"You want tea?" Elora asked.

"Yes. Whatever you're having."

"Monq has a *really* intriguing idea."

"I'm getting a strong intuitive feeling that I should leave now without asking what it is." Litha looked at Monq with unmasked suspicion.

"Before you go, you should know it's about Rosie," said Monq.

"So you *do* know her name!" Elora accused.

"Of course I know her name. She's a phenomenon. How could I not know her name?"

Elora stared blankly. "Sometimes I think you're the

biggest mystery in the whole of The Order and that's going some."

Litha took a chair at the table. "Where's Helm?"

"Playing Dungeons and Demons. Monq, tell her what you have in mind."

"Very well. Did you know that Sir Catch is on assignment with the tracker who's filling in for you?"

Litha pulled back as if she was examining Monq, then directed her attention toward Elora when she said, "No. I didn't." She sounded concerned.

"Well, truthfully, it's not widely known," he said. "In fact, neither of you are supposed to know. Technically."

Litha managed to look even more suspicious. "Then why are we sitting here listening to this, Dr. Monq?"

"You know the two of them have a romantic history?"

"Of course I know that."

"Well, then, the answer to your question is simple. I think the happiness of two young people is more important than Order protocol. Don't you?"

Litha glanced at Elora when she put a steaming cup in front of her.

"What are you thinking?" asked Litha.

"They're chasing an AWOL knight on a lost-cause mission of love. All the way to Paris."

"Oh." Litha took a sip of tea feeling sorry for the poor bugger, whoever he was, who was in the agonizing midst of unrequited love. She'd been there herself and wouldn't wish it on anybody.

"We were thinking…"

"We?"

"Mrs. Hawking and I."

Litha smirked at Elora. "Oh. You and Mrs. Hawking." Elora rolled her eyes. "But I'm guessing that wouldn't be you, Mrs. Hawking, and the Jefferson Unit Sovereign."

Monq readjusted his seat in the chair. "I don't think he should be bothered."

Litha laughed out loud. "Hmmm. I can see that."

"We," he motioned between himself and Elora, "were thinking that, if Glen and Rosie found themselves together in the City of Lights for long enough they might find their way back toward one another."

Litha looked at Elora. "How did you get roped into this?"

She rolled a shoulder. "I love Rosie. I love Glen. It didn't take much persuading."

Litha stared into her tea cup for a long time. When she looked up, her eyes went back and forth between the two cohorts. "You're not planning any interference beyond that? Making sure they're in the same place together for a while?"

Monq held his hands up. "Just that. Then we back away and let love do its thing."

"What is it that you want from me?"

"Well, background for starters," Monq said. "What happened?"

Litha sighed then did a little bobble head thing. "They were dating." She looked away and smiled nostalgically. "It seemed like Rosie was in love with Glen before she was born. The first word she ever said was Glen.

"Before she could even walk she would try to pitch

herself out of my arms, in Glen's direction. Sometimes I was afraid she was going to fall. Although I shouldn't have been. Now I know that she had the ability to stop herself from falling." Monq glanced quizzically at Elora, but didn't stop Litha mid-speech. "Glen would always get there in time to catch her. He'd take her in his arms. The two of them would laugh and she'd pat his cheek with her chubby little hands and squeal his name. It was cute as…"

Litha looked up and became embarrassed when she realized she was waxing maternal. She cleared her throat and continued in a more clinical tone.

"He babysat a lot when Storm was lost. I was gone so much searching. You know?" She looked up for confirmation and maybe absolution. Monq and Elora both nodded sympathetically. "And, gods, she grew up overnight. At least physically. I turned around twice and she was pubescent. That's when she began to be petulant about Glen."

"In what way?"

Litha sighed. "Glen was… how do I say this? Highly sought after by girls and equally receptive to their attentions. He didn't try to hide that from Rosie, at all, because he didn't see her as anything but the kid he was babysitting. Perhaps even as a little sister. She, on the other hand, believed she was in love. His dating was becoming more and more of a problem for her, while he didn't get why she was acting crazy.

"When we," she made a motion between Elora and herself, "decided that perhaps Rosie was old enough to date, we practically had to ritualize giving Glen permission to take her out."

"That's right." Elora chuckled. "We had a private candlelight dinner for four."

Litha nodded. "It worked. They were together, and by all appearances happy, right up until Glen was being inducted into knighthood."

"What happened then?"

"Rosie told him she didn't want him to accept commission as a knight. Naturally he told her that was ridiculous. She ended up giving him an ultimatum. She gave him four days to choose her over the job." Litha sighed. "It's not that it was just childish. It was also the worst case of self-sabotage I could imagine. When Storm found out what she'd done he blew a gasket. It was her first experience with having her dad be angry with her. Between not understanding Glen's need to accept the knighthood he'd spent half his life working toward and her father, well, you could say it was a perfect storm. And I don't mean that to be funny. There was nothing funny about it.

"She gave Glen a deadline and said that, if he didn't call to say he was choosing her over Black Swan, she'd disappear. Bottom line. He didn't call, at least not by the deadline. And she disappeared."

"You didn't know where she was?" Monq asked.

"My friend knew where she was and I knew that I could reach her if there was an emergency. But for whatever reason, she'd decided to go off on her own and I thought it was best to let her make her own choices. Sometimes we learn the most from our failures. Good parents get out of the way and allow their kids fall down so that they can learn to pick themselves up and keep going. At least that's what I think."

"So you hadn't seen her again in all this time?" Monq asked.

"No. I did. A few months after she'd left, she'd had a really bad experience where she'd been staying and came home distraught. Storm and I listened and reassured her that we would always be there for whatever support she needed from us and that she'd always be loved no matter what. Then she was gone again and I didn't see her until a couple of weeks ago.

"Half the reason why I took a leave of absence was to give her a purpose close to home so I could reconnect with her. So I wouldn't have to go for years between visits."

Elora nodded reassuringly.

Monq said, "What about Glen?"

"Glen had been close to our whole family. He'd practically worshipped Storm, and Storm thought the world of Glen. For the first year Glen called twice a month to find out if we'd heard anything from Rosie and if there was a way he could reach her. The next year the time between calls began to grow. For a while it was once a month, then once a quarter until he stopped calling.

"After he stopped calling, he also stopped returning Storm's phone calls, which I have to tell you, didn't sit well with my husband. Although he would never say so, I think it hurt his feelings. When Glen was transferred back here, he never reached out to us. That was hard. There was a time when he came to dinner every Tuesday night. Like family. We loved him."

She held up her cup. "How about another?"

"Sure," Elora said as she rose to pour another cup.

"That's all there was to it," Litha said. "If Rosie had been more mature and not put Glen in the outlandish position of choosing her or The Order, I would bet my last dollar that they'd still be together." She looked at Monq. "You believe in soul mates?"

He pursed his lips. "I don't know about that. I believe that, at any given time, there are multiple people in the world with whom any one of us could find love and happiness, but I also think that of those options, there is one that is the best match possible."

"For somebody trying to conjure a love match, that's just about the least romantic thing I've ever heard," Elora said.

Monq shrugged. "These two personalities settled on each other early and then missed out on the follow through. Now that I've heard the details of their history from a reputable source, I'm even more convinced that Sir Catch, at least, would greatly benefit from finding his way to forgiving Rosie."

"What is it that the two of you have in mind?"

"They believe their mission is to find Sir Falcon and bring him back. If he is actually headed to Paris to find Jean Etienne, and by extension, Genevieve Bonheur, we could ask Jean Etienne to apprehend and subdue Falcon. We could even have people transport him back here. But if Glen and Rosie believed he was still at large, they would continue looking. Subterfuge in the name of love isn't subterfuge. It's caring."

Litha exchanged a look with Elora.

"So the big question is this." Monq looked at Litha. "Would it be possible to create a decoy for Falcon that would fool a tracker? Something that would cause her to believe he was there? In Paris? Something that someone could move around from place to place?"

"Something that would lead them on a chase, you mean." Litha considered that for a moment. "It would be four-layered and tricky, because, not only would I need to create something that would suffice as his proxy, I would also have to mask his actual presence, essentially make him undetectable magickally. That and we'd also be depending on things of a mundane nature that are beyond my control."

"A cloak of invisibility," came a small voice from just outside the door.

"Helm!" Elora said. "Were you eavesdropping?"

Helm appeared at the doorway. "I was coming to the kitchen to get juice."

"How much did you hear?" Elora asked.

Helm's blue eyes twinkled in an eerily familiar way. "Some."

"Come here."

Helm crossed the room, stood by his mother, and put his hand on her gigantic abdomen. "How are the babies?" he whispered, trying to endear himself to his mother.

Elora couldn't help but giggle. "The babies are fine, but you, young elf, are in trouble."

"Why?"

"Do you know what confidential means?"

"No."

"It means that you can't tell other people what you know."

He looked around the table. "Like a secret."

"Exactly like that."

"So you want me to keep my mouth shut." He shrugged. "Okay. Can I have juice?"

Elora stared at Helm for a couple of beats. "You are your father's child."

Helm's eyes cut to hers sharply. "Is that a bad thing?"

She laughed. "No. It's the best thing in the universe."

He grinned as she pulled him in for a big hug. He got his juice out of the refrigerator then, on his way past Litha said, "If you can make a cloak of invisibility, I'd like to have one for my birthday."

Litha raised an eyebrow. "Better come up with something else because that's *never* going to happen."

"Aw," he said, mocking disappointment. He smiled when he looked back at his mother.

"Go," she said, "and no more listening in." When Elora was sure Helm was in D & D zone, she sat down and said to Litha, "So. Can you do it? A cloak of invisibility?"

Litha treated her co-conspirators to one of her rare demon-like smiles. "Close enough."

Elora looked impressed. "I'm so glad I'm on your good side."

Litha nodded. "I have to admit, it is the best place to be."

Monq broke in. "You said four-layered. What are the

other two pieces?"

"We need cooperation of both Jean Etienne and my father."

"Go on," said Monq.

"I need to get my dad to remove Falcon from this dimension so that Rosie's tracking crystal will lock onto the poppet. That's a big if because he's unpredictable. If he agrees, the last thing would be to get Jean Etienne to move the poppet around Paris to give them something to chase after. When they arrive at our destination of choice, Jean Etienne will douse the energy of the poppet by covering it with the, um," she dropped her voice to a whisper, "cloak of invisibility."

Elora said, "This plan is nothing if not elaborate. What can go wrong?"

Monq said, "Let me count the ways."

"I actually think that's a good idea," Elora responded. "Number one?"

"Jean Etienne could say no," Litha offered.

"He's French. Aren't they all about romance? Especially if he's feeling romantic toward Mme. Bonheur?" Monq asked.

"Hmmm. Comme ci comme ça," Litha said.

"So you think he might say no?" Elora asked. "Monq, you know him best."

"It's really impossible to predict. He's a virtually immortal vampire, not a man."

"Okay. Moving on. Number Two?"

"Deliverance could say no," said Litha.

Elora waved her hand in dismissal. "He never says no

to you, Daddy's girl. Number Three?"

"The couple might experience stress over not finding Falcon, which could cause either Glen or Rosie to be out of sorts and repel the desired result. Judging from what I've seen, right now they're already behaving like flint and steel." Litha and Elora waited for him to clarify that. "If they get too close together, sparks fly, fire starts, etcetera, etcetera. The last time that happened in my office, I had to replace the carpet. Again."

"Glen and Rosie ruined your carpet?"

Monq realized he was getting off topic so he waved his hand in the air as if to clear that question from the air. "Never mind. We have more important things to cover."

"Such as?" Litha asked.

"How to keep the Sovereign satisfied that progress is being made on Falcon's return, while keeping him from pulling the plug on our mission."

"I can fix that one," Elora said.

"How?" Litha and Monq both asked in unison.

Elora smiled. "Secret weapon."

"Don't be coy," Litha said. "Spit it out."

"Farnsworth." Elora nodded. "She can get stick-up-his-ass to do anything."

"She can?" Monq seemed bowled over by the idea of that.

"Yes."

"I don't know," he said. "Sounds risky. Letting Farthing in on this could knock the legs out from under the entire operation. He might just say no."

Elora pondered that while her fingers made clockwise

circular patterns on her rounded tummy as if she was soothing the twins. "I see what you're saying, but I have faith that Farnsworth can lead him to reason."

"Then we'd be in trouble," said Monq, "because there's really nothing reasonable about what we're proposing. It's quite mad and could get the lot of us in hot water with The Order, not to mention the young people who are being played like pieces in a game."

"It sounds manipulative when you put it like that," said Elora. Litha and Monq stared at her. "Okay. So it is. But hopefully the end result will justify the manipulation."

Litha joined in. "If this goes south, Rosie may not speak to me for centuries."

"Well, that would be bad," Monq said.

"Are you going to live for centuries?" The question came from a small sweet voice at the kitchen door.

"Helm! I told you not to listen in. I thought you were busy with your game," Elora scolded.

"I'm hungry and the talking is going on forever."

"Well, you have a point," Elora said. "What do you want for supper?"

"Macaroni and cheese."

"No."

"French fries and potato chips. With ketchup."

"No."

"Blackened tilapia and green beans."

"Yes!" She beamed. "We have a winner. I'll call it in. You can have some grapes to tide you over until it gets here."

"Popcorn." He bargained.

"No."

"Peanut butter and cheese crackers."

"No."

"You're not the boss of me. I'm the king."

Elora looked shocked. "Who told you that?"

"I heard you talkin' about it with Da."

Elora's eyes narrowed. "Your pointy little ears are starting to get too big. Even for an elf."

Seeing the look on his mother's face, Helm was beginning to think better of making a scene in front of company. "You gonna tell Da?"

"Depends. Am I going to hear any more about who's boss?" He shook his head vigorously. "Grapes."

Helm hunched his shoulders and trudged to the glass pedestal bowl that housed a selection of grapes like he was trying to survive a forced march. He pulled a bunch of seedless red grapes away from the stem then left the room with a smile so charming that all three adults were enthralled and sat staring after him when he'd gone.

"He's going to be a handful," Litha said.

"He already is! Thank the gods his father has a handle on things. It's like he can predict what Helm is going to say and do next." She chuckled. "And all hel may break loose when these two meet daylight and share an apartment with the..." She mouthed 'the king' and put it in air quotes.

Monq stood up. "I'm going to get ahold of Baka and let him know what's up."

"Tell him I said hi," Elora added.

"Is there going to be anyone associated with The Order who *won't* be in on this?" Litha asked.

"Don't be terse, my dear. You have magick to perform."

"I need to get in Falcon's apartment and get something of his," Litha replied.

"Very well. Phone call first. Burgling next."

Litha eyed the outrageous swell of Elora's pregnancy. "You think you can keep that together until after you talk to Farnsworth?"

Elora pressed her lips together. "I'd better go call now. Just in case. Although the timing isn't great because the Sovereign is likely off duty now. It would be a whole lot easier to talk to her about this when he's not around."

"Well, you'll have to weigh the options and decide."

"Maybe I can get someone to create a situation that he needs to attend to personally?"

"No. That's crazy," Litha said. "Instead of trying to get her alone tonight when he's not home, just invite her over here for tea. Have her tell him that you want to discuss your birthing options one more time."

"I could do that," Elora agreed. "Sounds plausible enough."

"Oh what a tangled web we weave," added Monq. Both women looked at him like they couldn't believe he'd just said that since he was the one who'd started the snowball rolling down the mountain. "What? I wasn't saying it in a bad way. Just an observation."

"Let's not ever forget who orchestrated this folly." Elora looked at Litha. "How long do you need to get your, um, things ready?"

Litha tapped her fingers like she was calculating. "Six hours?"

"You'll be done before the boys are back. They'll never be any the wiser," said Elora.

"If peewee really does 'keep his mouth shut'," Litha replied.

"He will. He's good at secrets." She paused. "With proper motivation."

"What would that be?"

"Brownie muffins." She smiled.

"Okay, then," Monq said. "We all have our jobs. Elora, you're on Farnsworth. Litha, you have hocus pocus duty. I'm working the Baka, Jean Etienne angle."

"Oh." Elora looked like she'd thought of something else. "While you're at it, call the Jeanne d'Arc Unit and tell them to give Glen and Rosie the Charlemagne Suite." Monq and Litha looked at her with a question mark on their faces. "Ram and I have stayed there when we were traveling with Helm. It's a two-bedroom tower suite on the Paris side and has a view of the Seine. They reserve it for special guests. Just tell the Operations Manager that Glen and Rosie are coming and that they're special guests."

Before bedtime all contacts had been made, agreements extracted, bargains entered into, and schedules synchronized. Naturally, the most intense bargaining was between Litha and Deliverance because, as everyone knows, demons are nothing if not determined to get the upper hand of a deal.

"I JUST NEED you to take him to your lair and hide him for a few days," said Litha.

"First of all, my home is not a lair. It's insulting for you to call it that. Second, what do you expect me to do with him?"

"Make him watch hours of *I Love Lucy* reruns. That's what you made me do." She pulled in her chin and looked at him as if seeing him for the first time. "In fact, how many people have been subjected to that experience? It could be the origin of the hel myth."

Deliverance smiled. "Good times."

"Right. What do you say?"

"I'll have to think about it."

"It's for Rosie."

"Bargaining with my granddaughter's happiness is out of bounds."

"I'm half demon. Nothing is out of bounds."

"Good point. I'll do it if you give me the one thing in all creation that I want most."

"What is that?"

"Time spent with you."

"Dad, you're going to make me cry."

"Not really."

"No. Not really."

"Just, you know, remember before Engel?" Deliverance screwed up his face. "Even his name is offensive."

"I like that his name means angel in German."

"Whatever. The point is that we used to wander the worlds together. You would shop while I would gas up. It was wonderful, wasn't it?"

"Yes. It was. I can manage lunch once a week."

"Three times a week."

"Twice."

"Done."

They both smiled knowing that it was a mutually satisfying deal.

THE ONLY THING left to be done was the creation of Litha's sympathetic magick props. Farnsworth, having willingly entered into the conspiracy with little coaxing required, let her into Falcon's apartment where she shopped for bits of things to go into her poppet and create a believable target for the family crystal. Nothing that he would miss, of course. A little hair from his comb. The dog ear portion of a page from a well-worn book. A note he'd written to Mme. Bonheur, but thrown in the trash. She shot copies of several photos with her camera, including the one of K Team winning the past year's Jefferson Unit rugby championship and was satisfied she had enough to create a shadow of his essence.

Before Glen and Rosie reached Paris, Deliverance would have Falcon secured in his lair, Litha would hand the poppet and cloak over to Jean Etienne, and Farnsworth would convince Farthing that the pursuit of love was a far higher good than routine administration.

Elora made one more phone call to the most romantic person she knew, Istvan Baka.

Chapter Seventeen

After Falcon managed to lose Sir Catch and The Order's current premier tracker, he'd gotten a whister ride to Manhattan then grabbed a cab to the private jet charter at Teterboro. He had no experience arranging for his own travels because the Operations Office had always handled logistics. Because of that lack of experience, he was somewhat surprised to find out that the company never had jets fueled up and ready for walk-ins. After insisting that they make phone calls on his behalf, he learned that there were no other long-range private planes available for *immediate* hire elsewhere.

"When will you have a ride for me?" he asked the impeccably sleek young woman behind the counter.

"Tomorrow midday. Will that be satisfactory?"

"No. It will not, but it doesn't look like I have a choice."

"Sorry nothing is available sooner, sir. How would you like to pay?"

"Cash."

Falcon expected the clerk to be surprised, but she was not.

She didn't bat an eye when she said, "That will be

$25,632."

He hitched his bag up onto the counter, unzipped it, counted out stacks of cash and placed them in front of her. The clerk calmly counted the cash, then handed him sixty-eight dollars in change.

"Thank you, Mr. Falco. We have a suite in the hangar that is sometimes used by clientele for layovers. It's available if you'd like to wait there. You could sleep or watch TV."

"Sure," he said.

She handed him a key. "Down this hall, turn right and you'll run into it. The refrigerator and bar are fully stocked with drinks and snacks. There's also a number to call for complimentary food delivery. Please make yourself at home until tomorrow. Someone will come for you when we're ready for departure. Is there anything else I can do for you?"

"Yes. I'll need a car to take me into the city on arrival."

"Very well." She gave a nod that was somewhere between professional and subservient. "That will be another one hundred forty."

Falcon handed over the sixty eight dollars he was still holding in his hand, pulled out another hundred, slapped it on the counter and said, "Keep the change."

He thought the clerk might crack a smile at that, but she did not. She simply nodded.

After pulling the strap of the bag, now somewhat lighter, over his shoulder, he walked in the direction she'd indicated. He supposed it couldn't hurt to start his quest with sleep in a real bed. He'd been sleeping in a hospital bed in a hallway. And though the popcorn was good film fodder, he wouldn't mind a decent dinner and the distraction of TV. He'd start out fresh, well-rested and well-nourished, so that he could spend the time in the air planning what he was going to do when he got to Paris.

He didn't have a plan beyond talking to Genevieve, if not to persuade her to choose him, then at least to make sure she was still certain about the choice she'd made to go with Jean Etienne. He didn't know what alternative he had to offer if she said no. He just knew that everything was well and truly fucked and that he had to do something other than going on with life as if the catastrophe hadn't occurred.

The thing that he could never have anticipated in a thousand guesses would be the thing that happened next. Somewhere between New Jersey and Paris, the dashing young knight simply disappeared from the plane without a trace. It would be a mystery that UFO specialists would be examining for decades thereafter.

GLEN MADE THE same error as Falcon. Having never arranged for a private jet before, he assumed one would be available, which would have meant Falcon would be in Paris in about eight hours including travel time on the ground.

Due to the miscalculation based on not having all the information, Glen and Rosie would arrive in Paris a full twenty hours ahead of Falcon.

Glen had requested a meeting with the Paris Unit Sovereign at around midnight. Middle of the night meetings were not unusual for vampire hunters since that would be near the beginning of their work 'day'.

Chapter Eighteen

Day One – Paris

THE GOOD NEWS was that the pill Glen took worked great. He arrived at the Jeanne d'Arc Unit with no dizziness, queasiness, headache, blurred vision, or other side effect.

The bad news was that Rosie had brought them out of the passes inside the Unit grounds and set off the alarms.

After explaining who they were, how they bypassed security, and presenting verifiable credentials, they were checked in and escorted to the Charlemagne Suite as requested by the Lady Elora Laiken, although they were not told that placement in the premier suite was a special request made on their behalf because, after all, discretion had been part of the request and, if nothing else, the French are consummately accomplished at two things: romance and discretion.

Glen and Rosie had both spent the past few years in environments that would not be considered luxurious by anyone of any standard. So each, in her or his way, appreciated the plush pad with its twenty-foot ceilings, beveled mirrors set in carved paneling, Venetian rugs, and Renoir paintings.

The crystal was quiet so Glen said, "Taking a nap. Knock if you get anything."

The suite phone rang at four. When Rosie picked it up, she heard Glen's voice on the line. He'd answered first, so she hung up. In a few minutes there was a knock on the door.

Glen was standing on the other side frowning. "Still nothing?"

"Nothing."

"Maybe I guessed wrong. About where he was going, I mean."

"I don't think so. Let's give it a little longer."

"That was Baka on the phone."

"Oh?'

"He and Mrs. Baka have invited us to join them for dinner. A welcome-to-Paris thing was what he said."

"So. Are we going?"

"Do you want to?"

"Well, yes. I've never been to Paris."

Glen cocked his head. "You haven't?"

"No. Why?"

"It just seems like you're, ah, well-traveled."

"I probably haven't seen as much of *this* dimension as you think."

He pursed his lips then said, "They want to pick us up at eight. That okay?"

Rosie nodded. "What did he say to wear?" She looked behind her at the armoire in the suite.

"He didn't say. Wear whatever you want. Who gives a shit?"

Glen stalked away like asking about clothes had set him off, leaving Rosie wondering what had happened.

Rosie opened the bar refrigerator and pulled out some mixed nuts and soda to tide her over until dinner. She ran clothing options in her head and eventually decided on black velvet leggings, a blood red silk tunic with a thin rhinestone belt and black thigh high boots. She pulled her hair up into a messy bun and secured it with a clip covered with diamonds and rubies. It amused her to know that no one would guess the stones in the clip were real and that the sale of the piece would render enough to buy a chateau in the French Alps. They would assume rhinestones to match the belt.

Glen didn't bother to knock on her door. At eight he just stood in the living room that separated their bedrooms and yelled, "Let's go. You're making us look bad."

Rosie opened the door and strode toward him with a smile. For a second his permanent scowl faltered as he let his eyes wander down to her feet and up again. But without a word, he opened the suite door and walked out, leaving it standing ajar behind him.

Rosie sighed thinking at least he didn't slam it behind him.

He'd already called the elevator when she arrived at the end of the hall.

"Wonder when they put in an elevator," she said, making small talk.

"Sometime last century," he quipped.

"Well, that narrows it down."

Glen and Rosie walked in silence until they were past

the second set of security gates where a limo was waiting, apparently for them.

Baka climbed out of the car. He shook Glen's hand and gave Rosie a kiss on the cheek. They renewed greetings with Heaven inside the car.

"Where are we going for dinner?" Rosie asked.

"Istvan made a reservation at Le Train Bleu. It's one of his favorites. I think it's Rococo hel. It's gilded, carved, molded, and frescoed to death, but Baka loves it. So what can I do?" She turned and looked at him adoringly, which made Glen hope it would be a very short dinner.

"Poor darling," Baka said to his wife. "You must suffer through an evening at one of the world's great eateries. How *will* you manage?"

Baka grinned when Heaven kissed his nose.

"I can't wait," Rosie said. "I've never been to Paris before."

Heaven's eyes went wide. "Noooo. Eat eez impouseeble," she said with a French accent, making fun of the fact that the French overuse the word 'impossible'. Rosie giggled. "In that case," Heaven continued in her own British accent, "let us make some recommendations of must-see's."

Rosie smiled. "I'd love that."

"How about you, Sir Catch?" Heaven asked Glen. "Have you been to Paris before?"

He glanced at Heaven before returning his attention to whatever was in the darkness outside his tinted window. "Yes, but not for sightseeing," he said drily.

"For vampire hunting, I suppose?" asked Baka.

Glen met his gaze. "That's right. Does that bother you?"

"Not at all. Though I'm certain it might if I was still a vampire." Baka smiled amiably. "I'm sure you're very good at your job. But of course, these days we do the same work, you and I."

"Tell me about Le Train Bleu." Rosie was eager to change the subject. Vampire hunting was not appetizing in the least.

Baka's smile remained fixed, but somehow seemed to become more genuine when his attention shifted to Rosie. "As my wife said, it is extremely ornate and, I admit, overdone by modern standards, but the historical style is part of its charm."

"Comes with the territory when you're married to a relic," Heaven teased.

Baka pretended to pinch her. "The restaurant is part of the train station built at the turn of the century."

Heaven interrupted, "He means the turn of the *last* century. He loses track."

"Thank you, love," said Baka. "It's a national historical monument. The walls and ceilings have forty-one paintings done by masters of the time. Gervex. Saint-Pierre. René Billotte. It's like dining in a museum."

"Baka is an artist. Did you know that?" Heaven said.

"No." Rosie smiled. "I didn't know that."

Glen didn't bother to acknowledge that anyone was speaking.

THE MAITRE D' called Baka by name and showed them to a

corner booth. Heaven sat and scooted toward the wall. Baka sat beside her, which meant that Glen had no choice but to sit close to Rosie across from the vampire and his wife, who was reported to be some sort of strange summoner of everything from goats to vampire. Looking at the couple making kissy faces across the table, he wondered if she also summoned happiness.

Rosie noticed that the room was crowded despite the fact that it probably cost a small fortune to dine there.

The sommelier appeared as soon as they were seated, looking as pleased as if it was his birthday. He allowed his gaze to touch everyone at the table before fixing on Baka. He asked if Baka wanted something in particular. Without hesitating, Baka asked if they still had a bottle of Romanee-Conti.

The man grinned in a way that made Rosie wonder if he got a commission on wine sales. After bowing slightly, he disappeared.

"I hope that's just for the two of you," said Glen. "We're working tonight. Or at least I hope we will be."

"Of course," Baka replied. He looked at Heaven. "We can make a splash all by ourselves, can't we?"

She gave a throaty laugh. "We're supposed to be working later ourselves."

"Well," he said, "then we'll have to finish dinner with some of their outrageously fabulous coffee which tastes like it was brewed in heaven."

At that he kissed his wife like they had just procured a room and were alone in it. Glen and Rosie watched the public display of passion, Rosie with amusement, Glen with disdain. When the waiter arrived tableside, he stood waiting politely for some time before clearing his throat.

Baka drew back with a roguish smile when he saw that Heaven's eyes were glazed and distant. "Haven't lost my touch," he whispered loud enough that Glen and Rosie could hear across the table.

"Would you like to see menus?" Baka asked Glen and Rosie.

"Since you know the place, I'm okay with having you order for me," Rosie said.

Baka looked to Glen who shrugged in reply. Taking that to mean yes, Baka ordered for the four of them.

"Duck foie gras with the crystallised pear. The leg of lamb with gratin Dauphinois. Rum baba with Malagasy vanilla. And espresso after." Heaven whispered something to Baka, who then said, "Raspberry cheesecake for the lady instead of Rum baba."

When the waiter left, Glen said, "It's a good thing our employer has deep pockets."

Baka smiled. "That is nice. But dinner tonight is *my* treat. I was hoping for news of American friends."

"He means Elora," Heaven said, rolling her eyes.

Baka stared at his wife. "That is *not* what I meant. I'm curious about all the people I came to know during my transition."

"Elora is having twins. Had you heard that?" Rosie asked.

"I had heard something about that," Baka said. "How is she?"

"Ready to pop. She's huge. And due anytime from

what I understand."

"How is your father?"

"Good, but tired of the knight grind. You know."

"Indeed I do."

Heaven leaned toward Baka and said something so quietly that Glen and Rosie couldn't hear. Baka laughed and then consumed his wife in a series of kisses that made the two of them seem much more like desperate teenage lovers than settled married couple.

When the foie gras arrived, they were still going at it.

Glen tapped the table nervously, not wanting to stare at them, not wanting to look at Rosie, and not wanting to stare at other diners either. Rosie, on the other hand, was rather captivated by the demonstration of married life at its best.

The Bakas pulled apart long enough to feed each other foie gras.

"This is embarrassing," Glen said under his breath so only Rosie could hear.

"Oh, I don't know. I think it's kind of charming and optimistic for lovers everywhere."

"Optimistic?"

"Yes. It says that married life doesn't have to be dull."

"Are you two sharing secrets?" Baka asked.

"Yes," Glen said. "You should try it sometime. Keeping private things private that is."

Baka laughed. "Didn't mean to ruffle sensibilities, old man."

When Glen stared at Baka like he was dumbfounded, Heaven chuckled and said, "It's something the cool kids said before the beginning of time."

Glen's scowl returned as he stared at the foie gras, thinking it didn't look edible. Rosie, on the other hand, was gobbling it down and making little low humming noises that got a reaction from Glen's traitorous dick.

Baka reached for his phone. "Excuse me. I'd hoped we could get through dinner, but…" He paused to frown at his phone. "We're needed elsewhere. Please stay and enjoy. Order anything else you might want. The tab is settled." Baka and Heaven slid out of the booth. He nodded at Glen and Rosie. "I hope I'll get to see you again while you're here in the city of love."

"We're sorry you have to rush off, but thank you for dinner," said Rosie.

"If I don't see you again, please give our regards to your family."

"Of course."

Heaven smiled at Rosie, "Please don't think us rude. Duty calls."

"We understand." Rosie smiled at her.

Glen remained silent, but watched Baka stop the maître d and say something to him. The maître d nodded in response.

"I hope he didn't just order drinks on the house and tell that guy that I would pay."

Rosie looked at Glen like she'd never seen him before. "What's the matter with you?"

"No idea what you mean."

"You're acting like a perfect stranger. The Glen I know would never be ungracious."

"The Glen you know is gone," he said, his tone completely void of emotion. "Thought you would have figured that out by now."

"Are we leaving?" Rosie asked with an unmistakable sadness over the way the evening had turned out. She hadn't realized that she was enjoying herself until Mr. and Mrs. Baka departed. Then the reality of the fuming thunderstorm that used to be Glendennon Catch settled around her like a shroud made of thick hemp dyed black.

Glen got up, walked around to the other side of the table and slid into the booth seat facing Rosie. "Might as well stay. We have to eat. And it's free. Supposedly."

The waiter punctuated the end of that thought by arriving to reset the table for two according to instructions from the maître d'. Glen watched every movement as if he was training for the job. Rosie wasn't fooled by his feigned interest. She knew he was trying to find something to look at that wasn't her.

"So," she said, "tell me what you've been doing since I saw you last."

Glen's first impulse was to snarl and tell her to fuck off and that, if she'd wanted to know, she damn well could have called, but before the ugliness left his lips he rethought it. Since there was nothing to do while they had dinner but talk, he decided he'd make the best of it.

"Moved around a lot."

"Oh? By choice."

"No."

"Oh. Well, what was it like?"

He let his gaze meet hers, long enough to confirm that

her green eyes still had the yellow and brown flecks in them. Long enough to see that she was undeniably the most beautiful creature alive. He hated her for that. He hated himself for making the choice to walk away from her. He hated the life he'd lived for the past five years. And he hated being left alone to have dinner with the last person in the world he wanted to sup with.

He took in a big sigh. "It was awful."

"I'm sorry. Did you make some friends though?"

He barked out a laugh that indicated the answer was no, just before the lamb arrived. When the aromas reached his nostrils, he suddenly had a hard time remembering why he didn't want to be there and made a decision that it wouldn't cost him anything to be civil to Rosie.

"This smells good."

"It does," she replied.

In between bites of what was perhaps the best dinner of his life, Glen sketched out a travel log of assignments, leaving out details about the seediness, the loneliness, and the stress of not knowing for certain that the people on his team could be trusted to have his back in a confrontation with vampire.

Rosie listened quietly but intently, trying to hear what was being said and discern what was being left out.

"You want coffee?" Glen asked. "It was ordered."

"Not really," she said just before her eyes went wide. She jumped a little in her seat.

"What is it?" Glen demanded.

"The crystal is awake. I guess I'll have to get used to that."

Without a word Glen stood and began walking toward the exit leaving her to follow behind him. She didn't know if people were watching the display of boorish behavior, but she felt humiliated.

Outside on the street, she said, "Do you want to take a pill and wait five minutes or take a taxi?"

Glen reached for the pill bottle in the pocket of his leather jacket. He looked at Rosie when his hand was withdrawn empty. He patted himself down and went through all his pockets, one by one, before finally saying, "Taxi it is."

Ten minutes later the taxi let them out in the heart of Paris night life.

Standing next to the curb after the taxi drove away, Rosie said, "You think he decided to go dancing?"

Glen shrugged and looked perplexed. It didn't make sense to him either and he wondered if Rosie's crystal could malfunction. But they were there so he was going to check it out. "Which way?"

The crystal led them to a cerulean blue building at 13 Boulevard Poissonnière with an alterna-style crowd milling about outside. The sounds of bass-heavy electronica drifted out into the street.

"In here," Rosie said.

Glen eyed the place. "You sure?"

Rosie cut her gaze at him sharply. "You just see to your own job, *Sir Catch.*"

He tightened his lips and started toward the door. That was the one of too many times Rosie had seen Glen turn his back on her and walk off. She considered going back to the Paris Unit without telling him, but decided it would be unprofessional.

Inside there was a sunken dance floor and an international crowd that felt reminiscent of the big techno-grunge clubs of London. The place was crowded even though it was early by club standards.

Glen looked at Rosie with eyebrows raised, clearly asking which way. She took hold of the crystal, but shook her head. He grabbed her bicep and leaned down to her ear so he could be heard above the music.

"Stay close to me. I can't look for him and watch out for you at the same time."

Rosie laughed with enough derision to be sure he caught the bite and pulled away. "I can take care of myself."

Glen nodded and turned in a slow circle looking for Falcon, carefully scanning not only the ground floor but the part of the mezzanine that was visible from below. Between the mirrors and the tiny spotlights that moved over the dancing crowd, changing color, size, and direction, he began to feel a little disoriented. He started through the gyrating crowd on the dance floor. Several pairs of feminine hands reached out to beckon him closer, but he gently shrugged each would-be partner away. When he reached the other side without a glimpse of their target, he turned to ask Rosie what the crystal had to say. She wasn't there.

He started back through the crowd the way he'd come and hadn't gone far when she came into view. She was dancing, sandwiched in between two guys who looked skungie enough to be on Z Team. His temper shot straight to white hot. Not because she was uber sexy and doing a provocative dance that involved touching in suggestive ways.

If not for the horde of moving bodies between them, he would have stomped over and jerked her away, but progress was as slow as trying to walk in waist-high ocean at high tide. By the time he reached her, he had lost control of his composure and the part of him that was werewolf. Fortunately the music was so loud that only those close by heard the distinct sound of angry canine growling as he passed. They quickly attributed it to imagination or one too many sense-bending beverages and forgot all about it.

Rosie was startled when she felt a strong hand encircle her wrist and yank her away from the pleasurable masculine sandwich she'd been enjoying.

She looked up into Glen's fury with surprise that quickly turned to anger that was all her own. "Growling?" she said. "Seriously?!? Have you lost your mind?"

"Have you lost yours?" he yelled in response. "You're supposed to be working."

"The crystal has gone quiet. He was here, but he's gone. So I might as well have a little fun."

"Fun?" Glen looked at the two boys she'd been dancing with in a way that made them both retreat in search of another partner. "When were you going to tell me?" he shouted. "You were just going to let me keep looking all night while you had public sex with strangers? Knowing he's not here?"

She pressed her lips together. "First, since when do you care who I dance with? Second, if you want to know something from me, then maybe you shouldn't always be turning your back on me and walking off. I don't owe it to you to follow."

"You're supposed to be working with me."

"Really? Are you supposed to be working with *me*?" Glen's angry panting had begun to slow and he wasn't showing quite so much tooth when he spoke. When no response was forthcoming, Rosie said, "I'm out of here. I'll let you know when I have a fix on him again."

And with that she vanished, leaving him to find his own way back to the unit. Alone. He'd forgotten how much he hated that she had the ability to do that in the middle of an argument.

He left the club still too angry to get a ride. So he walked around for a bit, hood up and shoulders hunched with hands in his pockets. It was a posture that had become familiar to his body. As he walked he began to take a good look at himself and realize that he'd been angry for so long he'd forgotten how to be anything else.

Sometime after midnight Rosie heard the suite door open and close. She looked at the clock out of reflex. She hadn't been lying awake waiting for him to come in. She just hadn't fallen asleep. At least that's what she told herself. She turned over, blinking slowly, calming her mind, and let her eyes close.

Chapter Nineteen

Paris – Day Two

GLEN HADN'T BEEN able to find the little tin of miracle pills that prevented travel sickness in the passes, so they had to resort to transportation human-style. The cab let them out at Bois de Vincennes, the largest park in the city. They followed a tree-lined avenue then took a meandering path ending at a boat dock.

"Well?" Glen asked.

"Over there." She pointed to a small island in the middle of the lake with a pillared Grecian gazebo rising on a hill above the grotto entrances.

Glen turned to the man in charge of canoe rental. "What is that place?" he asked in French.

"The Temple of Love," the man answered. "On Île de Reuilly."

Glen shook his head and laughed bitterly. Under his breath he said, "Of course it is. Swear to the gods this feels like a set up." He turned to the man. "Is this the best way to get there?"

"Oui. Which one do you want?"

"Which boat?" Glen looked behind him. The first one that caught his attention said *Se Leva* on the side.

Seeing Glen's fixation on that particular boat, the man said, "Oui. This one," and began untying the rope.

Rosie came up next to him. "Oh. The boat's named Rose. Cool. It's a sign."

"It's not a sign. It's a canoe. And Rose is not exactly a unique name."

The boat renter said something to Glen. "What did he say?" she asked.

Glen sneered. "He wanted to know if I was going to propose in the 'temple of love'." He made air quotes.

Rosie simply looked away and sniffed as if she was unaffected by Glen's spitefulness.

IT DIDN'T TAKE long to get to the halfway point because the lake wasn't big.

"You're not going to row?" Glen asked.

"No. You lost the pills. Now we have to get around human-style. So it's only fair that you provide the power."

Glen didn't really mind rowing. It wasn't hard. He'd just made the comment as an opportunity to be contentious. He stopped and looked around, noticing that the temperature and atmosphere were as close to perfection as it gets this side of paradise. The muscles held in a constant state of tension for years on end were beginning to relax in spite of himself. He didn't know if that was because of the gentle feel of the air, the beauty of the place, or, gods forbid, the presence of the woman at the other end of the canoe. He batted away the unwanted thought that, if things had turned out differently, the two of them might have been there in that very place, on that very day, enjoying a honeymoon.

"What are you thinking?"

Glen looked at Rosie. "I don't get out in the daytime often." He paused. "For obvious reasons."

"Because vampire are out at night."

He nodded. "When you think about it, it's kind of amazing, being able to see far away, knowing if something is coming for you in time to stop it."

Something in the way Glen expressed that filled Rosie's soul with sorrow. She was putting bits and pieces together like a puzzle and it was taking shape in a way that made Glen's life since she'd known him seem like hel.

"Most of us take that for granted. It must be awful having to live your whole life at night."

Glen didn't respond. He simply took another look around, picked up the oars, and resumed rowing toward the island.

THEY STOOD INSIDE the stone gazebo, turned a full circle, then descended the jagged steps to the grotto beneath the 'temple'. The natural formation was magical enough to distract them from their purpose for being there temporarily, but not completely.

"I just don't get it," Rosie said. "The crystal indicates that he was here. Now he's not only *not* here, but it would seem that he's not *anywhere*."

"We're being punked by your crystal. How am I supposed to report that to the J.U. Sovereign? 'Sorry. But he's not anywhere.'"

"We could respond a lot faster if you hadn't lost your

pills. Chasing him the human way puts us at a disadvantage."

"Well it wouldn't do much good for me to get within grabbing distance and have to stop to puke on the street either."

As Rosie looked at the crystal and shook her head, it came to life again. "Got something. If we go the other direction and take the bridge, we can probably get to a taxi faster."

"Leave the boat?"

"Why not?"

"Because it would be extra trouble for the boat guy."

"Leave a big enough cash tip in the boat so that he doesn't mind the trouble."

Glen seemed to internally debate that solution before weighting some money down with an oar. "I hope marriage-proposal guy finds that before somebody else." He climbed back out of the canoe and said, "Okay. Let's go your way. It'll be under a minute, right?"

"Yes."

Glen took her hand and placed her fingers between his leather belt and his jeans. "Hold on tight. Don't lose me."

She tightened her grip on his belt and smiled sweetly. "This time I won't, but the next time you turn your back on me and walk off, expect me to do the same to you in the passes."

Glen parted his lips to say something, but before he got the chance to form a retort, he was plunged into the passes. They emerged on the left bank of the Seine.

"Still got a signal," Rosie said. "Can you move?"

Glen was leaning over with his hands on his knees. He shook his head vigorously. Without thinking, Rosie put her hand on his back and patted in a way universally understood as comfort-giving.

"What are you doing?" he growled.

She jerked her hand away. "Sorry. I wasn't thinking."

By the time he raised his head and said, "All right. Let's go," the crystal had dimmed and gone quiet.

"Too late. He's gone."

Glen took out his phone, typed out a text then put his phone back.

"Reporting?"

He shook his head. "No. Telling Monq to overnight some more of those pills."

"Oh. Good idea. How are you feeling?"

"Halfway to okay." He looked around to get his bearings. He knew the center of Paris well enough to figure out where he was visually. "Left bank." Something seemed to get his attention. "I guess you're hungry."

"Yes. How did you know?"

He smirked. "Because you're always hungry unless you just ate."

"Oh."

"See that?" He pointed at people sitting on the bank of the river with pink balloons in front of pink pizza boxes.

"People eating pizza?"

"I heard about this. It's Pink Flamingo Pizza. You get a balloon with your order, then you can park your ass somewhere along the walk and they'll find you by bicycle delivery. Pink bicycles."

"Pizza sounds good." Glen smiled before he remembered he was supposed to be mad.

He quickly changed his expression but not so quickly that Rosie didn't notice. "You know, if you're having to work so hard at being angry, maybe you should stop."

He looked into Rosie's face and thought about what she'd just said. She was close enough that he could see the few faint freckles on her nose. He used to love those freckles.

She expected him to bury the hatchet, but the past three years all he'd had to hold onto was misery. Somewhere along the way it had become a part of him, a side that was admittedly shadow, but necessary for survival. Letting go would mean leaving a hole where the misery had been residing, a vacuum. And everyone knows that nature abhors a vacuum. It would rush to suck in unknown things to fill itself up including some that could tear your heart out and leave it shredded. Like love.

He stopped a guy going by on one of the pink bicycles and ordered pizza. They got a pink balloon and strolled along the river until they found a good place for people-watching. Glen had to admit that the city looked different when seen from the point of view of a person who wasn't hunting for vampire. It was beautiful and, he supposed, probably as romantic as some claimed.

Since the crystal was quiet, the two of them sat and ate pizza in silence until a guy walked by smoking a cigarette, wearing combat boots, white Jockey briefs, and a Nine Inch Nails tee shirt. When Glen looked at Rosie's face, he couldn't hold in the laugh that bubbled up any more than she could keep from laughing with him, but within seconds, he remembered that he didn't laugh, at least not in mirth, and looked away.

"You want to go back to the Unit?" she asked.

"The pattern so far is, when he shows up, it's around here. So it makes more sense to stay in the city center until we're tired."

"Okay. Sure."

They walked along the river at dusk until they came to a place near one of the famous bridges where couples danced the tango by portable music. Glen bought two cups of wine from a hole-in-the-wall vendor and they sat at a table where they could watch.

Rosie was clearly fascinated by the sensuous movements of people in everyday street clothes performing the dance of passion next to one of the most famous rivers in the world.

"Glen," she said without looking away from the dancers, "Paris is wonderful."

"Yes," he agreed. "It is." That was a revelation. Even though he'd spent months in Paris, he'd never thought it was all that. Before.

"Don't you wish you could do that?" she said, still staring transfixed.

"Do what?"

"Dance the tango."

"I can," he said offhandedly like it was no big deal.

She looked at him with wide eyes. "Shut up."

"No. Really. I went on a couple of dates with a teacher of el tango when I was in Buenos Aires. She taught me the basics."

"The basics."

"Uh huh."

"Prove it."

He cocked his head. "That's a challenge because you don't believe me or because you want to try it. Which is it?"

"Which answer will get me to yes?"

"Come on." As he stood, Rosie was amazed to see his body transform into the attitude of the dance. Drawing a slow arc in the air with a straight arm, he extended his hand to pull her from her chair.

"Oh my," she said, as she put her hand in his.

He put her left hand on his shoulder then spread his right hand between her shoulder blades.

"It's mostly about attitude," he said. "Pretending sensuality gets you halfway there." He guided her through some basic steps and within minutes they were dancing. "You're a fast learner. Not that I didn't already know that."

"That can't be a compliment, can it?"

She was sounding a little breathless. He didn't know if that was from the dancing or the contact, but he knew his own feverish feelings were coming from having the bane of his existence in his arms. He cursed himself for revealing that he knew tango and agreeing to the dance. It was chipping away at his armor. When he realized that, he stopped abruptly and stepped away.

"Let's get a taxi. Falcon's not out, but the vamps will be soon."

She dropped her hands. "Okay." The word conveyed

more disappointment than she'd intended, but she had been enjoying herself. Why pretend otherwise?

ROSIE LAY AWAKE pondering the question of whether or not it was possible to love two men. Her heart still hurt for the one she'd lost, but after five years she couldn't quite picture his face anymore. She questioned herself about whether or not she'd ever stopped loving Glen and concluded that she hadn't. He wasn't just her first love. He was a permanent part of her. It was pointless to deny that, but it was also pointless to want to rekindle something that she'd killed.

Glen was finished with her. He'd made that clear.

Chapter Twenty

Paris – Day Three

GLEN WAS IN the Unit mess talking with some of the Paris knights when Rosie came rushing in.

"Time to go?" he asked.

She nodded. "Did your package arrive?"

"Not yet."

They hurried to the Operations Office to get a car and driver on the double. Using the crystal, Rosie directed the driver straight to the largest park in Paris. They got out and ran in the direction indicated by the crystal until they came to a wall.

"What is this?" Rosie asked, then looking down she said, "Damn. He's gone."

Glen was staring at the wall. "I heard about this place. Le mur des je t'aime. The wall of I-love-yous."

Rosie looked up. The wall, which was the length of a short city block, was covered with I-love-yous written in every language in every alphabet. "Wow. That's a whole lotta love."

They hung around the park until evening then ducked into a sidewalk café for a late lunch or early supper. During the day Rosie had made stops at a crepe truck, an ice cream vendor, and a roasted chestnut vendor. Glen didn't see how she could possibly be hungry, but she said she was.

The weather was beautiful even as the sun went down. Rosie pulled a shawl out of her bag and wrapped it around her shoulders. It was more for fashion than necessity and also helped her blend in.

As they were deciding whether to head back to the Unit, the crystal weighed in and led them to the Palais Garnier, the famous old Paris Opera House.

Rosie read the marquee. "The ballet. Falcon's gone to the ballet? Alone? You're right. The crystal must be broken."

"Well, we're here. We might as well go in and see if he's here. If he actually sits down to watch, it might be our best chance to make contact."

"We can't apprehend somebody in the middle of the ballet."

"One step at a time. Let's find him first. Then we'll decide what to do."

Glen went to the ticket window and discovered that two mezzanine seats had been turned back in.

"That almost never happens," said the cashier. "You're very fortunate."

Inside the booth, but out of sight, Jean Etienne handed the cashier a large bill for her part in delivering the tickets to the right party. She put it in her purse and, when she turned back to thank him, he was gone.

"We're going to the ballet?" Rosie asked.

"Yes."

She stopped and grabbed Glen's arm. "Oh, shit! We're going to the ballet!"

"What's the big deal?"

"What's the big deal?"

"You've never been? In your life?"

"I've never been in my life. And I'm wearing jeans and a Free People thing."

Glen looked at her clothes. "You look fine."

"It's ballet at the Phantom of the Opera House." Glen chuckled whether he wanted to or not. "Shouldn't I be wearing an evening gown?"

"No. People don't do that anymore. Look around."

She did. People were dressed in street clothes which made her relax a little, but didn't quell the excitement in the least.

"It's Romeo and Juliet," she said.

"I know. I saw."

"Only it's contemporary times. They're doing it in modern clothes." She pointed at the posters.

"Yep. Jets and Sharks."

"What?"

"Nothing. What does the crystal say?"

"Oh." She pulled on the chain to bring it out of the bodice of her Free People thing. "It's gone quiet."

"What?"

"Yeah." She frowned.

"Well, we bought these stupid tickets so we might as well do this until you get another signal. I still think the blasted thing is broken."

WHENEVER GLEN LOOKED over at Rosie during the performance, he could see that she was riveted. By the last scene of the last act, wherein Romeo kills himself, Rosie was gripping the arms of her chair with tears streaming down her face. Minutes before the end, Glen pulled her up out of her seat, took her hand and led her out of the theatre, onto the street.

"What's this about? It's not like you didn't know how it was going to end." He reached up impulsively to wipe her tears away.

"You don't want to know."

He dropped his hand to his side. "I wouldn't ask if I didn't want to know."

Studying his face in the dim light, she thought she detected honest concern, something she hadn't ever expected to experience again. A commotion drew her attention away when people began pouring out of the opera house.

"Let's walk," she said, turning south toward the river. Glen kept pace with her, letting her choose the direction. She faced forward as she began to speak. "I asked Kellareal for a place to go where I could..." she paused, but continued walking, choosing words carefully, "where I could try to figure things out without people pushing and pulling."

"Who was pushing and pulling?"

"Well, Dad for one. When he found out what I'd said to you, he was livid. I hated that he was mad at me and didn't know how to respond. But more than that I hated that I was a disappointment to him."

"He said that?"

"Not in so many words, but the message was clear enough. You know, he's Black Swan to the marrow. So Kellareal agreed to help me locate a retreat. He took me to a dimension where somebody owed him a favor. They were a subspecies of hybrids he'd rescued and kind of adopted, I guess. I learned to work." She looked over at Glen for a second and smiled. "I tended bar."

Glen didn't try to hide his disbelief. "You did not."

She laughed. "I did. What's more surprising, I liked it. No. I loved it. Even the mindless sweeping, polishing, washing glasses part. All of it."

"Wow."

She took a deep breath. "I came to care for one of them. And he died."

Glen stopped walking and went as stiff as a board. "You're telling me you fell in love?" Even though it wasn't spoken, Rosie heard the whole question with her heart. What he was really asking was, "You're telling me you fell in love with somebody else?"

Rosie screwed up her face. She wanted to be truthful, but didn't want to be responsible for hurting Glen more than she already had. "I was very attached and prepared to be committed. It would have been impossible not to respond to someone who thinks you're everything." Glen winced, feeling the emotional bite of that even if it hadn't been intended that way. "He needed me and I loved being needed."

It started to rain lightly. After a couple of seconds Glen put his arm around her shoulders and guided her under the awning of a sidewalk café for shelter. For a long time they stood there in damp clothes, silently watching the rain fall all around them. The streets had instantly cleared of people and, sheltered as they were, even though temporarily, it felt like they could have been the only two people alive.

Finally Glen said, "How did he die?"

"In battle. Trying to rescue his younger brother who'd been taken prisoner." In an even quieter voice, she added, "I saw it."

"You mean you saw him die?"

"Yes."

He sighed. "Sounds hard."

"Yeah," was all she said.

"Rosie, regardless of what happened between us, I don't want you to think that I didn't need you. I did. Believe me, I've told myself thousands of times that, if I had a do-over, knowing everything I know now, I would have stayed with you."

Rosie looked at Glen sharply, her eyes shining in the darkness. "Don't ever say that. You were the one who was right! I was the one who was too young for a relationship." Her shoulders sagged because she feared Glen had been torturing himself, believing he'd chosen wrongly and she hated that she'd been the cause of so much grief. Words from the past echoed in her mind and she found herself saying, "Don't you get it? If everybody who could kill the monsters stayed home, where would we be then?"

There they stood in a swirling eddy of emotions that touched briefly on understanding, empathy, even forgiveness, and time seemed to slow down. Rosie felt the connection they'd both once taken for granted slide back into place and click like a high end star-chamber lock. When she raised her face to see if Glen felt it, too, he was turning away and stepping out into the street.

He'd hailed a passing cab and was motioning for her to come as he opened the car door. Glen gave the driver the address of the Jeanne d' Arc Unit.

When they were settled inside the taxi, Glen reached for his phone which lit the darkness. Rosie looked over and saw that it was a text from Farthing, but couldn't read it.

> FARTHING: ***Falcon is in custody. Transport will be available for return midday tomorrow. The Paris Unit will provide two knights to accompany you.***
>
> GLEN: ***Acknowledged.***

Glen put his phone in his jacket pocket. "They have Falcon in custody and ready for transport back to J.U. tomorrow. They've allocated two knights from this unit to make the trip." He gave a wry smile. "I guess they don't want to take any chances on me losing him again."

Rosie said nothing. She simply turned and watched the passing scenery out the window. By the time the cab pulled up outside the massive gates of Jeanne d' Arc Unit, the rain had stopped.

Glen paid the driver and gave his code to the guard at the gate.

After slipping through the side door reserved for pedestrians, Glen and Rosie walked the rest of the way in silence. When they reached the suite, Rosie hesitated, standing in the large center room that was shared by suite occupants. Glen brushed past her on the way to his bedroom.

"Glen." He stopped, but didn't turn around. "Do you think we…?"

He turned his head far enough that she could see his profile and said, "No," before continuing to his room and closing the door behind him.

Regardless of the discomfort of wet clothes and a chill, she didn't correct the discomfort or move from that spot. For some time after she'd been left alone she continued to stand there mulling over what had happened. For a moment, under that awning, she'd been foolish enough to think there was a chance of starting over. If she hadn't ruined their chances by instigating the physical separation, she'd done so by letting it drag on unresolved for years. Or when she confessed that she'd had feelings for someone else. It seemed there was an endless supply of ways to hurt Glen and pursue self-sabotage at the same time.

THE NEXT MORNING, after a night with a lot of thinking and little sleep, Rosie got up early. During the hours since Glen had walked away with a definitive, "No," she'd decided that it was pointless to make the trip back to J.U. Glen and the other two knights didn't need her to help return Falcon and every minute with Glen burned a bigger hole of grief into her solar plexus, knowing what she'd lost and that she'd done it to herself. And worse, to him.

SHE PACKED HER bronze-tinted, polished taffeta backpack, wrote a note for Glen, and left for Edinburgh. The preeminent tracker had use of an apartment at headquarters, a nice perk. She'd determined to throw herself into the job, figure out other ways of tracking besides relying on a temperamental crystal that worked intermittently. She'd find out what else needed doing and lose herself in the blessed distraction of work. If it was work that ended up benefitting someone, she'd be satisfied, if not happy.

ROSIE WASN'T THE only one who'd spent a sleepless night. Glen had tossed and turned and rolled and whipped himself and the bed covers into a tangled mess. In the darkness his mind saw Rosie closing her eyes and making yummy sounds as she tasted the Rum Baba at Le Train Bleu, looking like a Renoir painting in a rowboat with the Temple of Love hovering above her in the background, reading the Wall of I Love You's like it was the most beautiful thing she'd ever seen, watching the tango dancers with the transparency of an unclaimed lover who wanted more than anything to be consumed by passion, and shedding tears over a lost attachment, tears so powerful that the clouds opened up and cried with her.

He wondered if she'd thought about him over the years apart and, if she had, why she'd never called. He also wondered why he hadn't asked her that. He'd certainly had opportunity.

He made a decision that he was going to get up early, order a lavish breakfast to be served in the suite, and before they left Paris, ask her that one simple question.

Why hadn't she called? Just on the off chance that her answer might be something he could live with.

Feeling good about that plan, he set the alarm and drifted off to sleep.

Chapter Twenty-One

Paris – Day Four

He grabbed the alarm when it went off. He didn't think it would wake Rosie, but he wanted to have everything ready before she woke up. Kind of a surprise-I've-decided-maybe-I-don't-hate-you-as-much breakfast.

He called the kitchen, then showered and dressed quickly.

When he emerged from his room to wait for breakfast to arrive, his gaze went first to the door of the other bedroom standing open, then to the handwritten note propped up and left on the dining room table.

Glen.

It was so good to see you again. You don't need me to get Falcon back to J.U. I'd probably get in the way. Please take care of yourself.

Rosie

He crumpled the note in his hand.

Gone again.

Only this time he knew he had no one to blame but himself. She'd tried to reopen a line of communication between them, indicated that there might still be something there, and he'd shut it down every time.

He'd thought his pride was more important than what he really wanted. That thought brought him up short.

What *did* he really want? And the answer was as clear and definitive as a lightning strike. He wanted Rosie. He'd *never* wanted anything more, not even knighthood. For four days she'd been standing a breath away, demonstrating that reconciliation wasn't beyond his reach. In fact, it would have been easy. All he had to do was accept the gift being offered. But he'd been so caught up in thinking he wanted to punish her that he'd blown what might have been his only second chance. Four days in Paris with the woman he loved and he'd wasted it.

Standing alone in the main room of the Charlemagne Suite with a crumpled note in his hand, he said out loud, "Which one of us is being childish now?"

A knock on the door interrupted his thoughts. He assumed it was room service and opened the door to tell them to give breakfast to the dogs, but it wasn't the kitchen staff. It was two of the Paris Unit knights letting him know that the car was ready to take them to the plane where they'd be taking responsibility for Kristoph Falcon until he was handed over at Jefferson Unit.

"WHO HAS HIM now?" Glen asked in French.

The one named Frederique frowned slightly, but answered, "We weren't told that."

Glen said, "I'll get my stuff."

On the drive to the hangar The Order used for Paris

transportation, Glen sat silently looking out the window, devising a plan for another chance with Rosie. As soon as Falcon was taken care of, he'd be taking some well-deserved leave to go on a knightly quest. Only it wouldn't be vampire killing. What he'd be hunting was potentially so much more satisfying. A happily ever after.

THE CAR PULLED to a stop on the tarmac next to the jet that waited with steps lowered, beckoning passengers to board.

After exiting the car, the three knights waited, trading curious glances and looking around for some sign of their assignment.

Within a couple of minutes Deliverance popped onto the scene holding Falcon by the bicep.

The two knights who were unaccustomed to being around people who could pop in and out both jumped and reached for their chests reflexively as if to protect their hearts.

GLEN LOOKED FROM Falcon to Deliverance. "What are you doing with my runner, Gramps?"

"Don't call me that, Choker," Deliverance sneered. "What do you think? I've been keeping him occupied so that you could have a few days in Paris to win my granddaughter back." He looked around. "I take it by her absence that you blew it. Again."

Glen's jaw clenched. "This was a set up."

"More like an opportunity to get your head out of your ass. How's that going for you? I'm thinking you're still preoccupied with smelling poop."

"Who else was in on this?"

"Everybody who cares about you, shithead. And her. I can tell by the look on your face that opportunity knocked and you told it to go fuck itself."

Glen motioned to the Paris knights to take Falcon on board.

"Wait a minute." Deliverance stopped them. "I promised this kid that he'd get to talk to the vamp if he behaved himself and stopped calling Lucy stupid."

"Who's Lucy?"

"Not dignifying that with an answer."

"Which vamp does he want to talk to?" Almost immediately a wave of understanding replaced confusion on Glen's face. "Oh."

Deliverance opened his mouth to answer, but before he spoke, Jean Etienne popped onto the scene with Genevieve.

Falcon started to take a step toward her, but Frederique jerked him back.

"Gen." Falcon wanted to say more, but he was so overcome with emotion his throat closed up making swallowing hard, much less speaking. She looked different. Her skin was truly flawless. If she had pores, they were invisible. Her hair was brighter. The natural caramel highlights had turned a brighter shade of red. Her eyes weren't the ice blue of virus infected vampire, but they weren't brown anymore either. They were somewhere between a light hazel and amber. She almost seemed to give off light, like a visible aura, and looked more like a goddess or a human who'd been airbrushed by nature.

"Hello, Kris."

Falcon struggled for a minute, but found his voice. "How are you?"

"I'm well. But this is more about you. For all our sakes, you need to go back to work and get on with your life. Forget about our friendship. My time in the human world is over forever, but yours is not. Go home. Know that I'm happy and making an adjustment."

"An adjustment?"

Her smile was so glorious it almost brought him to his knees, but she also deliberately showed her very white and very pointed fangs. "I'm well cared for and learning new ways of doing things. I probably won't see you again after this, but I wish you the very best, as I always have." She glanced at Jean Etienne. "I hope you will allow yourself to find someone to love. Even if this hadn't happened, it would never have been me."

Falcon was trying to decide what to say when the vampire couple disappeared. As the knights pulled Falcon away, Deliverance said, "So long, kid."

They boarded the plane. Glen took one last look at Deliverance before putting his foot on the first step.

"What are you going to do now?" Deliverance asked him.

Glen stopped and looked back at Rosie's grandfather. "I'm going to get her back."

Deliverance smiled as he watched Glen go up, but before they had pulled the steps in, he was gone.

Chapter Twenty-Two

ROSIE DECIDED TO pay her mother a quick visit before moving into the headquarters apartment in Edinburgh.

When Litha emerged from her bedroom in the Jefferson Unit apartment, sleepy-eyed and dressed in a flannel robe, Rosie had been sitting at the kitchen table waiting for four hours.

"Tea?" Rosie asked. "The kettle's hot."

Litha shook her head. "Coffee." She headed straight for the pod brewer and said nothing more until she was holding a cup of Kona blend just under her nose, smelling the aroma and letting the steam touch her face. She sat down at the table in front of Rosie and waited.

"I'm moving into the apartment at Edinburgh."

"Oh?" Litha was deducing that meant that Paris hadn't gone as well as she and her co-conspirators had hoped.

"Yes, but first I thought I'd stop by for a bit of orientation."

"What do you mean?"

"Hit me with tracker tips. Tell me if the crystal came with a warranty. Stuff like that."

"A warranty."

"Yes. The blasted thing works when it wants to, which is seldom. Made me look like a fool at best and like I'm really bad at tracking at worst. And maybe I am."

"What happened in Paris?"

"I was supposed to locate Falcon so that Glen could bring him back here for debriefing. The French vampire found him first."

"I see. So how was it seeing Glen after so long?"

Rosie shrugged. "He's changed."

"And?"

"Not for the better."

"I see."

"I think I'm responsible for the change that's not for the better. I feel guilty. And my heart hurts. I think I ruined him."

"I see."

"You keep saying, 'I see', like you're the all-seeing eye."

"Do not be disrespectful to your mother."

"Okay. What else have you got in your bag of tricks for use tracking?"

"The demon crystal is usually your best friend. I showed you how to get into my magick room at headquarters. If you're looking for something unusual, not a person or creature, you can ask ancestors on your witch side. They'll help if they approve of the likely outcome *and* your motivation.

"Sometimes you have to get creative. But Rosie, you'll be a hundred times better than I ever was. You've got talent off the charts."

"If you say so." Litha smiled. "Everybody's mom thinks they're the best."

Litha shook her head. "If that was so, the world would be a better place. Sadly it's not true. Fortunately for you, it just so happens that your mom *does* think you're the best. Especially when you wear that look you've got right now, so much like your father."

It never failed to make Rosie smile that her mother took so much pleasure in seeing bits of Storm reflected through her. "About the apartment in Edinburgh."

"Uh-huh."

"Is there anything you want? I'd kind of like to make it mine. You know?"

"Let me get dressed and I'll go with you. There might be some photos. Stuff like that. Anything else you want to tell me about Paris?"

Rosie zeroed in on her mother, who raised her coffee cup and blinked a little too innocently as she underestimated her daughter's deductive skills. "You didn't."

"What?"

Rosie slumped back and chuckled at the ceiling. "Of course. It all makes sense. Baka and Heaven making out like horny adolescents at that outrageously romantic restaurant?" Her eyes widened. "The Temple of Love? The wall of I Love Yous? The tango? Romeo and Juliet? The pink flamingo pizza?"

"Pink flamingo…?"

"Gods. Could you have been any more obvious? I guess that makes us both look pretty stupid because we didn't figure it out, huh?"

"Well…"

"Whose idea was the suite?" Rosie held up her palm. "Wait. Let me guess. Auntie Elora." Litha closed her mouth. "Who all was in on it?" Litha pressed her mouth into a line. Rosie's mouth dropped open into a full-blown gape. "The crystal! How did you get the crystal to behave all wonky?"

Litha couldn't suppress a little smile of pride. "Well…"

"You've been a bad, bad witch. You're not supposed to use your gifts like that and you know it."

"Now listen here, young lady. As far as I'm concerned, trying to give you and Glen another chance to figure out that you belong together? I can't think of any possible use of magick that would be better."

"Promise me that you will cease and desist."

"All right."

"I'm serious. No more magickal meddling in my love life. Promise!"

"I promise," Litha grumbled.

"Gods."

"I'm sorry it didn't work out."

Rosie stared at her mother for several beats before pensively saying, "Yeah."

FALCON WAS ALLOWED to return to his apartment. He was also allowed freedom to go anywhere within Jefferson Unit, but not outside. He'd been fitted with a bracelet that looked a lot like a Fitbit watch except that, it wouldn't come off without special equipment kept under state-of-the-tech lock and key and it made Falcon easily trackable, every minute of the day, by the Sovereign, Dr. Monq, or *anyone* who possessed one of the tracking devices housed at the quartermaster at J.U.

"There," said Monq when the bracelet locked around Falcon's wrist. "There'll be no more running about until you and I have sorted out your feelings about what's happened and what you plan to do with the rest of your life."

"You can't hold me prisoner."

"Hmmm. Well, perhaps you didn't read the fine print of your contract with The Order. We can do exactly that, if you want to call premises-restriction 'being held prisoner'. You're in possession of too many secrets to go off half-cocked."

"Say what you want, but I do have a whole cock."

"Well," Monq chuckled, "your sense of humor is intact and that is very encouraging. The sooner you and I get started sorting out what's going on in your head, the sooner you can get on with the rest of your life, whatever that may be. When do you want to get started?" Falcon shrugged. "Very well. Be here for dinner at seven o'clock. And don't be late."

THE REST OF K Team was glad to have Falcon back, not for active duty, but back in the sense of alive and well and living at J.U. even if temporarily. They were also concerned, but not so much so that humor was out of the question.

Wakey said, "I've heard the phrase 'crazy in love', but you've taken it to a whole new level of unhinged, my man.

Like I keep telling you, there are more girls than you could ever do and you're the lucky son-of-a-bitch who's wanted by every one of them."

Falcon was patient with his best friend and let him prattle on, but Wakey was coming from the perspective of a person who'd never been in love. In short, that meant he had no idea what he was talking about.

ON THE FLIGHT across the Atlantic, Glen came up with the perfect backdrop for his do-over. He devised a way to kill two birds with one stone, meaning that he would get Rosie back and take a stab at calming the ever present, underlying storm in his soul at the same time. It was brilliant even if he did think so himself.

AFTER GLEN AND the French knights had turned Falcon over, Glen had gone straight to Rev's office and asked for time off.

"We're in the middle of a crisis," Rev said.

"I know, but I haven't taken leave for years. Since I've been a floater, I didn't even take grief absence when there was a death. Just buried people and kept on keeping on. Since I don't have family, I haven't taken holiday leave either. That means I have time off coming. Actually I have a lot coming, but I'm only asking for a month. For now."

"A month."

"Yes."

"Starting when?"

Glen looked at his watch. "An hour ago."

"Funny." Rev sighed. "I don't guess you want to tell

me what's so important that it has to be done right now?"

"It's personal. Sir."

"Of course it is." He blew out a big breath then pulled up his calendar. "You'll be back a month from today."

"Unless I put in a request for an extension, yes."

"Don't put any effort into trying to make this easier on me," Rev said, each word dribbling sarcasm as only the Sovereign could do. "All right. Be in my office one month from today ready for a new assignment."

"Unless..."

"Unless I receive a formal request for extension at least forty-eight hours before."

Glen grinned and left before Rev could either change his mind or begin adding more qualifiers and conditions.

ROSIE BREEZED INTO Simon's outer office wearing striped tights and a sage green silk shirt that made the green of her eyes pop like high beams. His executive admin, Margaret, an institutional fixture at Headquarters, was on duty. She looked up and smiled.

"Go on in," she said.

Rosie heard voices on the other side of the door. When she stepped inside, Glen's head swiveled toward her and he immediately got to his feet actually looking like he was happy to see her. And something else. Nervous maybe.

"Glen, what are you doing here?"

Simon answered for him. "This is your next job, Tracker. You're cleared to help Sir Catch with his project for as long as he needs you. Now I hate to hand you your hats and show you the door, but I have things pressing. So…"

Glen managed to drag his eyes away from Rosie long enough to say, "Absolutely. Thank you, Director."

Simon nodded.

Glen opened the door and waited for her to pass through. "We can discuss my, ah, project…" He looked around. "How about in the mess?"

Rosie looked completely confused. "Okay."

Glen moved toward the outer office door, again he opened it and held it for Rosie, smiling.

"Wow," she said, as she passed by. "Holding the door for me? Hel must have frozen over."

"That's what I heard," he said, still smiling.

"What's this about?"

"Let's talk about it over coffee. We could do it in your apartment if you prefer."

"No."

"You know I stayed across the hall from you for about six months."

"Really?"

"Yeah. When I was still a trainee. It was before you were born. Elora needed a dog sitter. Blackie and I were muy sympatico. So she got permission to bring me along."

"Really?"

"Yeah. I have great memories of being here. I spent my off time talking to people in every department about arcane stuff that wouldn't interest most folks. One of the best times of my life."

The version of Glen who was talking about good

memories was so much like the old Glen Rosie had known that it made tears prick at the back of her eyes. She sniffed and turned her head away, but Glen's werewolf senses picked up on the shift in mood and he heard the sniff.

"What's wrong?" he asked.

"It's not that something is wrong. It's actually a great thing that you seem so much like yourself. Your old self, I mean."

"Not the asshole you ran around with in Paris?"

She stopped and looked at him quizzically. Then at the same time they both said, "We'll always have Paris." Surprised by the synchronicity, they stared at each other for two beats and then simultaneously erupted into laughter.

When Glen had been babysitting Rosie while Litha was looking for Storm, they had watched the entire list of AFI's one hundred best movies of all time in order. The famous line from Casablanca had popped into both their heads at the same time.

When the unexpected burst of laughter faded, Rosie said, "What's this about, Glen?"

He responded by taking her elbow and gesturing toward the mess. The big room was practically empty at that time of day. Within seconds of sitting down at a quiet corner table, one of the wait staff was there to take their coffee order.

"So?" she asked.

"I need a tracker and I hear you're the best. As a perk of being a long time and faithful employee of The Order, I get use of the resources on request. In this case, that would be you."

She was curious, but made sure her face didn't give anything away. "What do you need to track?"

"Help me find out something about my family. Who they were. Where they lived. Why I ended up in foster care. You know, that kind of stuff."

Rosie's expression softened when she realized what he was asking. "Yes. Of course."

He gave a half nod toward her chest and smirked. "You get that crystal fixed?"

"Yes. It's fine now. Good as new. I may want to consult with a couple of people about the best way to proceed."

"Okay. How much time do you need?"

"Do I have a time budget?"

"Sort of," Glen said carefully. "I didn't quit. Just took some time off."

"I'll see what I can find out today and let you know tomorrow."

"Okay. Well, it so happens I'm in town overnight with nothing to do. Want to go to dinner?" Rosie was so unprepared for that, she just stared and blinked. "Blink once for yes. Twice for no."

She blinked. "Great." He stood up. "Seven o'clock. I'll find something fun." She parted her lips to object, but it was evident that his hearing was going to be highly selective. "Later."

He rushed away before she could say no. Which made her smile.

ROSIE TOOK THE elevator to the sublevel that archives shared with research. The girl who looked up when she approached the first obstacle to research looked like a casting favorite for librarian. She was cute but studious with a ponytail, glasses, and no makeup other than red lipstick.

"Hi, I'm…"

"I know who you are, Ms. Storm. You're practically Order royalty."

Rosie frowned. "Wow. Well, I don't know exactly what to say to that."

"What can I do for you?"

Rosie looked around wondering what might be offered other than research. "I was thinking research."

The girl smiled. "This desk is where the adventure begins. You might say I'm the face of research. At least today."

"Oh. Good. I need an intensive background on Sir Catch. Sir Glendennon Catch. Not his record with The Order. I need to reconstruct a complete bio, pick up a trail that leads to before he was placed in foster care."

The young woman sat up straighter. "I have to admit that's a new one. Not the sort of request we get every day. Or ever. I'll find somebody who can run it down. How soon do you need it?"

"Tomorrow morning."

She barked out a laugh, then quieted when she saw that Rosie wasn't smiling. "You're serious. Well, all right then. Let me see who might be able to put something aside."

"Thank you. You know I didn't mean to be rude, but I got sidetracked during introductions. What's your name?"

"Aggie Praetorius."

"Ah. Good name for a sentry."

Agnes rolled her eyes. "Like I never heard that one before."

"I'd like to meet the person who will actually be doing the research. Is that possible?"

Aggie ducked her head and giggled. "You sure?"

"Is there something I should know?"

"Well, the person I was going to ask doesn't exactly have good social skills." She looked around, leaned toward Rosie and whispered, "Aspergers." She looked behind her again, then nodded. "I can introduce you, but I'm warning you that you need to be thick-skinned."

"Why's that?"

"Because there's no brake between the brain and the mouth. He could say or do *anything*."

"I see." Rosie almost kicked herself. Ever since her visit with her mother she'd been saying, 'I see' even though she thought it sounded daft coming from her.

"You've been warned. It's up to you."

"Yes. I'll take my chances. I think I can manage someone who is, um, straightforward."

Aggie huffed out a laugh. "Straightforward," she repeated. "Come around."

She motioned for Rosie to walk to the end of the counter where there was a waist-high swinging door.

They walked through a maze of hallways with little offices staggered on each side so that the open doorways faced walls. Aggie stopped at one the size of a medium cubicle. It had an L-shaped desk with four large flat-screen monitors. In front of the monitors was a bespectacled young man wearing powder blue pajamas with yellow Sponge Bobs in the print.

"Here you go," Aggie told Rosie like it was a joke. "X. This is Ms. Storm."

He glanced over, pushed his glasses further up the bridge of his nose, and turned back to his work saying, "I told you I don't like to be called that."

"Sorry, Xavier. I need you to put what you're doing aside for the time being and help Ms. Storm."

"Put this aside?" He sounded incredulous.

"Yes," she answered.

"Impossible."

"No. It's not impossible," she said mocking patience. "It's quite possible. I have to get back to the front. Do your job and help the nice lady." Aggie looked at Rosie. "You think you can find your way back out?"

"I'm supposed to be the resident tracker. If I can't find my way out of the basement, I should be fired."

Aggie nodded. "Agreed. See you."

She retreated the way they'd come leaving Rosie alone with her assigned researcher.

"So, Xavier. Can I sit down?" There was a small side chair wedged into the corner. Xavier looked at the chair and nodded. "I need to construct a history for a knight who was placed in foster care at a young age. Can you help me find out something about his parents?"

"Who is it?" Xavier asked without looking at Rosie.

"Glendennon Catch."

"The werewolf."

Rosie was a little surprised that Xavier knew who Glen was. "He's actually a quarter werewolf. Or at least that's what we think. Do you know all the knights by name?"

"Yes."

"Well, that's impressive. There are a lot."

Xavier shrugged. "Where was the foster care?"

"Seattle."

Xavier's hands flew over the keyboard. The Order didn't house all the data in the world, but there wasn't anything anywhere that researchers couldn't access, with or without permission. Records came up on the screen along with a photo of a very baby-faced Glen that pulled at Rosie's heartstrings. It appeared to be an intake picture for documentation purposes. Rosie impulsively reached toward the screen, but snatched her hand back when Xavier spoke.

"He was two."

"Two," Rosie repeated, mulling over all the implications, that he really had no memory of family loving him, ever.

"There was a car crash," Xavier said. "Killed the parents. Didn't even injure him. The name embroidered on his blanket led them to his birth certificate, but the case went cold there. The parents didn't have ties to family. The father didn't have a birth certificate that they could find. The mother had papers, but they were fake."

"Fake," Rosie repeated.

"Yeah." He nodded without looking away from the

images quickly passing by on the screen, which were mostly text.

"How old were they?"

"Pretty young. He was twenty-four. She was twenty-two."

"Were they married?"

"Yes. They were working at a fishing lodge on Lake Quinalt." Xavier typed ridiculously fast and images flew by. "Makes sense."

"What makes sense?"

"If our guess about Catch's heritage is on the money, one of the parents was half werewolf."

"Go on."

"Halvies can express traits in unpredictable ways. It's not uncommon for a half werewolf to be able to shift and mimic being a full bred werewolf."

"So Glen's mother or father would want to live in or near the rain forest."

"Ding. Ding. Ding. Ding."

"Okay. Smarty pants. What else you got?"

Xavier shocked her by having a giggling fit over her use of the term smarty pants. When he calmed down, he pushed his glasses up on the bridge of his nose and said, "Do you like Sponge Bob?"

"Um, honestly, I don't know. What is it?"

"What is it?" Xavier looked like the question was a personal affront. He turned back to the search in a huff. "No. That's all there is."

"What about the name of the lodge where they were working?"

"Lake Crescent."

"People who were working there at the same time as his parents?" she pressed. Xavier didn't reply, but continued to look busy. After a couple of minutes, Rosie said, "Okay, Xavier. Give me some help here. Should I ask the question again?"

The printer came on behind her.

"The list is printing out," he said.

"Oh. Thank you."

She started pulling sheets out of the tray and reading through. Of the people who had worked at the lodge when Glen's parents were there, there were three who appeared to be alive. Xavier had provided current info on all three including where they lived at present, where and how they were occupied, and so on.

"This is perfect, Xavier."

"Can I get back to work now?"

"Can I get print outs of pictures of his parents?"

Xavier rolled his head and attacked the keyboard. When photos came out of the printer, Rosie grabbed them.

"*Now* can I get back to work?" he asked, sounding out of patience.

"Yes. It was nice to meet you. Oh, one more thing, just for my own curiosity. How did The Order find out about Glen?"

"You know, just like always. School test results are reported from everywhere. Anything unusual draws attention."

"And he was unusual."

"Duh. You know him, right? He's smart. I mean, not like me, but pretty smart just the same." He grinned. "You could call him smarty pants if you want."

Rosie smiled. "Okay. I might do that."

SHE SAID GOODBYE to Aggie on the way out and went back to the apartment she was trying to remake into hers, but still felt like her mother's with a couple of stops along the way. She grabbed coffee from the coffee service in the lobby and had the barista blend a custom concoction that involved coffee with squirts of crème brulee and classic syrup.

She also stopped to text Glen.

ROSIE: ***Where are we going? What should I wear?***

GLEN: ***The Witchery.***

ROSIE: ***OMGS. I've never been! What are you wearing?***

GLEN: ***What do you want me to wear?***

ROSIE: ***Sponge Bob pajamas.***

After a long pause without a reply from Glen, she typed again.

ROSIE: ***Wait. In case you're out trying to find Sponge Bob pajamas, I changed my mind. I'm thinking concert tee, combat boots, jockey briefs (white), and don't forget a Marlboro cigarette behind your ear.***

Glen smiled when he read the second text, remembering the guy from Paris.

GLEN: ***I've got an idea. How about jeans and a leather jacket.***

ROSIE: ***lol So. The uniform. Ok.***

Inside Litha's secret room, Rosie set some unscented votive candles in a circle around the ancient dragon that occupied the center of the room. She took a few more sips of yummy sweet coffee, then set the cup down before dragging a big floor pillow into the circle of candles.

She went through the preflight magick checklist even though her demon blood meant that she probably could have skipped it with the same result. She sealed the circle and erected mystic barriers that would protect her from interference by trickster elementals or misguided devils like djinn. When she was certain that her preparations were sound, she closed her eyes and summoned any available ancestor who was competent and wanted to help.

She closed her eyes and almost immediately found herself standing in a landscape of treeless hills undulating in varying shades of green underneath a cloudy sky. The land was unmarked by the ravages of technology and over-population.

A woman turned to face Rosie and smiled at her affectionately. She was so much like Litha that it was startling and, in fact, Rosie would have thought that it was her mother except for the pale skin and auburn color of her hair. Same green eyes. Same wild hair. Same air and expression.

She was wearing a long dress that whipped and billowed in the wind, with ribbons in her long hair that swirled out and around her like a fantasy painting.

"I'm Lapis."

"You look like my mother," Rosie said.

The woman smiled. "More truly, she looks like me."

"I give you that." Rosie thought it was pointless to ask if they shared blood. While it would have been entirely possible for a variety of creatures to adopt a glamour that would mimic the appearance of one of Rosie's kin, her inner sight would have detected such a deception easily. "Thank you for coming."

Lapis nodded and waited.

"I'm on an errand for a friend..."

Lapis laughed. "A lover, you mean."

Rosie came up short, not knowing exactly how to answer that. "In a way. Someone who has been a lover in the past."

"Go on."

"I want to help him learn what happened to his family. He has no one."

Lapis looked at Rosie as if she was being indulgent. "Blood ties are important, but they're not everything. Your young man has rejected people who love him and chosen to dwell in darkness."

Rosie considered the truth of that. "He did, but now he's reaching out."

Lapis paused for a minute then showed Rosie a phantom-like figure of a handsome man with long braided hair and sharp intelligent eyes with a striking similarity to Glen's. The effect was like projecting a movie onto a wall during the daytime. Rosie could see the man going about his business, but the scene was transparent enough that she could also see the background of rolling green hills behind it.

She walked toward Rosie and whispered, "Ashenabe", just before she faded and became part of the wind. The sound of the wind lingered for a second after Rosie's eyes jerked open.

"Thank you, Grandmother," Rosie said out loud. "I don't know which generation of grandmother you are, but thank you."

Rosie hastened through the ritual of undoing the circle she'd created, doused the candles, returned the floor pillow to its place, locked up, and practically ran to find Xavier in research.

She waved to Aggie. "Don't mind me. Just passing through," she said as she rounded the counter and passed through the half door.

Xavier was still at his station.

"Oh, thank goodness, you're here." He didn't bother to respond or look up. "I need you to find references to the word Ashenabe. It could be a person, place, or thing."

"I'm busy."

"Well, I know you are, but this will only take a minute."

"Busy means busy."

"Okay, Xavier, let's make a deal."

That got his attention. He looked up and narrowed his eyes. "What kind of deal?"

"What do you want?"

"You mean like three wishes?"

"Don't be ridiculous. Pick one thing."

He looked around. "I want a VIP pass to Comiccon in Brussels. Hotel. Limo. The works."

"Done."

"Really?" She nodded. "How do I know I can trust you? Never mind." He pulled an eyeball camera over, turned it on, and adjusted it so that it would record Rosie, then accessed sound studio recording software. "Now. Look at the camera and swear. Just be natural. You'll do great."

Rosie shot him a look that said he was getting stranger by the second, but faced the camera.

"I hereby promise to provide Xavier…" She looked at him, waiting for him to provide a last name.

"Puddyphatt."

Rosie hesitated, but began again. "I hereby promise to provide Xavier Puddyphatt with transportation, hotel, and VIP tickets for Comiccon Brussels in exchange for useful information."

"Excellent," he said as he swiveled the camera away. "What was it again? Ashenabe?"

"Yes."

Xavier typed something and said, "It's a werewolf tribe. They have a reservation in British Columbia."

"Werewolf tribe," she repeated. "Yeah. That's it! Thank you, X. You did great."

"Don't call me that."

She paused. "You know, when people call you X, it's because they like you and they're trying to express fondness."

"I don't like it."

"Okay. Later."

Rosie looked at her watch. It was after four. She had

less than three hours to find something to wear and get 'cleaned up'.

Glen hadn't indicated that it was anything more than friends having dinner, but she wanted to look her best regardless.

She exited the passes in the London Harrods designer dresses section and practically ran right into *the* dress. She almost laughed out loud because it was the perfect thing and she knew Glen would *love* it. Just the right combination of chic and hip.

It was a Moschino Smoking Lips mini dress, black virgin wool, with long sleeves and a figure-hugging silhouette, £365. She paired it with a Saint Laurent red leather biker jacket, £2,550, a black Saint Laurent wallet clutch, £950, and black Gianvito Rossi stiletto ankle boots, £560. It was a lot of money, but her salary was generous and with an all-bills-paid job, she could buy what she wanted. Of course, she could have just manufactured her own knocked off replicas, but Kellareal would somehow know and then she'd have to listen to the lecture about not misusing her abilities coupled with the lecture about the importance of keeping the economy flowing for the benefit of everyone.

She visited the makeup department and found a SUQQU red lipstick that matched the reds of the jacket and dress with the added feature of glowing in the dark. Plus, she figured, you couldn't go wrong with a lipstick brand that sounded like 'suck you'.

Back at the apartment she laid her purchases out on the bed and admired them while she ran a steamy bath.

Glancing at the time, she remembered to use unscented products because Glen's sensitive werewolf nose didn't appreciate artificial scents.

She dozed off in the tub and woke with just fifteen minutes to wrestle her wild hair into submission and get into the outfit that she hoped would make her look and feel pretty. He hadn't said if he was picking her up at her apartment or meeting her downstairs. She didn't have to wonder long because the door chime rang. Taking one last look in the full length mirror, she pulled open the door.

Glen's face made the shopping trip so much more than merely gratifying. He looked her up and down and let out a long low whistle.

"Wow. Were you expecting somebody else?"

Her responding blush thrilled him all the way down to the carpet because he knew she'd gone to some extra trouble. For him.

He stepped back so she could exit, then after she closed her door, he reached down, took the red leather jacket from her hand and held it for her to put on. The gesture was such a contrast from the way she'd been treated when they were hunting for Falcon that she grinned.

"What's funny?" Glen asked.

"Nothing. Well, actually. No. Nothing."

"Come on. What were you thinking?"

"That I like gentleman Glen."

He looked over at her as they strolled down the hall toward the elevator. "I was a dick, wasn't I?"

She smiled. "I'd like to argue, but yes."

"Yeah." He looked dejected and she felt responsible for ruining the mood.

"Hey," she said. "Let's pretend that we haven't seen each other for years. Hi, Glen. How have you been?"

He smiled. "Lousy. Miserable. Wretched. Forlorn. Heartsick. Lonely. Bereft."

"That's all?"

"I could go on."

Rosie knew that he was telling the truth and that the honesty of their time apart was part of the new leaf he'd turned over. "There's always tomorrow."

"Wait a minute. We haven't gotten through tonight yet." She laughed. "Maybe I can turn things around."

Rosie was stunned by that outright declaration, but it answered the question about whether dinner was a date or a business meeting.

Glen smiled warmly and pushed the elevator button.

"So," she said as she stepped into the elevator, "seven is kind of early for dinner out. Does this mean you're getting old?"

His smile grew even warmer. "It means I have something else planned for after dinner."

Images sprang to Rosie's mind. As she imagined what that might be a flush rose in her cheeks to complement the reds of the dress, jacket, and lips.

Glen laughed. "I wasn't thinking that, but I'm definitely receptive."

"So what is it we're, um, doing after dinner?"

"Nuh-uh. It's a surprise."

"You know I'm not that into surprises."

"Sure you are. Everybody likes surprises when they're good ones."

"And you know I'm going to think it's a good one?"

With hands in his pockets, he leaned into her space and gave her a conclusive, "Yes."

ROSIE WAS GLAD to see the car was waiting just outside the front entrance. In tennis shoes The Witchery would be an easy fifteen minute walk, but doing it in stiletto boots would take all the fun away.

Glen helped her out of the car at the door to the restaurant. She heard him tell the driver that he would text a few minutes before they were ready to be picked up. Inside Rosie quickly realized that The Witchery was every bit as beautiful and magical as people said it was. As they were being shown to their table, she noticed women's eyes lingering on Glen a few seconds too long to qualify as casual interest and she was glad she'd gone to some extra trouble to dress like it was an occasion.

She ordered Loch Duart salmon. He ordered Cairngorm venison. They shared some truffle mac and cheese and topped it off with Tonka bean crème brulee with white chocolate palmiers.

With Glen relaxed, open, making eye contact, and appearing emotionally engaged, they quickly fell into a rhythm of dialogue that felt familiar.

"You look like a million bucks tonight."

"I'm glad you think so because that's pretty close to what this cost," she said, looking down at her clothes.

"No matter how much it cost it was worth every penny."

"Ooh. That was extra rich and creamy smooth. Have you been practicing lines since the last time I saw you?"

"Seriously. No. It came out that way because it's what I really think."

"In that case, thank you, Sir Catch." She mouthed the 'Sir'.

Conversation between them was easy. They shared their individual reactions to realizing that Paris was a set up.

"So how did they fool the crystal?" he asked.

Rosie cocked her head. "I was so busy trying to process the fact that so many people had thought it was okay to meddle in our business that I didn't get the details."

"How many is so many?"

Rosie laughed. "I didn't get that either. But you know that, if Mom is up to mischief, Auntie Elora is always in the middle of it."

"I think his holiness, the great Reverence Farthing was in on it, too. Had to be."

"If he was, then add Farnsworth. It's unlikely that Dad and Uncle Ram didn't know, even if they didn't participate."

"Deliverance. And Jean Etienne."

"Baka! And Heaven!"

"Gods. What do you think made them do it?"

"Mom said all those people thought we belong together," Rosie answered honestly.

Glen nodded slowly, eyes glittering. "Always liked your mom. Wise and smart. Very smart. Also crafty." He took a sip of coffee and, noticing Rosie's flush of embarrassment, decided to change the subject. "So. Name the best dinner you ever had in your life."

Rosie looked around. "This one, of course."

"All right." Glen rolled his eyes. "Silk shouldn't call the vampire killer extra rich and creamy smooth."

The waiter came up just as Glen said that. "Vampire killer? Like Buffy?" he gushed. "I *love* Buffy. This summer I'm going to California to take the Buffy tour. You know Torrance, Santa Barbara… I can't wait. You're Americans, right?" They both nodded. "Have you taken the Buffy tour?" Rosie and Glen both shook their heads no. "Well, you should. I hear it's great! I own all the DVD's. Watched them thousands of times." He gave a small sigh before remembering where he was and recomposing himself. "I'll be right back with your check."

When he left they both broke into a grin and laughed silently.

"I don't know why I'm laughing," Glen said. "There's nothing funny about vampire."

"No. But there's something funny about waiters who are saving their money to travel halfway around the world for a Buffy tour."

"Okay. So ask me."

"Ask you what?"

"Best dinner ever."

"What was your best dinner ever?"

"Pink Flamingo Pizza."

Rosie's eyes widened. "Why?"

"I think that was when I first started to realize I was

kidding myself about getting along without you. So, no matter what we say about all those nosy people not minding their own business, it worked. At least for me."

Rosie's beautiful bow lips pulled into a captivating smile. "For me, too."

Throughout dinner she felt torn about whether or not to tell Glen she had information about his family and maybe a lead on someone who was still alive. She didn't want to withhold, but she didn't want to ruin the evening either, especially since he'd clearly gone to some trouble and had expectations, or hopes, for the way things would go.

She'd folded the photos of Glen's parents and put them in her purse, just in case the time felt right at some point. It was a tricky and sensitive subject.

She watched Glen pull out his phone and text.

"Just letting Remy know we're ready for him."

"Are you ready to tell me what's next?"

"So impatient."

"Give me a hint."

"All right. You're going to get a chance to work off some of that crème brulee."

Rosie blinked. "We're going to a gym?"

Glen laughed as he stood and held out his hand. "Come on."

Remy was standing next to the car waiting to open the door for her. They drove south on Pleasance for just over five minutes and then turned into the University of Edinburgh.

"This is getting more mysterious by the second," Rosie

said.

Glen chuckled. "You're gonna love it."

When the car stopped, Glen said, "It's a short distance. Over there." He pointed toward the buildings arranged around a green in the shape of a U. She looked at the old stone walkways and looked at her heels.

"I don't know," she said. "Do you have the pills?"

"No. I can either carry you or you can meet me over there via poof travel. But first, you won't need your purse thingy or the jacket. Remy will look after your stuff."

"Remy?" she said, leaning down so she could see his face.

"Yes, madam," he replied.

"Are you taking responsibility for my 'stuff'?"

"Yes, madam."

She left her purse and jacket in the backseat, smiled at Glen and vanished.

Glen made it to the spot where she waited in less than a minute.

"So now are you going to tell me what we're doing here?"

He took her hand and led her into the building at her back. As they neared the doorway where Glen was obviously headed, she heard music and saw the poster. *The Edinburgh Tango Society.*

She came to a full stop and grinned. "No. Way."

Glen returned her grin and gestured toward the door. "This. Way."

"Tango in Edinburgh. Nothing will *ever* surprise me again." The room was large and had a wood floor. It was apparently where dance was taught at the school. "You know this dress was not chosen with tango in mind, right?"

Glen looked down. "If I grab your thigh and hitch your knee over my hip, I'll make sure you're pulled tight enough that no one will see panties."

"What makes you think I'm wearing panties?" She giggled when he almost stumbled. "So this is why we were having early dinner?"

"Yeah. At eight they dim the lights and the DJ starts playing musica in tandas con cortinas."

She looked at her watch and started to say it was eight. "It's…" Before she finished the thought the lights went down and the sultry tones of tango began surging through the sound system like a magical audio aphrodisiac.

"It's not as romantic as the Seine, but…"

"Shhh. It's so much more romantic because this time you want to do this. With me." She looked up. "Don't you?"

"Gods yes."

He took her right hand in his left and extended her arm then flattened his palm against her back between her shoulder blades. It wasn't an erogenous zone, but between the low lights, the music, the nearness of her partner, and the musky scent that she'd known intimately as uniquely Glen, she nearly swooned.

His face was inches away when he began to move, guiding and controlling. He brought her even closer and spoke to her in low tones, so close that she could feel his breath, sometimes on her face, sometimes in her ear, which sent her body into overdrive and meant she wasn't having to pretend sexual intensity.

"The tango is mostly walking, but doing it like you would if you were stalking prey, like you wanted to sneak up on them so that by the time they knew what you were after, it would be too late. Every muscle is tense while pretending laziness at the same time. It's sexy. Sensual, but it's also playful and vibrant." He stopped to show her how to spin and come back to his embrace then showed her how to fall into him, trusting that he would catch her. "I will always catch you," he whispered in her ear.

Something about that hit a nerve. She stepped back suddenly and pushed at his chest. "You'll always catch me? Just a few days ago you were letting doors slam in my face."

He dropped his chin and looked straight into her eyes. "Give me a do-over. And I'll do the same for you."

She searched his face and saw the sincerity. "You better mean it."

"I do."

"Or I'll drop you in the passes."

He chuckled. "I'll be good. I promise."

She stepped back into him and they began to dance. "How good?"

"If you want to find out you're going to have to do something about all that red, red lipstick. It's gorgeous on you, but I have a feeling it wouldn't look that good on me."

"You're saying you want to kiss me?"

"Oh. Yeah."

Rosie felt everything that was capable of clenching clench in unison as a response to that declaration. She looked at his lips, remembering that he was an awesome kisser and decided that was exactly what she wanted, too.

"You want to go?"

"Only if we're going to be at least this close," he pulled her in tight, "wherever we're going next."

"So you want kisses and tightness?"

Glen narrowed his eyes. "This isn't a demon negotiation, is it?"

She laughed. "No. But now that you mention it…"

He twirled her around and leaned back so that he was balancing most of her weight. It was so intimate that it was almost like having sex in public.

His breath blew in her ear when he said, "You have me at a disadvantage. You could ask for anything you want."

"Anything I want?" Rosie asked, her voice sounding far away even to her.

"Anything." He grinned as he dipped, showing her how to balance her weight on one leg while the other slipped between his.

"Let's go," she said.

He stood up abruptly and noticed that Rosie's face was as flushed as the smoking lips on her dress.

"I'll meet you at my place," she said.

"What? Wait."

"I'm going to get the lipstick off. If it will come off," she added. She pulled him over to the side of the room, where they wouldn't be noticed. "Don't forget to bring my stuff. Okay?"

"Well," he began, but she was gone. He said under his breath, "I guess that's what happens when you fall in love with a demon."

At least he wouldn't have to make up some story for Remy. Employees of The Order were used to unusual occurrences. Thank goodness.

Twelve minutes later Glen was knocking at Rosie's door.

When she answered, he held out the clutch bag and red leather jacket. She grabbed them and threw them over her shoulder before pulling him in for a kiss. She was still wearing the dress, but she was barefoot with lips free of lipstick and moisturized, and she'd let her hair down.

Glen kicked the door closed as she shoved his leather jacket off his shoulders. He plunged his hands into her wild hair and grabbed both sides of her head so that he could plunder her mouth exactly the way he'd wanted to for all the years they'd been apart. When he pulled back he said, "I missed you."

"I missed you, too," she said breathlessly.

He pulled her in for another kiss and started maneuvering her toward the bedroom at the same time.

It was at that moment she realized she needed to tell him what she'd learned about his family. She owed it to him to not have him wait unnecessarily for another day.

"Stop. There's something I have to tell you."

Glen looked confused. "What?"

"Um, let's go sit down."

"What?" he repeated.

"You want coffee?"

"No. I don't want coffee. I want you. In bed. Under me. Right now. What's going on that's more important than that?"

"I found out some things about your family. I didn't want to interfere with the nice night you planned, but I don't think I ought to keep it from you any longer. If you find out tomorrow that I knew something and didn't tell you, well, it wouldn't be the best premise for starting over."

Glen stared at her for a few beats. Everything about his demeanor changed. "You have grown up." She remained quiet, not really thinking that warranted a response. Glen ran his hand through his hair. "Am I going to want coffee?"

"Maybe. Or whiskey?"

"That bad?"

"No. It's just information, not bad news."

"Coffee."

"Won't take long."

Glen sat down at the little table for two and watched anxiously as she padded around the tiny galley kitchen making two coffees.

After a few minutes they both had steaming cups sitting on the table between them. Rosie had gathered the pages that she'd taken from Xavier's printer, along with the photos she'd carried in her purse.

Glen looked wary and anxious with a touch of sadness thrown into the mix. His eyes were fixed on the pages she held in her hand.

"You survived a car crash when you were almost three,

but your parents didn't. I have their pictures, if you want..."

Glen reached over and took the photos from her hand, then looked at them like he'd found the holiest relic of myth and legend. She watched as he reverently ran his thumb over the replica of his mother's face.

"The authorities tried to find your extended family, but the investigation led nowhere."

"What do you mean?" He looked up then shook his head. "They didn't have any family?" Rosie hesitated and Glen picked up on it. "The guy in research says your mother's ID was counterfeit. Maybe she had family and didn't want to be found."

Glen stared at Rosie with his eyes out of focus, like he was far away and trying to process that. He looked down at the photo of his father. The resemblance to Glen was noticeable.

"And what about...?" His voice sounded a little rough.

"Same thing. The ID had been manufactured."

"So it wouldn't be something like witness protection because the IDs would be real."

"Yeah." Rosie nodded. "They were working at a fishing lodge on the edge of a national park in Washington State. We found some of the people who worked there at the same time." She handed him the other pages. "We could go look them up. Maybe ask them if they remember your parents?"

Glen didn't respond other than to read through the information once, then twice, then three times.

"There's something else," Rosie said.

Glen's head jerked up, a tiny spark of hope in his eyes. "Tell me."

"I had a brief encounter with, um, a departed loved one."

"Departed? You mean dead?"

"Bluntly put, yes."

He shook his head. "I'm beyond being surprised at anything. What did the departed say?"

"She showed me a vision and gave me a name. Ashenabe. The quirky guy in research told me Ashenabe is a werewolf tribe in British Columbia. It might be my imagination, or wishful thinking, but I thought there might be a family resemblance."

Glen's lips parted and hope, not just a vestige but full-blown hope claimed his face. He stood up. "We have to go there." He looked at his watch. It was nine o'clock. "What's the time difference?"

Rosie opened her laptop and typed in a search. "Seven hours earlier. That's two o'clock in the afternoon there. You got your pills?"

He grinned, reached inside his jacket and produced a little rectangular tin, which he rattled as a response.

"Wait a minute," she said, then put her hand to her forehead. "I don't know why I didn't think of this. Well, I do know why I didn't think of it. I lost faith in Granddemon's crystal because I thought it was misbehaving in Paris." She was wearing it simply because the safest place for it was around her neck. She pulled it out and looked at it. "I need to change clothes and you need to take a pill. What do you want me to wear to meet your family?"

When Glen looked at her she could see that question had made his eyes red with unshed tears and she wanted to envelope him in a cocoon of the love and nurture that he'd missed growing up. She reached for his hand, wishing she could turn time back and make up for every slight and deficit, but knew that wasn't possible. All she could do was love him in the present the way he'd always deserved to be loved.

The move to Edinburgh had been her practical approach to moving on with her life, when she'd believed Glen had shut down possibilities in Paris. When he turned up with reconciliation in mind, it hadn't taken much to convince her that he was worth a gamble. She'd already been primed and was more than ready.

"Never mind," she said, squeezing his hand. "I'll find something." She started to get up then said, "Oh. I've got one more thing." She reached for the last photo. She walked around to Glen's side of the table and leaned over so they could look at the photo of him as a toddler together. "Is that not the most precious thing you've ever seen?"

Glen stared at the photo for a full minute with Rosie's face next to his shoulder. When he turned toward her, they were barely more than an inch apart. His eyes immediately went to her lips for a split second before he covered her mouth in a kiss that was part relief, part gratitude, and part devotion. He pushed back his chair and pulled her onto his lap without ever breaking the kiss.

She pulled back and smiled. "You want to get reacquainted first?"

He chuckled. "I can't believe I'm going to say no, but when we get 'reacquainted', I want to be focused on that and just that. Right now I can't think about anything except the fact that I might have a relative out there who, ah…"

"Who wants you." She finished the sentence.

He nodded. "Yeah."

"Okay. I'm changing."

"Not too much," he said playfully.

It was both wonderful and weird how quickly Rosie had begun feeling comfortable with Glen. She hoped he was serious about another chance for them because, at the moment, she couldn't imagine wanting anything more.

The place where they were headed was roughly the same latitude as Edinburgh. So she reasoned that the temperature would be much the same, give or take precipitation, humidity and wind variables. She didn't really have to worry about being too cold or hot because she could direct her body to control its response to externality, but she didn't want to wear a yellow polka dot sundress to a blizzard either.

So she wiggled into some dark blue skinny jeans that had enough give to be comfortable, a white long sleeve tee for an under layer, and a forest green cashmere Henley. She topped it off with an Irish wool infinity scarf that was a camouflage print in the same value of green as the Henley, on a tan background. She realized she didn't have any hiking boots, so she went into her closet, turned off the light, closed the door, and wished hiking boots into existence, giving Kellareal a silent and not *completely* insincere apology.

When she came back into the kitchen, she found Glen still holding the photo of his mother. It made her breath catch, but she summoned a bright smile.

"I'm ready. How about you? Has your pill kicked in?"

He looked her up and down and didn't miss the boots. "Yeah. You look… good."

She cocked her head to the side. "You sound surprised."

"No. I'm just nervous." He pulled her onto his lap again. "When I started this, it was just an excuse to get to work with you again and show you that I'm done being…"

"A dick."

His head came up and he met her eyes. "I was going to say clueless. I thought this was a good way to insure a second chance because I know you've got a soft heart. I knew that, if you thought it was for a good cause, you wouldn't turn me down." He put his face in her neck and sniffed. "You smell so good."

She pulled his face up so that she could look at his expression and read him. "You're going off topic. You started this hunt for your family to get a second chance to work with me, but…"

"But I didn't think you would really find something. I feel thrown for a loop. I'm, I don't know. Scared?"

Rosie melted at that. "I'm going with you. And I'll always catch you."

Glen hadn't expected that kind of declaration so soon. He figured he might have to spend years earning her trust back. "You promise?"

"I do. Now, are you ready?"

"Kiss me first."

Chapter Twenty-Three

THEY STEPPED OUT of the passes in an old growth forest on the edge of a partially cleared settlement with log buildings that blended well enough with the surroundings to probably be invisible by satellite.

"All good?" Rosie asked Glen.

He grinned. "Modern pharma. It's magic." He looked around and took a big breath to steady his nerves. "So. This is the place?"

"Crystal says yes." He slanted a look in her direction. "No. It's working. Really."

They both froze when they heard a growl behind them, deep and rumbling as a distant thunderstorm.

"Move slowly," Glen said so quietly it was almost a whisper. Rosie did as she was told, turning around at the same speed as Glen, not faster or slower, though she was prepared to make a flaming shish kabob of the growler if necessary. They faced a very large wolf, over two hundred pounds, whose lips were drawn back from his extremely impressive teeth.

"My. What big teeth you have." Her Auntie Elora had told her stories when she was growing up.

"Rosie. Let me do the talking," Glen said while trying

to keep his lips from moving, as if that was the thing that would calm the creature.

"Okay. Go ahead."

He thought she was being a tad too flippant, all things considered, but then again, she probably didn't really understand fear. At least not fear of being harmed bodily.

After a few seconds thought, he said, "Take me to your leader?"

Rosie almost fell down laughing, which did cause the wolf to stop growling. His ears also pricked forward from curiosity. "Take me to your leader? That's the best you could come up with?"

She took a step toward the wolf. "Look. We're here on family business. He's one of you." She pointed at Glen. "I would have thought somebody with a snout that big would have figured that out."

"Rosie! Insulting the werewolf is probably not the best strategy here."

The wolf had stopped snarling. He'd raised his nose and was sniffing the air in Glen's direction. In a display of magic that was impressive even to Rosie, the canine body stretched and reshaped into human form in one fluid and effortless movement. Before them stood a perfectly beautiful, and quite naked, man.

"I do smell something familiar," he said to Glen. "Who are you?"

"That's what I'm here to find out. I don't know who my family is, but either my mother or father was connected to this place."

"What makes you think that?"

"I made him think that," said Rosie.

The handsome werewolf, who appeared to be in his early thirties, took time to appreciate how Rosie looked from the perspective of two-legged form. Rosie noticed the man's coloring was very similar to Glen's and his eyes held the same mixture of menace and amusement. Though she tried to direct her attention away from his muscular form, she couldn't help noticing that, even in the cool weather, he was endowed like Glen as well.

"I'm Hunter." He gave Rosie a grin that would have to be described as wolfish. "And you are?"

"Taken," Glen said.

Hunter looked at Glen and raised an eyebrow. "Maybe you *are* one of us."

Rosie turned toward the settlement and pulled the crystal from under her tee. "That way," she said.

"She's my tracker," Glen said to Hunter.

Hunter smiled at Rosie again. "Something we have in common."

Since Glen had warned the wolf off and he was persisting, it was time to be more insistent. So he released his own surprisingly loud growl.

Hunter was so startled he took a reflexive step back then laughed out loud. "Message received. What's your name?"

"Glendennon Catch."

Hunter's smile faltered as surprise danced over his face, but he quickly recovered the cocky facade. "I'm right behind you." His upright form collapsed into his wolf and he bumped Rosie's hip with his nose.

Glen snarled again which made Hunter crouch on his front feet and wag his tail like he was a puppy wanting to play. Glen looked at Rosie. "Weird." He motioned toward the buildings and said, "After you."

People looked on with open curiosity as Hunter followed Glen who followed Rosie right through the middle of the cluster of log buildings toward a smaller one off to the side. Smoke was curling from the chimney, which was a good indication somebody was home. She turned to Glen. "That's it."

He stopped at the base of the two steps that led up to the porch. "I'm not sure what to ask."

She nodded. "Talk with your heart."

He thought that advice was as good as any. So he climbed the steps, knocked softly on the door, and stepped back. Rosie saw that Hunter had followed. He was keeping his distance, but also keeping an eye on the two of them.

The door opened to reveal the man Lapis had shown Rosie in the vision. He was much better looking than his phantom self and the family resemblance seemed more pronounced in full color.

The man took his time looking Glen over before saying, "Who are you?"

"Glendennon Catch. I'm following a lead, hoping to find someone who can tell me about my family."

The man's eyes grew a little misty just before he grabbed hold of Glen and pulled him into a crushing bear hug. Glen was too surprised to move.

Rosie was riveted by Glen's reception, but was jolted out of her preoccupation when a deep voice close to her ear said, "Looks like you came to the right place." Hunter chuckled.

Rosie said, "Why don't you go find some pants?"

He sniffed the air close to her body. "Not human. Witch?"

"Partly. If you want to know more, get dressed first."

He grinned. "Modest? Or shy?"

"Neither. I'm committed to a jealous man."

He laughed. "All right, but I have to say that a lady asking me to put pants *on* is a novel experience."

"I'll bet." Rosie turned her attention back to what was happening on the porch.

She wished Hunter would have been quiet so that she could have heard what was said between Glen and the man in the doorway. When she looked that way again, Glen was pointing at her, then motioning for her to join him.

"Come in, young woman," said the man. "Let's have some coffee and figure this out together."

"Rosie," Glen said, "this is Deep."

"Hello," she said.

When they stepped inside the cabin, they saw an old woman sitting by the fire who appeared to be in her late seventies, a striped wool shawl over her shoulders. She was smiling, but said nothing.

"This is Emma," Deep said. "My wife." Rosie and Glen both reacted noticeably, but tried to cover their surprise for fear of appearing impolite. "She's in pretty good health for her age, but her mind sort of comes and goes. Have a seat." He motioned to the leather sofa and chair. "I have a fresh pot just brewed. How do you like your coffee?"

"Black," said Glen.

"Lots of sugar," said Rosie. "And cream. Lots of cream. If you have it."

Deep chuckled. "You hear that, Emma? The girl likes her coffee same as you used to."

Glen and Rosie sat down on the sofa, but didn't have to wait long for Deep to return with coffee.

He handed a mug to each of them and sat down in the big chair. "You're kin to me. No doubt about that."

"I've lived my whole life thinking I didn't have any family. So, please don't take this wrong, but how do you know?"

"Even if I didn't have eyes, I can smell." Laugh lines formed around Deep's eyes when he smiled. "Then when you told me your name…"

The door opened and Hunter walked in without knocking, but clothed, Rosie noted, in jeans that would have been fashionably worn if Hunter was the kind who cared about fashion, and a charcoal gray Henley that made the pale gray of his eyes even more prominent. He walked over to the old woman, bent down and gave her a kiss on the cheek.

"Hunter, sit down and help us sort this through." He motioned to Hunter. "This is our son."

As Hunter sat on the stone hearth, Glen said, "We've met. Sort of."

"Hunter," Deep said, "this is Glendennon Catch."

"I heard," Hunter said.

Deep cleared his throat. "So you say you don't have

any family."

"From what I've learned recently, my parents were killed in an accident when I was two. The authorities couldn't find any family. So I went into the foster care system."

"You just now began looking?"

Glen looked down at his hands. "I'd always thought that, if I had any family who cared about me, they would have shown up before now." Deep nodded, looking both sad and thoughtful. "I have pictures of my parents."

Glen withdrew the folded photo-copies he'd received from Rosie.

Deep took them and stared for a long time before passing them over to Hunter.

Sitting back with a deep sigh, he said, "There's a whirlwind of feeling in my heart. I've just learned that my son has passed beyond the veil. I've suspected as much for a long time, but wasn't sure until now." He looked at his wife. "I'm glad she's beyond caring. I would hate to imagine what this would do to her." He glanced at Rosie before focusing on Glen again. "Your father's name was Catch."

Deep looked away for a moment with a wistful smile. "Got the name as a pup because he caught fish in the air." He chuckled. "Most amazing thing you've ever seen. I would take him out on the water on a pontoon. He would change into wolf form and crouch on his haunches. If a fish jumped anywhere near, he'd leap into the air almost like he could fly, catch the fish in his jaws before it reentered the water, and swim back to the pontoon." He looked at Hunter. "We'd have to pull him up, of course. But it was entertaining as a circus act. When he decided to live in the human world, I suppose he chose to use Catch as a surname. To fit in."

He looked at his wife, who, so far as Rosie could tell, hadn't moved a muscle. "Emma's family name was Glendennon."

Glen looked at Rosie for her reaction. She gave him a little encouraging smile and reached for his hand.

"So you're my…"

"Grandfather," said Deep. "Hunter, here, is your uncle."

Hunter gave Glen a little smile. "Guess it's a good thing I didn't eat you."

Deep ignored him. "So, Glendennon…"

"Glen."

Deep nodded and looked at his wife lovingly. "Emma, this is our grandson, Glen." Turning back he said, "We're glad you found us. I wish we had known about you. If we had, no power on Earth could have kept us from you."

Rosie heard Glen's breath hitch and she knew he was struggling to keep from breaking down. Going from believing no one wanted him to learning that people would move mountains for him was a lot of change to assimilate.

"Why did he leave?" Glen asked.

"Oh, he wanted to go down to the human world. Find out what it was like. I guess he must have fallen for a human." He looked at Emma. "Can't blame him. That's what I did."

“So my father could shift, um, into a wolf?”

Deep laughed quietly. “Oh, yes. I think your question must mean that you don’t?”

Glen shook his head. “I can smell emotions and I have the vocal cords for making sounds that humans don’t make. I might be a little quicker than most humans. But that’s about it.”

“To me the most important thing about you is that you’re Catch’s son. Welcome home.”

THEY LINGERED FOR hours listening to stories about Glen’s father. It was clear that both Deep and Hunter had loved and respected him and grieved when they’d been cut off from contact and news of him.

Glen found that the idea of a grandfather who appeared to be not much older than he took some getting used to, but not as much as might be expected. Rosie sat next to Glen, quietly supporting the blood reunion, pleased that his quest had led to something resoundingly positive.

At length Glen asked, “Why did he stay away? Had you had a falling out?”

“Oh, no,” said Deep. “I couldn’t answer why. I wish he hadn’t.” His eyes warmed when he looked at Glen. “For so many reasons.”

WHEN THEY ROSE to leave, Deep pulled Glen into another hug and made him promise to visit often. Glen caught Hunter winking at Rosie which meant that, before their departure, Deep and Hunter got to hear that Glen was telling the truth about having the ability to snarl like a full wolf.

"Settle down," Hunter said in a placating way. "I'm just flirting. I would never take what's yours, nephew."

"You got that right, wolfman," Rosie said.

"See?" Hunter held up his hands. "Everybody agrees the witch is yours."

AS THEY STEPPED out of Deep's cabin, snow was starting to fall in flakes so big the icy patterns were almost visible to the naked eye.

Rosie said, "Maybe he stayed away to protect your mother. I mean there had to be a reason why her ID was fake."

Glen nodded. "Maybe sometime we'll look up some of those people who worked at the lodge. Find out what they know." He smiled at Rosie with a twinkle in his eyes. "But not today."

She caught his meaning. "Your pill still working?"

Glen looked at his watch. "Yeah. I should still be good."

"What a day, huh?"

"Yeah. What a day." He smiled. "Thank you. This means…" He seemed at a loss for how to finish that sentence.

"I know. No explanation necessary."

"You hungry?"

"Have we met?"

He laughed. "Surprise me."

WHEN THEY EMERGED from the passes, Glen looked around.

"This is your apartment."

"Yeah," she said with a predatory grin.

"Thought you were hungry." He returned her grin as she removed her scarf and cashmere sweater.

"I am, but I've got some stuff in the refrigerator. We can eat later. Let's celebrate now."

She pushed his jacket off his shoulders and ran her hands under his shirt, coming in contact with bare skin. His abs tightened as he jerked back. "Oh my gods. Your hands are like icicles."

"Forgot to warm them up." She pulled her hands away, laughing. "I'm going to jump in for a quick hot shower. Don't go away," she purred. Pointing to the bedroom, she said, "You can wait for me in there if you want."

Rosie hurried to turn the shower to hot and wiggle out of her boots and jeans. She clipped her hair on top of her head to keep it from getting completely wet and stood, shifting her weight from foot to foot, impatiently waiting for the water to heat.

She took a shower in record time using the unscented soap because she remembered that Glen's nose was ultrasensitive, dried off, and threw on a midnight blue silk robe. When she opened the bathroom door, heavy steam wafted into the bedroom.

The bedside lamp was on, illuminating Glen lying on his back. The sheet was pulled up just high enough to expose the waistband of black cotton boxers. Otherwise, he was bare.

Rosie had known that he had filled out from years of claiming manhood and, no doubt, Black Swan workouts, but she hadn't seen the rippled and defined expression of that carved into the flesh until that moment. He was beautiful enough to be the centerfold of a gay magazine.

He was luscious. He was inviting. He was a fantasy come to life. He was also snoring with a volume that could only be achieved by a person with a werewolf's vocal attributes.

Thinking back, she realized that he'd lost a night's sleep and had also had an emotionally exhausting day. The pleasure of seeing him asleep in the bed she currently called hers quickly overrode any disappointment she felt about the sexual encounter she'd been anticipating. She turned out the light and crawled under the covers. When she laid her head on his chest, his arm immediately came around her and everything about that reflex, even in sleep, felt so right.

With a slight mental adjustment, Rosie fell asleep even with the rumbling snoring occurring just inches from her ears.

The next time she opened her eyes, filtered daylight was streaming through the south-facing windows. She was turned on her right side with a very large, very warm body spooning her from behind, alternating little kisses with little licks and delivering intermittent nips so light that they produced no sting.

"Hmmm," she said, wiggling back to indicate receptiveness and bring her in even closer contact. He responded by pressing back, revealing unmistakable evidence that her bedmate had ideas for how they might spend the morning.

The hand, at the end of the arm that was wrapped around her waist from behind, came up to palm her breast and that prompted an echoing, "Hmmm," from him.

She smiled to herself, feeling her nipple harden from the light friction of his thumb. Turning around to face him, she smiled like she was delighted with herself. "Good morning."

"Good morning," he answered with a lazy smile of his own.

She reached up and ran her hand over the stubble that had formed on his face. He answered by playfully rubbing his face the wrong way against her shoulder.

"Ow," she protested. "Stop."

"What will you give me if I do?"

"What do you want?"

"You. Forever."

"Deal."

He grinned. "That was the easiest deal made with a demon in the history of demons."

She grinned. "Probably. Just remember I have all kinds of creative ways to make you sorry if you make me mad."

"You can't threaten me."

"Why not?"

"Because I'm friends with your parents."

"Since when? The way they tell it, you stopped returning calls. And texts. And emails."

"Yeah. I did. But I fixed it."

"When?"

"Between Paris and Edinburgh."

"How did you fix it?"

"Groveling."

She nodded. "I believe you because I know from experience that groveling works with them." She reached for his waistband. "Now that we agree on what the rest of our lives…"

He stopped her. "About that."

"What about that?"

"When we were at my grandparents' house?"

"Yes?"

"It was a clarifying moment. The consequence of mating somebody of a different species."

"The age difference."

"Yeah. I know none of us know how long we'll live, but it's almost a certainty that you will outlive me, by a long time, even if I live three times as long as most humans."

Rosie searched his face. "You're worried about how I might feel if you're old and I look the way I do now."

He nodded slightly. "I think you should give it some thought."

"Okay." She smiled and rushed in for a kiss.

When she released him, he said, "You're sure you've thought this through?"

"Absolutely. If you turn into the cryptkeeper, I'll hire somebody to go down to the basement and check in on you once every few days."

Even though he was sure she was joking, he looked a

little stunned. "Has anyone ever told you that your sense of humor is unusual?"

She laughed. "I was just kidding. I'll feed you oatmeal myself and I won't put you in the basement unless you start to smell."

"Good gods, Rosie!"

"Glen, I'm kidding! Really. Why don't you just relax and think about the here and now?" Her tone changed to seductive. "If you want me to reward you with maple sugar in your oatmeal when you're old, you need to give me a reason to dote on you now."

"Do you know what incorrigible means?"

"Must have sex now?"

He grinned as he pulled the tie of her robe to loosen it. "Yeah. That's it."

He treated her to one of his long slow almost-better-than-sex kisses and reminded her of why he was unforgettable.

He pulled the silk away from her body and threw it in the general direction of the foot of the bed. Pushing the sheets out of the way, he took his time looking his fill at how Rosie's body had changed, marveling at the fact that the changes were for the better. Her breasts were fuller and heavier and her hips flared more from her waist. But the best thing was the womanly expression she wore on her face telling him that his lover knew who she was and what she was doing.

Rosie preened in response to the pleasure she saw in Glen's eyes and pulled on the waistband of his boxers indicating that she wanted them off. He was still struggling with compliance when she took his cock in her hand. He instantly forgot what he'd been doing and froze except for the soft growl that rumbled in his chest. That response was a stimulus that went straight to Rosie's core as if Glen's vocal cords had invisible fingers.

Coming together, skin to skin, for the first time in so long, Rosie's body recognized Glen and responded like it had been hours, not years. She was cast into an acute state of euphoria. Glen shared her eagerness to cut foreplay short. He put up a front of weak resistance, but when Rosie wanted something, she was a force not to be denied and Glen was just as eager to experience being joined with Rosie. She was his drug of choice. She always would be. So without much of a protest, he surrendered and slid into her slick channel, knowing that she was immune to both disease and pregnancy unless she wanted it.

She moaned when he entered her fully and he wasn't entirely sure it was a pleasure response.

"What's wrong?" Glen looked concerned.

She needed time for her body to adjust to the stretching and the invasion.

"It's just been a really long time. Years." He pulled out. "No. Don't go away. Just take it a little bit slow at first."

He reentered, taking his cues on how to proceed from her. When she began moving with him, he increased his pace until he was sure the sounds she made *were* pleasure responses.

"I think this feels better than it's supposed to," he said breathlessly.

"It's supposed to feel this good. When you're with the

right person."

He kissed her long and deep as he continued to thrust slowly, savoring the moment he'd thought would never happen again. When he pulled back, he looked into her eyes. "Do you love me, Rosie?"

"Of course. I loved you before I could walk."

"It was hel without you. You know that? There's nothing in life more important than being with you. Nothing will ever come between us again."

"I know. So shut up and make love to me."

They spent at least half of Glen's leave in bed. Rosie responded to a few small tracking jobs, but they were easy and she was never gone long.

Chapter Twenty-Four

With the help of pills that Glen called magic, Rosie delivered him to a command performance meeting at Jefferson Unit. She was going to take the opportunity to visit with her parents while Glen met with the J.U. Sovereign, Reverence Farthing.

Glen was standing in front of the Sovereign's desk after the admin had been told to show him in. Farthing was on the phone, but he made a motion for Glen to sit. When he hung up, he said, "Dratblasted vampire."

Glen was thinking that, even without knowing the context, he couldn't have said it better, himself.

Rev looked up at him. "Sir Catch."

"Yes, sir."

"How was your time off?"

Glen tried to suppress a grin, but just couldn't. "Good."

"You certainly give every appearance of being refreshed, relaxed, and ready to go back to work."

Glen's face fell. He'd been so caught up in the deep and abiding pleasure of Rosie that he hadn't given any thought to work or his future with Black Swan.

"Well," he began, "I…"

"We're not sending you back out as a floater."

"You're not?"

"No. In fact, Monq has launched a worldwide campaign to overhaul our policy on substitutions."

"He has?"

Rev nodded. "Seems he thinks you, especially you, got a raw deal from us."

Glen couldn't argue with that, but was curious as to why they thought he'd gotten a raw deal. "Why's that, sir?"

"Why does he think you especially got a raw deal? Did you know that before you the longest anybody had ever lasted as a floater was two years?"

"No. I didn't know that, sir."

"And it's no wonder. It was conversations with you that brought it to our attention. Really says something about your character that you beat the record by two and a half times." Glen's only response to that was a deep sigh. He didn't really feel like being congratulated for it. "Here's the thing."

Glen was glad that the Sovereign was getting around to 'the thing' because the discussion was beginning to make him uncomfortable.

"I'm retiring. Long and short is I need a replacement. I'll be honest. I offered it to Storm, not because he's more qualified, mind you. Just a matter of tenure. But whenever things die down enough for him to move on, he just wants to grow grapes. And maybe more children." Rev shook his head as if to say that was a damn shame. "So I'm offering the position to you. You know it. You've done it. Damn fine job of it, too. Jefferson Unit would be fortunate to have you in this chair. What do you say?"

Glen sat staring at Rev for several beats. He couldn't have been more stunned if lightning had just struck and paralyzed his tongue.

"Catch?"

"Yes, sir?"

"Are you with me?"

Glen took a deep breath. "I am. It's just… That's the last thing I guess I was expecting to hear when I reported. I was pretty sure I was being fired."

"Well, you're not. So what's your answer?"

"The only thing that keeps me from saying yes on the spot is that I promised myself I would never make another career move without taking Rosie into consideration. I need to run it by her."

"Send her a text. Time's wasting."

"Yes, sir."

GLEN WALKED PAST the admin's office into the hallway outside the Sovereign's suite.

> GLEN: ***Can you come to the hallway outside the Sovereign's office?***

Within three seconds of sending the text, Rosie was standing in front of him holding her phone.

He smiled. "I think I've actually gotten used to that."

"What's up?"

She could see that he was trying not to smile. "I just got offered the Sovereign's job. Here. At Jefferson Unit," he whispered.

Rosie squealed with excitement for him and leapt into his arms, legs straddling his waist.

"Madam," he said, "this is conduct unbecoming a Sovereign's wife."

"Well then, if you want me to behave, you better hurry up and make me a Sovereign's wife."

"Deal." He grinned, looking years younger than when she'd first seen him on her return to Jefferson Unit. He'd been damaged and scarred, but his core was indomitable.

Rev heard the muffled squeal outside his offices and smiled, thinking sometimes things do turn out the way they're supposed to.

GLEN AND ROSIE were married at Jefferson Unit at two in the afternoon so that all active duty knights could attend. Sovereign Reverence Farthing officiated. He was empowered to marry, although he'd never done it before and thought it a fitting end to an illustrious career.

The Lady Elora Laiken, not to be outdone, went into labor as soon as the groom kissed the bride. Beautiful twin girls were delivered in the infirmary, with perfectly shaped elven ears and a smattering of white blond hair. Rammel, never ashamed to emote, shed tears of joy as he posed for photos holding one in each arm.

He also vowed to tell the new Sovereign that he was retiring from vampire hunting as soon as Glen returned from his honeymoon. It was looking as if there would always be more vampire, but more time to spend with his growing family could not be manufactured.

GLEN AND ROSIE took a two week honeymoon to Paris. Among other things they revisited the places they'd seen while looking for Falcon and discovered that Paris was even more magical when seen through the eyes of lovers. One of the things Glen enjoyed most was inviting Baka and Heaven to dinner at Le Train Bleu and forcing them to watch he and Rosie engage in hot make-out sessions between every course.

The newlyweds were offered the Charlemagne suite at Jeanne d'Arc Unit, but chose instead to take the top floor at the Auberge du Jeu de Paume in Chantilly. Glen was well-armed with pills so that transportation was never a problem.

They agreed that their next vacation would be a cross-dimensional tour of exotic experiences unavailable from the corner travel or tourist agency.

AFTER THREE WEEKS of intensive dinner conversations with Monq, Falcon was cleared to return to work.

He stopped by the Operations Office on the way to mess one day to request travel home for his mother's surprise birthday party being arranged by his older brother. When he stepped inside, there was a young woman standing, facing the door as she read something lying in front of her on the counter while her auburn bangs obscured most of her face.

She looked up with clear amber-colored eyes so exotic they could only be called arresting and flashed a brilliant smile. "Hello. Can I help you?"

Falcon dragged his eyes away as fast as humanly possible, looked around nervously, and frowned. Without making eye contact, he said, "Where's Farnsworth?"

"Retired. Didn't you hear? I'm Gretchen Galen from the San Francisco office. I work here now. You can call me Great. Short for Gretchen."

She waited for Falcon to tell her his name and state his business, but he did neither. He just walked out, leaving her wondering if it was something she'd said.

"I was just kidding about the 'great' thing," she called after him, but he'd already disappeared.

Swanpedia

SECTION 1: *Characters*

Ainsley – Black-on-Tarry horse groomer / handler. (8)

Archer "Magman" – Ralengclan scientist, Stagsnare Dimension. In charge of deciphering Monq's research, particularly regarding interdimensional travel. (3,5)

Ariel – Deliverance's mother. (2)

Baph – Angel Wolfram Storm's private nickname for the loan shark, Richard Shade (5)

Baka, Heaven – Wife of Istvan Baka. (9)

Baka, Istvan – An ancient vampire, prisoner and advisor to The Order of The Black Swan. (Series)

Balkin, Stefan – The male vampire character in a romance novel written by Istvan Baka under his pseudonym, Valerie de Stygian. (3)

Barrock, Bolstoi "Bo" – Jefferson Unit Trainee, Glen's Assistant. (5,7)

Blackie – The big Alsatian dog that Elora befriended, tamed, trained, eventually becoming her pet and protector. (Series)

Blackmon, "Prune Face" – Young Storm's teacher. (2) Alternate dimension version. (5)

BlueClaw – Stalkson Grey's native ShuShu friend. (4)

Blytheness, February "Rue" – Past life specialist assigned to Edinburgh. American originally from Boston. (3)

Bonheur, Genevieve – Farnsworth's assistant in the Operations Office. (7) Operations Manager turned vampire (9)

Borrini, Matteo – Anthropologist, University of Florence whose discoveries are cited in a memo read by Mercy. (7)

Brachen, Agent – Canadian security agent put in charge of Song and Duff. (6)

Brandywine, Litha – "Witch tracker. Employed by The Order. Renamed Litha Liberty Brandywine. Daughter of Deliverance. Wife of Storm. Mother of Rosie. (2,7,9)

Brave – Human prince of demons. Real name "Bruce". (*Prince of Demons*)

Caelian, Sir Chaos "Kay" – Berseker from South Texas. Member of B-Team. Storm's partner. (Series)

Caelian, Skulda "Squoosie" – Kay's older sister closest to his own age. (2)

Caelian, Urda "Urz" – Kay's oldest sister. (2)

Caelian, Verdandia "Dandie" – Kay's middle sister. (2)

Catch, Glendennon "Glen" – Rookie trainee. Dog walker. (1,2,8) In charge of Elora's rescue. (3) Candidate for Jefferson Unit sovereign. (4) Acting sovereign Jefferson unit. (5) Sovereign (7)(Series)

Cheng – Member of D team (8)

Chorzak, Kellan "Spaz" – aka Spazmodoc and The Voice of the Fray. Announced the skirmish with Stagsnare aliens at Jefferson Unit. (5,7)

Copeland, Miles – Music teacher to Kevin Durry as a gift along with a violin from Ram. Character named after one of Victoria's favorite music industry professionals, elder brother of Stuart Copeland, POLICE. (8)

Crisp – Jefferson Unit's mess maitre'd (Series)

Cufaylin, Brother "Cufay" – Cairdeas Deo monk who "adopted" Litha. Also, a monk by the same name was a resident at the Cozio Monastery in Romania in the 15th century and was Baka's benefactor and employer. (2,3,4)

Culain – One of the Council. (6)

Cyon, Hal – Owner of the Halcyon Bar. (5)

Darnell, Gordy – The hunter who alerts Liam O'Torvall to the fact that he'd seen a child alone in the heart of the New Forest, but wasn't able to track him down. (8)

Dart – Callii Demon. Brave's boyhood friend. (POD 2)

Deliverance – Incubus from Ovelgoth Alla. Subspecies of Abraxas demons. Son of Obizoth (father) and Ariel (mother). Nephew of Pandora. (2,4,7,9) Also appears in Carnal, Exiled 1.

de Stygian, Valerie – The pseudonym under which Istvan Baka writes vampire romances. (1,3)

der Recke, Dankvart – One of the two founders of The Order of the Black Swan (1)

Doc Lange – Physician at the clinic at Edinburgh headquarters. (3)

Dorthan, Cleary – Royal tutor for Ram in New Forest. (8)

Driftmaker "Drift" – Elder of the Elk Mountain tribe of werewolves (4)

Durry, Kevin – Driver in whose truck the young Ram and Liam O'Torvall hitched a ride to the palace at Dublin. (8)

Elsbeth – Jefferson Unit nurse. Elora's first female friend in Loti Dimension. (1,8)

Etana – One of the Council. (6)

Falcon, Kristoph "Kris" – Jefferson Unit Trainee. Along with Rolfe Wakenmann, he was the first person to be decorated for bravery while still a trainee for courage in the Battle of Jefferson Unit against Stagsnare Dimension assassins. (5,7,9)

Farnsworth, Susan – Operations manager at Jefferson Unit. (1,8) Engaged to Sol Nemamiah (4) Married to the Jefferson Unit Sovereign. (7) Operations Manager (9)

Farouche – Ralengclan assassin. Second in command to Archer "Magman" (5)

Farthing, Reverence Foster "Rev" – Sol's reincarnated identity (7,9)

Fennimore, Sir Dirk "Fenn" – Black Swan knight from Jefferson Unit. Had been considered as 4th member before Elora. (1,5,7,8)

Finngarick, Mick – Torn's deceased father. (4)

Finngarick, Torrent "Torn" – Elf on Z Team. From Dunkilly, Donegal, Northern Ireland. (4,5,7)

Finrar – The angel Kellareal's disguise as an elf hermit. Tells Glen and Rosie the story of the origins of the elf fae war. (6)

Flame – Dolmen wolf pack female. (3)

Fortnight – Member of D team (8)

Forzepellin, Robert "Glyphs" – aka Bob. Z Team member. (5)

Gaia – Aelsong's assigned roommate when she first arrived Edinburgh. (2,3)

Galfae and Galfin – Twins who fathered the races of elves and fae. (6)

Gheorghita – Baka's first wife from his life as a mortal. (1)

Grey, NightCloud "Cloud" – Stalkson Grey's daughter-in-law. (4)

Grey, Stalkson (King) – "The alpha of the Elk Mountain werewolves. (2,3,4) Also a central character in the New Scotia Pack series.

Grey, Windwalker "Win" – Son of Stalkson Grey. Heir apparent to the Elk Mountain Reservation werewolf pack. (4)

Grieve, Haversfil – Prince Duff Torquil's male secretary. (4,6)

Gustafsven, Gunnar "Gun" – Z Team member. (5,7)

Hallows, Sir Ruddy – Eighteenth century Black Swan knight who discovered/captured Istvan Baka and transported him to Fort Dixon. (3)

Hannyran, Able – Elfen teenager who guided Kay to Ram's New Forest cottage. (3)

Harvest, Sinclair "Sin" – Trainee transferred to Jefferson Unit. Peer of Falcon and Wakenmann. (7) Knight. Member of K Team (9)

Hawking, Aelsblood "Blood" – Ram's older brother. King of Irish Elves. (2,8)

Hawking, Aelshelm "Helm" Laiken-Storm – Son of Ram and Elora. (3)

Hawking, Aelsong "Song" – Princess of Irish Elves. Ram's sister. Psychic employed by The Order. Principal character in A Tale of Two Kingdoms. Wife to Prince Duff Torquil of Scotia. (2,3,6,8)

Hawking, Ethelred Mag Lehane – Ram's father. King of Irish Elves. (2,6,8)

Hawking, Sir Rammell "Ram" Aelshelm – Oldest member of B Team. Elora Laiken's partner. Prince of Irish Elves. (Series)

Hawking, Tepring – Ram's mother. Queen of Irish Elves. (2,6,8)

Helena – Baka's third wife. (3)

Heralda the Dark – One of the Council. (6,7)

Hillknocker, Tommy – Guard on duty at the New Forest gate when Rammel's father, the king, arrived. (8)

Huber Quizno – One of the Council. (6,7)

Igvanotof, Minister – Bulgarian Minister of Antiquities. (7)

Innes, Peyton – Duff Torquil's friend and solicitor. (6)

Javier – One of a group of young, French immortal vampire who are "real" immortals. (4,5,7)

Jean-Etienne – One of the "real" vampire immortals. Baby sitter for the group of French adolescent vampire. (4,9)

Jorge – Partner of Reverence Farthing (Rev), killed in the line of duty in Brazil. (7)

Jungbluth, Count – One of the two founders of The Order of the Black Swan (1)

Katrina – Sir Chaos "Kay" Caelian's love interest. (1) fiance. (2,7) wife.

Kellareal "Lally" – Litha's mysterious angel friend who helps Stalkson Grey with relocation. (4,5,7) Also appears in Carnal, Exiled 1.

Kilter, Hogmaney – The constitutional scholar consulted regarding the succession to the throne of Irish Elves. (6)

Laiken, Lady Elora – The heroine of the Black Swan saga. This is her story. (Series)

Landsdowne, Sir Basil Wrathbone "Lan" – K.I.A. member of B Team. Ram's former partner. Had occupied the apartment given to Elora when she was released from the infirmary. (Series,1,8)

Lapis – Litha's grandmother. Witch in Spirit World who speaks to Stalkson Grey. (4,9)

Lapsrain "Rain" – Stalkson Grey's late wife. Mother of Windwalker. (4)

Lefrick – Istvan Baka's vampire partner who reinfected him in *A Summoner's Tale.* (3)

Logature, Arles – Mediator of the elf fae peace talks. Human disguise worn by the demigoddess, Etana. (6)

LongPaw – Elder of the Elk Mountain tribe of werewolves. (4)

Luna – Virgin kidnapped from Cult of Vervain by Stalkson Grey. (4) Also appears in the New Scotia Pack series as the homeopathic wise woman.

Madelayne – Elora's cousin. Her best friend in Stagsnare Dimension. (1)

Magnus, Caliber "Cal" – Mercenary Temp Sorcerer (1) Adventurer (POD 1)

Margaret – Director Tvelgar's executive administrator. Long time institutional fixture at headquarters in Edinburgh. (5)

McBride (Baka), Heaven – Istvan Baka's wife. The summoner from *A Summoner's Tale.* (3,9)

Ming Xia – One of the Council. (6,7)

Mironescu, Marilena – Baka's second wife. (1)

Monq, Thelonius C. – Elora's tutor in Stagsnare Dimension who sent her off world in a pre-experimental transport device. (1)

Monq, Thelonius M. – Black Swan's head scientist, stationed at Jefferson Unit. (Series)

Mossbind, Brother – One of the seven monks of the Cairdeas Deo Order that raised Litha. Mossbind was the resident homeopath. (4)

Nance, Dr. – Headquarters doctor on staff in Edinburgh treating Elora during her pregnancy. (3)

Nememiah, Sol – Title is Sovereign. Administrative head of the Black Swan Knights at Jefferson Unit. (Series)

Nibelung, Gautier "Ghost" – Black Swan knight considered to replace B Team member, Lan. KIA. (1,8)

Nightsong, Rafael "Raif" – One of Z Team knights. Will not use his last name. Glen calls him the "Black Knight". (5,7)

Obizoth – Deliverance's father. (2)

O'Malley, Ren – Black-on-Tarry craftsman. Patriarch of the family known for making fine bows and arrows in the New Forest village. (8)

O'Moors, Harefoot "Harry" – Stray Irish werewolf captured in London and adopted by Stalkson Grey's tribe. (2,4,5) Also appears in the New Scotia Pack series.

O'Torvall, Liam – Serves informally as mayor of Black on Tarry. Was Rammel's guardian when he stayed in the New Forest cottage as a boy. (1,3,8)

O'Torvall, Moira – Liam's wife. (3,8)

Pandora – Ariel's sister. Grand Mother, Cult of the Moon Vergins, Throenark Dimension (4)

Peregrination "Perry" – Callii Demon. Brave's friend and chief of security. (POD 2)

Pietra – Flight attendant. (7)

Point Wolf – Dolmen wolf pack look out. (3)

Pottinger, Rosie – Litha's mother, the apothecary's daughter and Deliverance's lover. Elora Rose Storm's, aka Rosie, namesake. (2)

Puddephatt, Richard J. – Oxford professor who knowing the history of the Danu resolved the question as to the difference between elf and fae. (6)

Puddephatt, Xavier – Headquarters researcher with Aspergers. Helped Rosie locate Glen's family. (9)

Ragnal – One of the Council. (6,7)

Randeskin, Sir – One of the Black Swan knights Storm encountered during the time when he was stranded in Halcyon Dimension. (5)

Rathbone, Alder – Lan's uncle. Recruits Rammel into Black Swan. (8)

Ravin, "Lana" Atalanta – Heroine of *Prince of Demons* Trilogy. (POD Trilogy)

Rejuvenata (Luna) – Luna's name given to her by the Cult of Vervain (4)

Renaux, Mercedes "Mercy" – aka Dr. Renaux. Historian / archeologist teaching at Columbia. Principal character in *Solomon's Sieve.*(7)

Rodgers, Mr. "Tums" – The vice principal at young Storm's public school. (2) Alternate universe version. (5)

Romescu, Helene – The female character in a romance novel written by Istvan Baka. (3)

Rothesay, Lft. – Stagsnare Dimension commander in charge of the first wave of assassins who attacked Elora in *A Summoner's Tale.* (3,5)

Rystrome, Pvt. – Ralengclan soldier, Stagsnare Dimension, assigned to first wave team of assassins. (3,5)

Shade, Richard "Dick" – Loan shark. Privately called "Baph" for Baphomet by Angel Wolfram Storm. (5)

Shakespeare – Author of the dark play, "A Season in Hell". (3)

SilverRuff – Alpha of the werewolf colony established by migration a thousand years earlier. (4)

Stalking Shadow – Stalkson Grey's late father. (4)

Stalkson Grey (wolf) – Named after the king of the Elk Mountain werewolf tribe. The alpha of the Dolmen pack of wolves that live in the New Forest, Northern Ireland. (3)

Stavna – Baka's eldest daughter. (3)

Storm, Angel Wolfram – Storm's counterpart who must learn to impersonate him perfectly. (5)

Storm, Elora Rose "Rosie" – Daughter of Storm and Litha. (4,5,9)

Storm, Engel Beowulf "Storm" – B Team de facto leader. (Series)

Storm, Evangeline "Eva/Birdie" – Storm's mother and Rosie's grandmother "Birdie." (5)

Tarriman – Part of the Stagsnare Dimension assassination project. The seventeenth test subject used in Archer's interdimensional transport experiment. (5)

Theasophie – One of the Council. (6)

Torquil, Duff "Duffy" – Prince of the Scotia Fae. (2,3,4,6)

Torquil, Lorna – Duff's mother. Queen of Scotia Fae. (6)

Torquil, Ritavish – Duff's father, King of Scotia Fae. (6)

Tvelgar, Simon – Director of The Order's headquarters office at Edinburgh. (2,3,7,9)

Wakenmann, Rolfe "Wakey" – Jefferson Unit Trainee. (5,7) Knight (9)

Widow Brennan – Tutors Ram on plants, cooking, and playing stringed instruments when he was a child in the New Forest. (8)

Yanev, Professor – Bulgarian professor from Sofia University. Supervisor of the vampire dig. (7)

Zajac, Zutsanna – A dinner companion seated next to Elora who is working on a "top secret" project seemingly related to Elora's interdimensional transport. (1)

SECTION 2: *Terms, Places, Things*

abraxas – Type of elemental fire demon. (2)

Angland – England in Loti Dimension. (3)

Ashanabe – Werewolf Tribe in British Columbia. (9)

B Team – A.K.A. Bad Company. Black Swan's elite unit of knights stationed at Jefferson Unit, Fort Dixon, New Jersey. (Series)

Black on Tarry – The New Forest, Ireland village preserved in pre-technology living. (1,8)

blithemoss – An herb grown on Throenark by the Cult of Vervain for healing purposes. (4)

British Columbia – Western Canadian province where Duff and Song planned to live. (6) Site of Ashanabe werewolf tribe. (9)

Briton East India Company – Baka's shipping concern. (3)

Cairdeas Deo, Order of – Order of monks who raised Litha in Sonoma. (2)

Cape May, New Jersey – Location of Farnsworth's beach house. (7)

Coeur d'Alene – Idaho city near Elk Mountain werewolf tribe. (3,4) Also mentioned in New Scotia Pack Series.

Council – A group of misfit adolescent deities who were, given the planet and it's dimension as a group project; (Culain, Etana, Rager, Heralda the Dark, Ming Xia, Theasophie, and Huber Quizno.) (6)

Derry, Ireland – Seat of the Elfdom. Palace home to Rammel Hawking's family. (1,2,6,8)

Drac Unit – Nickname for Romanian Unit that housed Baka's prison. (1,3)

drayweed – herb that alters fetus gender, Throenark Dimension (4)

Dublin – Irish city. University, banking, and tourist trade. (8)

Dunkilly – Fishing village on Atlantic Coast of Ireland. The site of Mick Finngarick's wake. (5)

Edinburgh, Scotia – Site of Black Swan headquarters. (Series)

elf tales – Fairy tales told by Elora to Touchstone during his hospital recovery. (1) Renamed elf tales at Ram's insistence, retold and adapted by Ram when Elora was comatose. (8)

Elk Mountain, Idaho – Reservation. Location of Stalkson Grey's tribe of werewolves. (2)

Faroe Islands – First stop on Aelsong's and Duff's elopement flight. (6)

Field Training Manual – "#1 The plural of vampire is vampire." The FTM is the vampire hunter's resource guide. It contains information about vampire, their habits and proclivities, and also outlines rules of procedure and conduct expected from Knight of The Order of the Black Swan. (1)

Fort Dixon – Fictitious New Jersey military base that provided cover and the protection of a no-fly zone for Jefferson Unit. (Series)

frenalwort – herb that alters fetus gender, Loti Dimension (4)

gold – The universal currency. The only commodity accepted for trade across all worlds. (3)

Great Paddy – Reference of undetermined origin and uncertain meaning as used by Rammel Hawking (Series)

Great Vampire Inversion – Name given the era when it was believed that the vampire virus would be cured. (2)

Grunwald Unit – Black Swan unit near Berlin, Germany. (8)

Guadalupe River – Hunt, Texas site of two B Team weddings. (2)

Halcyon Bar – Where Storm worked when he was lost in another dimension. (5)

Halcyon Dimension – Home of Angel, Storm's counterpart. (5)

incubus – Male sex demon. (2)

Jeanne d'Arc Unit – Paris installation of The Order of the Black Swan. (9)

Jefferson Unit – Prominent facility of The Order housing active Black Swan knights, a training facility, and the largest scientific labs. (Series)

Sublevel 1 – Classrooms, media center, server rooms, administration, all offices except for operations which was off the Hub.

Sublevel 2 – Research labs, Monq's suite, training simulators, firing ranges.

Sublevel 3 – Fitness center, sparring, pool.

K Team – aka Kid Team, as named by Ram. Kris Falcon, Rolfe Wakenmann, Harvest Sinclair, Kellan Chorzak (9)

Laiwynn – Elora's clan. (1)

London, Angland – Shopping. (2,9)

Loti Dimension – The reality called "Earth" by humans. (2)

Lunark Dimension – Where the Elk Mountain tribe's ancestors had migrated. (4)

Manhattan – New York City peninsula. (Series)

Marquise de Rambouilet – The Paris salon established by Catherine de Vivonne for French nobles who were patrons of the arts. (3)

New Elk Mountain – New settlement of werewolves who migrated from Loti Dimension. (4) Also in New Scotia Pack series.

New Forest, The – Northern Irish nature and culture preserve. Home of the Black-on-Tarry village, the royal hunting cottage retreat, and the wolf dolmen. (1,2,3,8)

Notte Fuoco – Manhattan night club where B team sets up an undercover mission to track down vampires. (1,8)

Ovelgoth Alla – Home dimension to Deliverance. (2)

Palio di Sienna – Horse race held in the center of town (Sienna, Italy) twice a year. (2)

Ralengclan – Rival Briton Clan from Elora's home world, Stagsnare Dimension. (1,5)

Rio de Janiero – Brazil city where Sol's corporeal host died. (7)

Shamayim Super Dimension – The afterlife. (7)

Shrifthet Dimension – Where authorities gave Elk Mountain boys a VISA for thirty days to find brides. (4)

Sienna, Italy – Site of Litha's disappearance. Gateway to Deliverance's lair. (2)

Solomon Nemamiah Medal of Honor – Given to Falcon and Wakenmann for courage under fire. (5)

Sozopol, Bulgaria – Site of the vampire dig. (7)

Stagsnare Dimension – Elora Laiken's dimension. Home of the Laiwynn and Ralengclan. (1,3)

The Norns – Kay's three sisters named after The Norns of Norse myth. (2)

Transylvania – Site of the Romanian Unit where Baka was held prisoner. (1,3)

Throenark Dimension – Home of the Cult of the Moon Vergins. Where Stalkson Grey snatched Luna. (4)

Washington Square – Common Manhattan visual. (9)

White Fang – Baka's contact name in Elora's cell phone. (1)

Z Team – aka Zed Company. Misfits transferred from Marrakesh to test Glen. (4,9)

I'm an Indie author, which means that nobody pays me to write. I put my work out there and let readers decide what you want available to you.

You can help me stay in business and write more books by buying only from authorized book retailers and leaving a review on Amazon.

I invite you to keep up with this and other series by subscribing to my mail list. I'll make you aware of free stuff, news, and announcements and never share your addy. Unsubscribe whenever you like.

Also browse more from my library at the end of this book.

Victoria Danann

SUBSCRIBE TO MY MAIL LIST

http://eepurl.com/bN4fHX

Website

victoriadanann.com

Black Swan Fan Page

facebook.com/vdanann

Facebook Author Page

facebook.com/victoriadanannbooks

Twitter

twitter.com/vdanann

Pinterest

pinterest.com/vdanann

AUTHOR FAN GROUP

facebook.com/groups/772083312865721/777140922359960

New York Times and USA Today
Bestselling Romance Author

Winner BEST PARANORMAL ROMANCE SERIES –
Knights of Black Swan
three years in a row!